DEADLY PASSIONS . . .

The macabre dance between her and Gabe had begun, really begun, on Christmas Eve. With one kiss under that damned mistletoe.

Until that kiss, she'd believed that she could control the confused, contradictory emotions Gabe Hunter roused in her. Until that Christmas Eve, she'd been able to deny his hold over her. Then he'd trapped her against the wall, held that dry, withered twig over her head, and taken her mouth with his.

All right, she'd had too much to drink. And yes, she'd been feeling homesick and lonely, like everyone else that night. Still, she shouldn't have let him . . . devour her. She shouldn't have arched into him when he'd dropped the mistletoe and dug his hands into her bottom to cant her hips to his. Dammit, she shouldn't have gasped when her blood raced and heat streaked like molten fire into her lower belly.

He'd heard her gasp. Exulted in it! When he'd raised his head, his blue eyes had glittered with the knowledge that she wanted him every bit as much as he wanted her.

DUTY
AND
DISHONOR

by

MERLINE LOVELACE

AN ONYX BOOK

ONYX
Published by the Penguin Group
Penguin Putnam Inc., 375 Hudson Street,
New York, New York 10014, U.S.A.
Penguin Books Ltd, 27 Wrights Lane,
London W8 5TZ, England
Penguin Books Australia Ltd, Ringwood
Victoria, Australia
Penguin Books Canada Ltd, 10 Alcorn Avenue,
Toronto, Ontario, Canada M4V 3B2
Penguin Books (N.Z.) Ltd, 182-190 Wairau Road,
Auckland 10, New Zealand

Penguin Books Ltd, Registered Offices:
Harmondsworth, Middlesex, England

First published by Onyx, an imprint of Dutton Signet,
a member of Penguin Putnam Inc.

First Printing, October, 1997
10 9 8 7 6 5 4 3 2 1

This book is dedicated to the
men and women
who served in Vietnam.
No further words are needed.

ACKNOWLEDGMENTS

With special thanks to:

Brigadier General Jerry Dalton, USAF (Ret.), for his extraordinary generosity in sharing his time and insights into the PAO's role at MACV.

Colonel Virginia Pribyla, USAF, SAF/PA, for not batting an eye when I called to ask who would convene her court-martial if she were charged with, ohhhh, murder.

Major James Pasierb, USAF, Chief of Public Affairs for the Air Force Office of Special Investigations, for his invaluable assistance.

Lieutenant Bill Price, Oklahoma Police Department (Ret.), for his expertise in combat triggers and 110-grain Super Vels.

And, most especially, to

My husband, Colonel Cary (Al) Lovelace, USAF (Ret.), with whom I've shared one war, two careers, and almost three decades of adventure and romance. Thanks for the memories, my love.

ONE

When her intercom buzzed that bright December afternoon Julia Endicott had no idea that the simple message her secretary delivered would change her life forever.

"General Titus wants to see you, ma'am."

Julia's lips curved into a wry smile as she surveyed the crowd huddled around the worktable in her Pentagon office. "Right now, I suppose?"

"When else?" Maria replied cheerfully. "His exec is holding on the line, waiting to confirm your availability."

"Tell him I'm on my way."

Julia hung up and closed the leather-bound notebook she'd been scribbling in. Rising, she waved the others to remain seated.

"I want you all to keep working the media release on this base-closure list. Hard! Pete, you get on the line to the Senate liaison office. We need to know the minute the list gets voted out of subcommittee. Use my hotline."

"Will do, Colonel." The tall, thin captain in wire-rimmed glasses reached for the phone on the console behind the desk.

Notebook in hand, Julia headed for the door. "Donner, make sure the Installations folks coordinate on the economic-impact numbers we'll give the media. There were two different sets of figures floating around the halls when we worked the initial hit list last week."

"Right."

"The rest of you finish working the Chief's statement. The draft he approved addresses most of the major issues, but I want an update on the closure schedules and estimate of jobs that will be lost."

She paused at the mirror behind the door to tuck an errant strand of silvery blond hair into the smooth twist at the back of her head and straighten the tab collar on her blouse. As deputy director of Air Force Public Affairs, she'd met with the vice chief of staff often. She didn't feel it necessary to don her service dress jacket with its rows of colorful ribbons and shiny silver eagles on each shoulder to answer his call. She satisfied herself with simply smoothing her slim, navy skirt over her hips and freshening her lip gloss. When Julia dropped the gloss back into her purse, her fingers brushed the small, silver oak leaf pinned to the lining. As always, the feel of rank insignia her father once wore gave her a sense of comfort.

"I'll be back as soon as I can," she assured the group at the conference table.

Swiftly, Julia walked the echoing hallway of D-ring, the second of the Pentagon's five concentric rings. The offices of the director and deputy director of Public Affairs were on the fourth floor of the five-sided building, just minutes away from the executive suites on the outer ring. Uniform walls in an uninspiring shade of muddy cream stretched endlessly before her, broken by rows of glass-fronted doors and broad corridors that intersected the rings at regular intervals. Deemed the Puzzle Palace by some long-forgotten wit, either because of its confusing layout or because of the complex issues of national defense its occupants grappled with daily, the Pentagon was a familiar maze to Julia.

After two tours within its granite walls, one as an eager, energetic young captain and now as a more seasoned colonel, she had learned her way around the corridors of power. While most officers avoided a second tour at the Air Staff like the plague, hating the long hours and never ending stress, Julia thrived on the fast pace and the adrenaline-pumping issues. Of course, she didn't have a spouse or children waiting at home while she put in so many endless hours, or the worries about the high cost of living in the D.C. area that made a Pentagon assignment seem like a punishment to many. Over the years she'd had a few close brushes with marriage and one early, broken engagement. Of late she'd put most of her energy into her career.

It helped that she was good at her job, damn good. Having joined the Air Force as a young, incredibly naive journalism grad, she'd spent the last twenty-four years learning how to frame the military's triumphs and tragedies for public consumption. She'd also earned several early promotions in the process, and one or two wrinkles that skillfully applied makeup kept hidden. So far.

General Titus, the Air Force's second-in-command and Julia's gruff mentor, had hinted that she was heir apparent for the director's position when her boss retired next year. When that happened, Julia doubted if all the makeup in the world would disguise the pressures of the job. Still, promotion to one star would be worth a few more character lines.

General Endicott.

Julia K. Endicott, Brigadier General, USAF.

Julia Endicott, Director of Public Affairs, United States Air Force.

The title had a nice ring to it, she admitted with a grin, turning left onto Corridor 8. Her grinned softened into a small private smile as she thought how proud her father would have been to see silver stars on her epaulets. Lieutenant Colonel Paul Endicott hadn't lived to see his daughter commissioned as a lieutenant, let alone pin on her eagles so many years later. He'd died while she was still in school, but she knew she was close to fulfilling his dreams for her.

A few more steps brought her to E-ring, the prestigious outer circle that housed the offices of the most senior civilian and military executives. The tile under her feet took on the resonance of marble. Oak pillars defined the long stretch of hallway that made up the Air Force's locus of power. Life-sized portraits of former secretaries and chiefs of staff of the Air Force stared down from paneled walls.

She speared a quick glance at her favorite, General Curtis LeMay. Bristling with medals, he held his famous cigar in hand. She'd once heard the crusty old warrior speak at the Air War College and had admired his blunt honesty. He'd never held a job he felt qualified for, LeMay claimed. Circumstance and chance had always thrust him forward. Just as they had Julia.

Halting outside the door to the vice chief's suite of offices, she drew in a deep breath. For all his support of her career over the years, General Titus had a temper that matched what remained of his fiery red hair. He didn't suffer fools gladly, and had been known to throw generals and captains out of his office with equal ruthlessness. Not for the first time since her summons a few moments ago, Julia wished she'd had just a little more time to finalize the press release on the pending base-closure list. It was such a touchy political issue, impacting so many people's lives. Every word of the release needed to carry just the right blend of concern and assurance. She was sure the vice chief would ask her about its status.

Letting the air out of her lungs slowly, Julia opened the heavy wood-paneled door. The general's executive officer rose to his feet.

"Afternoon, ma'am."

"Afternoon, Dave. Hello, Norma."

The executive assistant returned her greeting cordially. A pleasant-faced woman whose grandmotherly appearance hid a razor-sharp mind and a tenure that stretched back through six vice chiefs, she kept the general and his exec both straight. While Norma buzzed her boss to let him know of the colonel's arrival, Julia queried the exec.

"Any idea what the boss wants to see me about, Dave?"

The exec shook his head. "No, ma'am."

"Well, I've got my trusty brain-book with me," she replied with a smile, holding up the leather notebook that went everywhere with her. "If I don't have all the facts and figures on whatever he wants to know right here, I'll eat this sucker."

Norma's smooth voice carried over the exec's laughter. "The general's ready for you, Colonel Endicott."

Nodding in thanks, Julia pulled open the heavy inner door. Her heels sank into plush blue carpet as she stepped into an executive suite with a magnificent view of the Potomac. Rare December sunshine streamed through the tall bank of windows to her left. The bright sunlight illuminated the glittering array of memorabilia from three wars arranged on the built-in shelves that took up one entire wall.

Only after she'd stopped before the general and snapped him a crisp salute did she notice the unsmiling man in civilian clothes standing quietly a few feet away. Wondering who he was, Julia waited for General Titus to wave her to one of the elaborately carved chairs in front of his desk, as he normally did. The ebony elephant chairs had been gifts from the Ethiopian government to an illustrious previous occupant of this office. As Julia had discovered, the elaborately carved, uncushioned chairs were uncomfortable as hell for anyone who had to sit in them for any length of time. She suspected General Titus kept them in his office for just that reason.

To her surprise, he didn't invite her to sit down. Under thick red brows sprinkled with touches of frost, his blue eyes held a cool reserve.

"Colonel Endicott," he said finally, his voice terse, "this is Special Agent Ted Marsh of the Office of Special Investigations."

Her heart sinking, Julia turned to the tall, wide-shouldered man in the three-piece gray suit and discreet red tie. Oh, Lord, she wondered. What was going down now?

As the Air Force's investigative arm, the OSI worked all kinds of nasty stuff. Everything from drug smuggling to child molestation to old-fashioned cloak-and-dagger spy rings fell within their purview.

With the base-closure list pending, her boss out of town, and half the Public Affairs staff on Christmas leave, the last thing Julia needed was for some sensational case to hit the front pages of the national press.

"Special Agent Marsh," she acknowledged with a small nod.

"Colonel Endicott."

The fact that she couldn't interpret the closed expression in his gray eyes bothered her. After two decades of dealing with a frequently disdainful and hostile press corps, she'd learned to size up people at a glance. Marsh, with his hard, lean face and gun-metal eyes, defied easy categorization.

She turned back to the general, her nerves tingling at the tense atmosphere in the room. Whatever had made these two men look so grim meant long, late hours for her and her staff tonight. So much for the leisurely dinner she'd planned with friends at Georgetown's newest watering hole.

When the heavy silence seemed to stretch interminably, Julia ventured a comment. "I take it the presence of the OSI means that you wanted to see me about something other than the base-closure list."

As hints went, that was about as unsubtle as a colonel dared to be with a four-star general. General Titus didn't respond.

Seriously alarmed now, Julia's nimble mind raced through the possible disasters that could have put such a stark look in his eyes. None of the catastrophic scenarios she imagined, however— from mass casualties as a result of an aircraft crash to a loss of a nuclear warhead—came close to preparing her for what he had to say.

He leaned forward, bracing both palms on his desk. "I've just spoken to the chief and to the secretary of the Air Force. With their concurrence, Colonel Endicott, I am relieving you of all public affairs duties, effective immediately."

His words were so unexpected, so absurd, that Julia didn't fully absorb them at first.

"You are now assigned as special assistant to Colonel Richards, head of the Issues Group."

His message finally penetrated her stunned mind. My God, he was serious! Reeling with shock, Julia gaped at him.

"I—I don't understand."

The man she'd always thought of as her mentor regarded her coldly. "You will be remain with the Issues Group pending an Article 32 investigation to determine whether you should be charged with murder."

"With what?"

"Murder, Colonel Endicott. Wrongful death, as described in Article 118 of the Uniform Code of Military Justice."

Julia stared at him blankly. She shook her head, trying desperately to force her brain to process the information it was being fed.

Murder?

Wrongful death?

The words reverberated in her head, having no basis in reality. Slowly, painfully, she drew herself up.

"With all due respect, sir, just what the hell is going on here?"

A muscle twitched at the side of the general's jaw. At any other time Julia might have worried about this sure sign that he was holding himself in check with great effort. Now she was too stunned to care.

"The State Department recently negotiated a new cooperative agreement with the government of Vietnam. A provision of that agreement included return of several sets of unidentified remains."

"What does that have to do with me?"

"One set has been positively identified as belonging to Captain Gabriel Hunter."

The leather notebook slid from Julia's grasp. It hit the carpeted floor with a dull thud that echoed in the sudden silence. Lifting wildly trembling fingers, she pressed them against her lips, trying unsuccessfully to hold back the hoarse cry that ripped from her throat.

"Gabe? Oh, my God, Gabe!"

General Titus leaned forward, his mouth compressed to a thin, taut line. "Before you say anything else, Special Agent Marsh will advise you of your rights."

His voice sounded as though it were coming

from a deep well. Julia heard the ripples of sound, but they bounced off the wall of her shock.

They'd found Gabe!

She didn't turn, didn't move, as the special agent stepped forward. Her wide, unseeing eyes were fixed on the winter sunlight streaming through the windows. A distant vision shimmered in her mind, of tropic greenery and shellpocked walls.

"Colonel Endicott, I must advise you that you're the prime suspect in Captain Hunter's death."

As if her head was too heavy for her neck, Julia turned slowly to face the OSI investigator. She opened her mouth to speak. No sound emerged. She swallowed painfully, then tried again.

"Why?" Her voice was little more than a whisper. "Why am I a suspect? Captain Hunter disappeared after a Vietcong ambush during the 1972 Easter offensive. He was listed as MIA, then KIA more than a dozen years ago."

Marsh hesitated, glancing at the general as if to confirm how much he should reveal. Julia's stricken gaze turned to General Titus. The vice chief stared at her for a long moment, then nodded to the special agent.

"Captain Hunter was ambushed," Marsh said flatly, "but not by the Vietcong. A farmer found his remains in a shallow grave just a few yards off the road leading from Saigon to Long Binh."

The foul taste of nausea rose in Julia's throat. A

face shimmered in her mind. Laughing, arrogant, incredibly handsome.

"A bullet was lodged in Captain Hunter's skull," Marsh continued. "Another in his chest cavity. A ballistic analysis has determined that they were a very special kind of bullet, Colonel Endicott. Super-Vel, 110 grain, jacketed hollow points, to be exact."

Julia's nails dug sharp, deep grooves in her palms. She knew what was coming next. Her face frozen, she stood rigid while her world crashed down around her.

"The recovery team found a pistol buried in the grave with Captain Hunter. A Smith & Wesson Model 19, with a rosewood grip and a combat trigger. The serial number matches that of the weapon you obtained special permission to carry with you into Vietnam . . . the same weapon you reported missing the day after Captain Hunter disappeared."

She had to respond. She had to say something. Anything. Clenching her hands into fists to hide their trembling, Julia ran her tongue over dry lips.

"The Smith & Wesson was stolen from my room at the women's quarters." She forced the words out one by one. "A military policeman investigated the theft. One of the *mamasans* took the gun, he thought, although he couldn't prove it."

The planes of the investigator's face seemed to flatten, harden. He leaned forward, holding her eyes with his.

"The recovery team also found a St. Christopher medal among Captain Hunter's effects."

Her medal! Oh, God, her medal! A ragged moan rose in Julia's throat. She caught herself before it fully escaped. Marsh's eyes flickered at the muted sound, but his voice remained impassive as he delivered the final blow.

"The medal has been identified as one you were given as a gift the night you arrived in Vietnam. We have statements indicating that you put it on that night and rarely, if ever, took it off."

For the first time fear began to seep into Julia's veins. Like an icy mist it curled through her body and slowly, so slowly, replaced the shock that held her immobile.

Her weapon and her medal. What else had they found? What else?

"At this point," the agent informed her, "I'm required to read you your rights. General Titus will act as witness. Then I'll escort you to a private office so my partner and I can take your statement."

Julia nodded. She didn't trust herself to speak.

The investigator reached into his inside coat pocket and pulled out a laminated card. He didn't refer to it as he spoke the formal phrases. No doubt he'd performed this small task too many times to need the prop.

"You have the right to remain silent. You have the right to consult with an attorney."

Gabe!

"Should you decide to answer our questions, your comments may be used in a court of law."

Julia heard the investigator's words but didn't absorb them. A single, desperate cry echoed through her mind, drowning out all else.

Damn you! I thought I was free of you!

"If you'll come with me, Colonel."

With a start Julia realized that Marsh had finished reading her rights. His face revealed no hint of emotion, no acknowledgment that he'd just shattered her world. She turned to General Titus. Her one-time mentor might have been carved from stone.

"You're dismissed, Colonel."

The curt order cut through Julia's numbed mind like a blade. Without another word she brought her arm up in a salute and left his office.

The general's exec said something to her, but his voice didn't register. Nor did the secretary's pleasantry as Julia strode past her desk. She stepped into the corridor, then stopped abruptly. Still dazed, she couldn't remember where they were supposed to go next.

Special Agent Marsh gestured toward a door across the hall. "This way."

When they entered the small, private conference room, the single occupant rose. The statuesque black woman wore a well-cut wine-colored wool suit and a white silk blouse that could have tagged her as a senior civilian of some authority, but her face held the carefully neutral expression of a professional investigator.

"This is Special Agent Barbara Lyles," Marsh said. "She's assisting me in the investigation of Captain Hunter's death. If you'll be seated, Colonel?"

The OSI agents waited until Julia had taken a chair, then seated themselves opposite her. Lyles retrieved a small tape recorder from her briefcase. Setting it on the table, she activated it with a touch of a polished nail.

"Thursday, 22 December, 1545 hours," Marsh stated succinctly. "Interview with Colonel Julia K. Endicott, conducted by special agents Ted Marsh and Barbara Lyles."

The tape whirred for a second or two.

"For the record, Colonel, let me state that you've been apprised of your rights and have waived the requirement to have an attorney present at this interview."

Julia refused to allow the fear now coiling through her like a living, malevolent creature to show in her face. Belatedly, her instinct for self-preservation began to assert itself. Forcing herself to speak slowly and deliberately, she countered his statement.

"For the record, Mr. Marsh, I retain the right to ask for an attorney any time I feel it necessary."

Something glinted in his alkaline eyes. Surprise, Julia guessed, although it was gone before her still stunned mind could interpret it. He pulled a small notebook from his suit coat and laid it on the table.

He didn't refer to it. As with the formal Miranda advisement, Special Agent Marsh obviously had the facts down cold.

"We've been conducting an investigation into Captain Hunter's death since his remains were identified several weeks ago. The purpose of this interview is to determine your awareness of and involvement in the events leading to his disappearance on or about June 12, 1972. I'd like to begin with your account of your relationship with the deceased."

Julia's chin lifted. Across the surface of the conference table her gaze locked with the investigator's.

"I didn't have a 'relationship' with the deceased."

"Then how would you describe your association with Captain Hunter?"

The question pierced Julia's wafer-thin control. She closed her eyes, fighting a rush of long-forgotten emotions. How could she describe what she'd felt for Gabe? How could anyone understand the fatal fascination she'd felt for the man who'd left his imprint on her soul?

Julia didn't understand it herself.

She never had.

Nor had she been able to fight it. Not from the first moment she'd stepped off the plane that terrible and glorious October and Gabe Hunter came swooping into her life.

Two

October 5, 1971,
Tan Son Nhut Air Base, South Vietnam

Grainy-eyed from lack of sleep and tingling with a mixture of nervousness and dread, Second Lieutenant Julia Endicott joined the stream of two hundred men and three women exiting the Pan American 707. As she stepped onto the metal ramp, the sights and sounds of South Vietnam slammed into her with stunning impact.

Hot, heavy, humidity sucked the air from her lungs and raised an instant film on arms left bare by her short-sleeve two-piece uniform. Already sticky from her twenty-two-hour flight, Julia raked a hand through her shoulder-length hair to lift the heat from her neck. Through the haze shimmering above the runway, she caught a faint smudge of purple mountains rising up to touch rolling black thunderclouds. The storm had just passed, she saw, and left a steamy network of puddles evaporating in the morning sun. A line of verdant foliage marked the edge of the cleared space at the end of the runways, but most of the objects within her immediate line of sight were tinted with the colors of war.

Helicopters in camouflage blacks and browns lined the taxiways in untidy rows, dwarfed by big-bellied C-130 cargo planes. A monstrous C-5, the Air Force's newest transport, was parked on a nearby apron, its nose lifted to allow a stream of armored personnel carriers to rumble out of its cargo bay. Across the runway, rows of fighter jets carrying both U.S. and Republic of Vietnam markings huddled under concrete shelters. Military vehicles, crew buses, and fuel trucks scurried like ants along the runway. Their black exhaust added to the tang of aviation fuel that hung on the air like an acrid curtain.

As Julia followed the slow-moving line of passengers down the metal stairs, the roar of fighters revving up battered her eardrums. She'd heard that Tan Son Nhut was the busiest airport in the world. Observing the whir of activity all around her, she believed it. A small shiver darted down her spine as she stepped onto the tarmac.

She was here.

Despite her mother's fears, her fiancé's objections, and her own occasional doubts. Despite the fact that President Nixon was withdrawing more U.S. ground combat forces every month, determined to end the war that had claimed so many American lives—including her father's.

She was here.

Instinctively, her hand slipped inside the black leather purse slung over her shoulder. Her trembling fingers found the silver oak leaf pinned to the inside lining. She rubbed her father's metal rank insignia for courage as she headed for the bus that sat patiently, its windows lowered to allow the muggy October moistness to circulate. Her stomach lurched when she saw the wire mesh covering the open windows. From her father's letters, she knew the purpose of that mesh screen. It was intended to keep hand grenades from being tossed inside the moving vehicle.

A sudden squeal of tires yanked her attention from the bus. Julia and the rest of the new arrivals spun around as a jeep screeched to a halt a few yards away. The driver, an Air Force captain sporting a luxuriant mustache well outside of regulation limits, swung his legs over the side and levered himself out of the open-sided vehicle.

"Hey, Lieutenant!" he shouted, his deep baritone carrying easily over the roar of aircraft engines.

A tall, gangly Army officer, standing next to Julia with shiny gold bars on the collar of his khaki uniform shirt, looked around. Hesitantly he took a step forward. The pilot waved him back into line.

"Not you. The one with the legs."

Julia stiffened. Her mouth thinning, she watched the captain approach. Tall and broad-shouldered, he filled every inch of his green flight suit. Even if she hadn't seen the embroidered wings on his chest, the unmistakable swagger in his walk would have told her that he was a pilot. With his jaunty mustache, sun-streaked blond hair, and blue eyes glinting with deviltry, he exuded an air of cocky assurance. The epitome of a sky warrior, Julia thought wryly. She knew the breed.

Although he outranked her, she made no move to salute him when he stopped in front of her. As an Air Force brat, she possessed an ingrained respect for military customs and courtesies. After the captain's crack about her legs, though, she didn't consider that he rated any courtesies, military or otherwise.

He didn't appear to mind her breach of service etiquette. His mustache lifted to display gleaming white teeth as he raked her with a glance of blatant male interest.

"Welcome to Vietnam, Endicott. I'm Hunter, Gabe Hunter." His grin widened, creasing his tanned cheeks. "Before you ask, it's short for Gabriel. I'd better give you fair warning, though, I'm no angel."

"I wasn't going to ask," Julia replied coolly. "And I didn't need the warning."

He laughed outright and reached for her overnight case. "Now that we've got the rules of engagement out of the way, let's go."

She swept the case behind her hip, out of his reach. "Go where?"

"On your welcome tour." He waved a hand in

the direction of the jeep. "Gabe Hunter and his welcome wagon at your service."

She hung back, not quite trusting the gleam in his blue eyes. "Do you perform this welcome service for everyone, Captain Hunter?"

He looked offended. "Of course not! But you don't think any self-respecting air commando would let a sweet young thing like you step off a plane and wander around unprotected."

So he was a Special Ops type. That explained the unexpected welcome, Julia thought ruefully. Special Ops constituted a small, select community. She'd grown up in that community and had almost reentered it through marriage before this assignment to Vietnam had come through. She might have known that her fiance's connections—her former fiance's connections, she amended with a pang—would reach even here, some five thousand miles from his home base in the Florida panhandle.

"I should've guessed Dennis would arrange something like this," she murmured, half to herself.

"No one like ol' Dennis for arranging things," Hunter agreed.

He took her arm to escort her toward the jeep. His fingers were warm on her bare skin, and more than a little possessive. Frowning, Julia pulled her arm free.

She climbed into the vehicle as gracefully as her short skirt and wobbly heels would allow. Although she wore the blue and white pin-striped uniform well within the regulation two inches above her knees, its slim skirt wasn't made for high steps and low seats. She caught Hunter's assessing glance and tugged the hem of her skirt down to cover as much of her thighs as possible.

He tossed her overnight case into the back and folded his muscular frame into the driver's seat. Shoving the gears into reverse, he draped an arm over Julia's seat and thrust the vehicle back in a wide arc, away from the plane.

"By the way," he said casually, his breath a warm shock of sensation on her cheek, "who's Dennis?"

She leaned away from the circle of his arm and sent him a hard look. Unrepentant, he grinned at her and dropped his arm to wrap a fist around the gear shift. He let the clutch out, and the jeep leaped forward.

"All right, hot shot," Julia shouted over the ear-splitting roar of a jet taxiing toward them on the parallel ramp. "Just who the heck are you?"

"I told you, I'm Gabe Hunter." He waited for the fighter to roll by before speeding across the ramp toward a cluster of sand-bagged buildings. "World's greatest gunship driver."

"And you're not the Angel Gabriel. I got all that. What I didn't get was why you came out to meet me at the plane."

He whipped the wheel left, spinning the vehicle off the apron and onto the wide expanse of concrete that led to the aerial port building. Julia clutched the seat with both hands.

"Your sponsor mentioned that you were arriving

in-country today," he tossed out when the noise behind them died to a manageable level. "I decided to come check you out. You check out pretty good, Endicott," he added, waggling his sun-bleached brows in an exaggerated leer.

The laughter in his blue eyes won out over her irritation at his high-handedness. Against her better judgment, almost against her will, she let an answering smile curve her lips.

"You check out pretty good yourself, Hunter. Too bad I'm not interested."

"Sure you are, sweet thing. You just don't know it yet."

She didn't bother to argue. From long experience she knew how difficult it was to dent an air commando's ego, much less his confidence, with mere words. She'd send him on his way as soon as he pulled up at the terminal.

Her fine shoulder-length hair whipped her cheeks as the jeep dodged streams of moving forklifts loaded with web-covered cargo pallets. Tucking the stinging strands behind her ears, Julia forgot the man beside her and drank in her first glimpse of the war that was slowly tearing apart the social and political fabric of the United States.

Transportation specialists in baggy green fatigue pants, their backs bared to the hazy sun and shoulders streaked with sweat, manhandled tons of stubborn cargo onto wooden pallets. The U.S. servicemen worked side by side with slender, dark-haired troops

whom Julia guessed were their Vietnamese counterparts. The Vietnamese soldiers, her father had
written in one of his letters home, were fierce fighters
and tireless workers—when they wanted to be. Much
like the Americans he commanded, he'd added.

The Vietnamese troops worked with almost grim
intent, Julia saw, as if desperate to get the incoming
war material re-palletized and shipped up-country.
She understood their urgency. President Nixon's
determination to conclude the long-stalled Paris
peace talks and take America out of this endless
conflict meant they had to stockpile all they could
now, before their allies pulled out.

Julia was so absorbed in the drama displayed on
the tarmac that she didn't realize the jeep had
driven right past the entrance to the squat, sand-
bagged terminal building. She twisted in her seat,
frowning, as the busses disgorged the first waves of
passengers from her flight.

"I think that's where I need to go," she told
Hunter.

"I've already taken care of all your in-processing."

"They'll need my orders," she protested.

"I got a copy of your orders from a buddy at Personnel and passed them to one of the guys working
the processing line."

"But my duffel bag . . . " She waved toward a
pallet of green, sausagelike bags formed in neat
rows beside the entrance to the terminal. "I'm supposed to take it through Customs."

"No sweat, kiddo. I filled out a Customs declaration for you."

Julia gave a little huff of exasperation, not quite believing this guy was for real. His brows lifted at the sound.

"You didn't have anything to declare, did you?"

"No, but . . . "

"You're not trying to smuggle in some grass or acid? Something the dogs might hit on?"

"Of course not," she snapped.

"I didn't think so," he said smugly, "not Iron Man Endicott's daughter."

Julia's annoyance at his presumption vanished instantly. "You knew my father?"

"He was my squadron commander during my first tour, back in '67. I rotated home a couple of months before he was shot down."

Hunter either didn't hear or chose to ignore the rattle of her swiftly indrawn breath.

"Your old man was one tough bastard," he continued with a crooked smile. "Threatened to court-martial me over a slight difference of opinion regarding a target of opportunity."

A familiar hurt closed Julia's throat at the memory of her father's uncompromising views of black and white, right and wrong. There had been no shades of gray in Lieutenant Colonel Endicott's world, no room for indecision or hesitation when it came to doing one's duty.

If Julia had inherited her dark green eyes, pale blond hair, and inquiring mind from her mother, she'd been gifted with her father's sense of loyalty and honor. That sense of duty was why she'd turned down a fellowship to Cornell's prestigious graduate school of journalism. Why she'd broken ranks with her increasingly strident antiwar peers and accepted a commission in the Air Force. Why she was here now, over Dennis's strenuous objections. Lieutenant Colonel Paul Endicott hadn't finished his tour in Vietnam. Julia would finish it for him.

Hunter broke into her painful thoughts. "The day after your father kicked my ass but good, I had to put my crippled bird down at a base that was taking hits from an entrenched mortar battery. Your father was flying a goony bird then, one of the old, converted AC-47s. He dropped out of the clouds and went after that mortar crew with guns blazing."

"Did he get them?" Julia asked quietly.

"Made one pass and blew the sonsofbitches into the next province," Hunter confirmed cheerfully. "Best piece of airmanship I've ever seen, before or since. He was one fine pilot, your father."

Julia sank back against the seat. "Yes, he was."

"Which is why I figure I owe you dinner."

It took a few seconds for his comment to sink in. "What?"

"I'm taking you to dinner, Lieutenant. Like in thick, sizzling steaks and fine old cognac. To celebrate your first night in Vietnam."

Julia glanced up pointedly at the low-hanging morning sun. "I hate to be the one to break it to you, Captain, but it's a long time until dinner."

"No sweat. I'll give you a guided tour of the territory first."

Julia's lips twitched. Evidently it didn't seem to occur to Gabe Hunter that after twenty hours strapped into a cramped airline seat, her knees jammed almost to her chin, she might prefer a hot shower and a clean bed to a day spent in his company.

"I appreciate the offer, but I'm— Watch out!"

With a colorful oath, her self-appointed driver swerved to avoid a three-wheeled motorcycle. The vehicle sported a roofed compartment over the rear wheels that held two side benches and several uniformed personnel. The whole contraption was decorated with gaudy, colored streamers and strings of paper rosettes. It putt-putted past them, trailing a plume of black exhaust.

"What's that?" Julia asked.

"A hop-tac. The local version of a cab. It also doubles as a hearse when necessary. A few piasters— Vietnamese dollars—will get you anywhere you need to go on Tan Son Nhut. A few more will take you to the raunchiest bars on Tu Do Street, in downtown Saigon."

"That's good to know."

At her deadpan expression Hunter's mustache tipped upward. "Sorry, I forgot about ol' Dennis. You never did answer my question. Who is he?"

"My fiance."

The pilot glanced pointedly at her ringless left hand. Julia shrugged, not exactly sure why she felt the need to explain.

"We both decided it would be better to put the engagement on hold for a while. A year is a long time to spend apart."

A hell of a long time, Dennis had said angrily when she returned his ring. People change in the course of a year, especially in 'Nam. He hadn't wanted her to go, had made no pretense of sympathizing with her reasons for volunteering. She couldn't avenge her father's death, any more than she could change the course of the war.

Maybe not, Julia had agreed quietly. But maybe she could understand both by going to Vietnam.

"A year is only as long as you want it to be," Hunter tossed out, pulling her attention back to him. "Most people start counting backward from three hundred and sixty-five the day they get here."

"Didn't you?"

"Nope." His white teeth gleamed under that ridiculous mustache. "I live every day as hard as I can. And I intend to live today with you, Lieutenant Endicott."

Julia thought of all the reasons why she should insist that he take her to the room her sponsor had waiting for her in the women officers' quarters. She was tired. She was dirty and wrinkled and slightly overwhelmed by the mere fact that she'd finally arrived in Vietnam. She needed sleep, badly. She needed to iron a fresh uniform to wear when reporting in for duty tomorrow. She had to find out *where* to report in for duty. That much at least Captain Hunter could do for her, Julia decided.

"Can you show me where Military Assistance Command, Vietnam, is?"

"MACV? Can do easy, Lieutenant. We'll make it the first point of interest on your tour of the base. Hang on to your seat."

Julia wasn't surprised that Hunter knew MACV's location, or that he proved to be such an entertaining tour guide. She suspected that he treated most of the women who stepped off the plane from America to one of his private tours. She had to admit, he made a lively companion as he wheeled her around the sprawling base.

Everywhere they went, she saw evidence of the war. Quonset huts and mobile, relocatable facilities the Americans had thrown up to accommodate their presence in-country crowded next to flimsy wooden buildings and crumbling stucco structures left from the French colonial days. Sandbags surrounded the lower half of most buildings. They protected the occupants and helped contain the debris if the structure took a direct hit from incoming rockets, Hunter explained casually.

MACV, headquarters for all U.S. military operations in Vietnam, occupied a huge, hangar-like building on the far side of the base. Julia craned her neck as they drove past its fenced complex. That was where she'd work for the next twelve months, unless Dr. Kissinger's negotiations achieved peace before she completed her tour of duty.

She was still trying to memorize the layout of the sprawling base when Hunter made a right turn and swept past a gate. Armed sentries waved them through; then the high walls of stucco topped with jagged glass and concertina wire were behind them. Ahead stretched a hundred or more yards of ruthlessly cleared no-man's-land.

"Hey, wait a minute," Julia protested, cringing in her seat. A feeling of naked vulnerability swept over her at the sight of that cratered, wire-strewn stretch. "I'm not sure I'm ready for this."

"This is the best time to see Vietnam," Hunter assured her. "Before your job and your American prejudices have had time to set. While your mind is still fresh."

"My mind feels anything but fresh right now."

She glanced around the open space nervously. She half expected to hear the crack of sniper fire at any moment. The war might be winding down, but

American troops still came home in body bags every day.

"Look, I really don't think this is a good idea."

"Trust me, Endicott."

"Give me one good reason why I should. I don't even know you!"

"You will, sweet thing. You will."

Julia swallowed her retort as he swung into the opposite lane to pass a string of motorbikes. Horns tooted raucously. Drivers shook their fists and shouted insults. Hunter cut back into his lane a half second away from a collision with an oncoming truck.

"Lord, I hope you fly better than you drive," Julia gasped.

"Honey, I fly better than I do just about everything." He threw her the slashing grin she was beginning to recognize as his personal trademark. "Except kiss, maybe."

"I'll take your word for that."

Within moments the cleared zone gave way to a tumble of shacks and thatched huts that formed the outskirts of Saigon. As they neared what had once been the shimmering pearl of the French colonial empire, Julia saw the devastation that more than twenty years of warfare had left. Many of the city's outlying buildings were in rubble, victims of rocket or sapper attacks. Those that still stood carried scars in the form of broken windows or cratered walls.

But despite its wounds downtown Saigon teemed with life. Narrow streets crowded with tawdry bars and tattoo parlors soon gave way to wider, tree-lined avenues. Hondas carrying anywhere from two to five people darted around buses and cars and the occasional plodding bullock cart. The stench of diesel fuel mixed with the heady scent of flowers and burning joss sticks from Buddhist shrines.

Eyes wide, Julia drank in the startling contrasts that Saigon presented. Broad boulevards and curved-roofed temples. French street signs and American cars. Western-style mini-skirts and flowing, high-necked silk tunics worn over black pajama pants.

Having trained as a journalist, she tried to catalogue the images that filled her mind, but they were too contradictory, too unfamiliar to capture coherently. She wasn't sure whether she was seeing an Asian city with a patina of European culture, or something caught between the old and the new, belonging to neither.

"That's the Continental Palace," Hunter informed her, sweeping a hand toward a ten-story building on the corner of the main, flower-filled square. "It's headquarters for those *bo chi* who are still in-country. They can charge the bar girls as well as the drinks at the terrace bar to their expense accounts."

"Okay, I'll bite. Who are the *bo chi*?"

Hunter swerved around a corner, cutting off a heavily laden bicycle. The two-wheeled vehicle tipped to one side and dumped a towering basket of produce into the street. A black-clad cyclist shook her fist as the jeep swept past.

"Number ten American! You for sure one fuck-fuck driver!"

Ignoring the shrill insults, Hunter wheeled through the streaming traffic. "*Bo chi* are foreign correspondents, Endicott. The esteemed journalists you'll be dealing with for the next year, if we stay in the war that long."

Julia flicked him a quick look, but saw no sign of the animosity most military personnel felt toward the press corps. In that respect Gabe Hunter stood apart from the many other officers Julia knew. By now she had a sneaking suspicion he stood apart in more ways than that. She'd never met anyone with quite his measure of sheer brass.

It was only when he left the crowded streets behind and drove south, out of the city, that Julia finally experienced the country her father had described in his letters. Here were the endless rice paddies. The water buffalo harnessed two in tandem, pulling heavily laden wooden carts. The women in conical straw hats and the thin, wide-eyed children.

This was Vietnam, once the rice bowl of Asia. A land of thick, impenetrable jungles and sweeping mountains, of lush vegetation and industrious people. The war seemed far away from this quiet, peaceful scene ... until the jeep rounded a bend and the scorched remains of a farmhouse loomed directly ahead. Grim-faced Vietnamese picked through the blackened rubble.

"The Vietcong laid a rocket on it last night," Gabe explained in answer to her look. "They were after a truck convoy en route to Chu Bai and missed."

"A rocket attack? This close to the city?"

His mustache lifted at the squeak in her voice. "Not to worry. You're safe enough. Charlie usually only operates at night."

His breezy assurances didn't calm Julia's jumping nerves. She couldn't quite believe she was in an open jeep, riding through countryside that had sustained a rocket attack mere hours ago. Her scalp tingling, she was about to insist Hunter turn the vehicle around and take her back to the base when he pulled up at a roadside stand. Two Vietnamese women squatted beside a low fire, patiently rolling a mixture of rice and what looked like vegetables in cabbage leaves. Hunter swung out of the jeep and strolled around to the passenger side.

"Come on, Lieutenant." He held out his hand to help her out of the vehicle. "You're about to experience your first Vietnamese meal. *Kemshi*, rice, and cold green tea. That's all a body needs to ward off hunger, disease, and diarrhea ... or bring them on, depending on the strength of your stomach."

Julia hesitated, reluctant to leave the illusory

safety of the jeep and even more reluctant to put her hand in Gabe's. Some deep, ill-defined instinct warned her that once his fingers closed over hers, he might never let go.

"You only go around once, kid."

His eyes glinted with a challenge she couldn't refuse.

"That's true for most of us," Julia muttered, slipping her hand into his. "I'm beginning to wonder about you."

By the time Gabe delivered Julia to the two-story wooden building that housed the women officers, eight hours later, she was limp from exhaustion, yet strangely exhilarated. Her mind whirled with her first impressions of Vietnam, and her stomach grumbled from a combination of highly spiced *kemshi* and a steak grilled to perfection. Fine, aged cognac warmed her veins, adding to her near stupor. She stumbled getting out of the jeep, too tired even to lift her legs. Hunter caught her before she tumbled to the ground and swept her into his arms.

"I love it when women fall all over me," he murmured, his breath warm in her ear.

"I'll just bet you do."

Dipping, he reached for her overnight case. Julia clutched at his neck for balance. Her body slid into his, damp heat fused to heat.

"Hunter, put me down."

"Relax, Lieutenant." He strode toward the

opening in the white wooden fence that surrounded the women's compound. "I know the
way."

"Why doesn't that surprise me?"

Bone tired, she let herself relax against him. Seconds later, she jerked upright as a series of catcalls
and whistles filled the night air.

"Way to go, Hunter!"

"Attaway, Ace."

Her face heating, Julia made out a group of men
and women clustered around a rickety picnic table.
The table was set on a cement slab bounded on three
sides by two-story barracks buildings and a long,
low building Julia guessed housed the latrines. A
string of light bulbs, most of them burned out, was
draped from balcony to balcony and provided dim
illumination for the narrow patio area.

A tall, lanky officer in tiger-striped fatigues lifted
a beer in salute. "That's a new record, Gabe, even
for you. Less than ten hours in-country and she's
already in your arms."

At Julia's hissed instructions, her escort let her
slide out of his arms. Embarrassed, she tugged at
her uniform jacket to straighten it.

A woman stepped out of the shadows. Dark-
haired and doe-eyed, she wore baggy green
fatigues that still managed to display a lush, well-
rounded figure. A silver bar glinted on each collar.

"Hello, Julia," she said with a small smile. "I'm
Claire Simmons. I've been waiting for you."

Dismayed, Julia extended her hand. "I'm so sorry. I didn't know you were waiting."

The lieutenant's smile softened into one of genuine warmth. "That's okay. When Gabe said he was picking you up at the air terminal, I knew you were in good hands."

"You got that right," Hunter concurred with a lazy grin. Wrapping an arm around Claire's waist, he pulled her against his side. "The best hands this side of the Pacific."

With careless grace he bent and brushed her lips with his.

Surprise held Julia stock still. It was followed swiftly by disgust that she'd made herself such an easy mark. She should have known better than to fall for the pilot's cocky grin and smooth line. Obviously, Gabe Hunter lived up to his name.

Claire disengaged herself from his embrace a moment later, her face flushed. Digging into the pocket of her fatigues, she pulled out a small box.

"I got you a welcome gift."

Hesitantly Julia opened the box. Inside was a tiny silver medal strung on a delicate chain. She lifted the oblong disc, trying to identify the engraved image in the fading light.

"It's a St. Christopher medal," Claire explained with a shy smile. "He's the patron saint of travelers. We Catholics pray to him to keep us safe while we're away from home."

Julia wasn't Catholic, nor was she particularly

superstitious. But she wasn't about to turn down any offer of safekeeping. Slipping the chain over her head, she tucked the small disc inside her uniform. The medal felt cool and smooth against her sticky skin.

"I hope St. Christopher watches over you while you're here."

Claire Simmons's sincerity and warmth touched Julia's heart. "Thank you."

"You're welcome. Hey, you must be exhausted. Your duffel bag's already in your room. Come on, I'll show you to your super deluxe suite." Ignoring the hoots of laughter her comment engendered, Claire took the overnight case from Hunter's hand. "It's not much, but it's all yours . . . except for the rice bugs and the geckos, of course."

Julia followed her up a flight of stairs, then along a narrow balcony to a corner room. Glancing down into the courtyard while her sponsor jimmied a key into a flimsy, slatted wooden door, she caught the casual salute that Hunter tipped to her.

She turned her back on him. A moment later the wooden door creaked open, and she stepped into the eight-by-ten room that would be her home for the next twelve months.

THREE

With the intensity of a hawk marking its prey, Special Agent Ted Marsh surveyed his suspect.

"So you knew from the first day you arrived in Vietnam that Captain Hunter was involved with Lieutenant Simmons?"

Colonel Endicott seemed unaware of his scrutiny or his prompting. Her wide, unfocused eyes stared at the small window behind him. They were distinctive eyes, the investigator noted dispassionately. A deep, shadowy green, with a network of lines radiating from their corners, imperceptible to any but the closest observer.

Those tiny lines gave Marsh the mental edge he needed with this suspect. They made her more human to him, less perfect than her smooth sweep of silvery blond hair, flawless skin, and high cheekbones would indicate. As he studied the face across from him, Marsh began to understand Captain Hunter's fatal fascination with this woman.

"Colonel Endicott?" he prompted.

She blinked. A frown drew her brows together. "Sorry. What did you say?"

"I was just confirming that you knew Captain Hunter was involved with Lieutenant Simmons from the first day you met him."

"Yes, I knew."

Marsh tapped his pencil on the table, measuring the cool, clipped response. This woman was tougher than she looked. A hell of a lot tougher.

They'd been at it for over an hour now. He'd listened intently as she described her first meeting with Hunter, had drawn her out when she faltered in her narrative. With a skill mastered during his twenty years in the investigative business, Marsh had subtly encouraged the subject to reveal far more of herself than she realized. The picture she'd painted of a determined, idealistic second lieutenant's arrival in Vietnam fit the detailed profile Marsh had put together on Julia Endicott the day after he took over this case.

The only child of a career Air Force officer, she'd graduated from college with honors. At a time when many of her classmates were shouting protests and throwing blood at men and women in uniform, she'd accepted a commission upon graduation and volunteered for Vietnam right out of Officer Training School. After her year in 'Nam, she'd served at a number of bases and risen rapidly through the officer ranks. She'd held some very impressive command and staff billets, and excelled in them all, according to her efficiency reports.

Despite the wealth of detail Marsh had extracted from her personnel files, he still didn't have a feel for the woman behind the officer. Why hadn't she ever married? Where was the passion behind those cool, enigmatic green eyes? She'd unleashed that passion once, if even half the details Marsh had uncovered about her and the deceased were true. Trying to understand her, he picked up the questioning where he'd left off.

"Were you surprised that Captain Hunter would spend an entire day with you when he was seeing Lieutenant Simmons on a regular basis?"

The ghost of a smile twisted her lips. "Surprised? No."

"Why not? From what you've told us, Captain Hunter came on to you pretty strong from the moment you stepped off the plane. Didn't it bother you that he'd put the make on one woman while seeing another?"

Her smile took on a mocking edge. "You've never done that, Mr. Marsh?"

"We're not talking about me here, Colonel."

She acknowledged the hit with a small nod. "No, we're not."

Beside him, Barbara Lyles stirred. She was a good agent, one of the best, which was why Marsh had requested her for this case. She'd played her role as the listener and observer well this past hour. He sensed Barbara's interest as Julia Endicott lifted her chin and responded to his query.

"In answer to your question, it didn't bother me that Gabe—that Captain Hunter spent so much time with me on my first day in-country. It's part of the air commando's code, or at least it was back then, to hustle anything in skirts. Everyone knew the rules, and no one got hurt as long as they didn't take things seriously."

"But someone did get hurt. Very hurt."

She met his look squarely. "Not by me."

Marsh fought a reluctant admiration for the woman who faced him across the conference table. In his experience, few Air Force personnel gave coherent statements when confronted with serious charges. For the most part, they weren't hardened criminals. They stuttered and stammered and eventually tripped themselves up with their own contradictory stories. Or they were so shaken that they refused to talk at all without an attorney present. In the last hour, however, Colonel Julia Endicott had done no stuttering or stammering. She'd pulled her professionalism around her like a cloak and answered every question he had put to her. Her low, throaty voice—not at all the voice of a senior officer, at least none that Marsh had served under— had steadied by imperceptible degrees.

He admired her composure, but it sure as hell made his job more difficult. He'd let her set the pace, let her tell her story in her own words. She'd grown comfortable with him, he decided. Too comfortable. He needed to throw her off balance.

"Apparently the woman you knew as Lieutenant Simmons wasn't quite as familiar with the rules of the game as you were."

"What do you mean?"

"Just that the recovery of Captain Hunter's remains seems to have generated some painful questions she doesn't have the answers for."

He caught the faint, reflexive jerk of the colonel's head. For the first time a crack appeared in her facade.

"When did you speak with her?" she asked.

"Last week, after the final autopsy and forensic reports came in. She took the probable cause of death hard."

When Colonel Endicott drew in a swift breath, Marsh didn't so much as flick an eyelash. But his pulse began to pound with a familiar heaviness.

"The fact that the St. Christopher medal was found with Captain Hunter's remains really distressed her," he added deliberately. "She's the one who identified it for us."

"Oh, no!"

The low exclamation set his blood to hammering. He felt the way he did during sex, eager to reach the breaking point but determined to hold back in order to coax the response he wanted.

"Claire told us that she'd given you the medal

your first night in Vietnam," he said softly, his eyes
on her face. "You've just confirmed that."

He paused, waiting for her to comment. She kept
silent. The opaque green eyes hid her thoughts
from his searching gaze. The predator in Marsh was
poised to swoop in for the kill.

"She said you put it on right then. You got
another chain, a longer one, so the medal wouldn't
show with your uniform, and always wore it."

"Yes, I did."

Once more her gaze drifted to the window
behind him. Marsh hardened his voice, forcing her
attention back.

"She told us that she couldn't imagine how Captain Hunter could have been in possession of that
medal. Unless . . . "

He let the unfinished phrase hang on the air
between them. With a sudden tension in his gut, he
watched the blood drain from Julia Endicott's face.

"Are—are you saying that Claire thinks I . . . ?"
She stopped, fisting her hands together tightly.
"Did Claire say that I killed Gabe?"

"No," Marsh replied truthfully, "she didn't say
that."

Her eyes burned with a sudden intensity. Then
she thrust back her chair and stood. Both Marsh
and his partner scrambled to their feet. Standing
ramrod straight, Colonel Endicott faced them
across the expanse of polished wood.

"I'm terminating this interview here and now."

He wasn't about to let her go. Not now. Not when he sensed that he was close to breaking through. "I'm not finished with my questions, Colonel Endicott."

"I'm finished with my answers. For the moment, anyway."

Marsh rocked back on his heels, allowing no sign of his disappointment to show on his face. The vulnerable woman of a few moments ago had vanished. In her place stood a senior officer.

"I take it this means that you intend to consult with an attorney?" he commented.

"I should," she replied with a touch of bitterness. "I certainly should. But first I want to see Claire."

"I'm sorry, I can't allow that."

Placing both palms on the table, Julia Endicott leaned forward. Shadows no longer darkened her green eyes. They glittered with swift, sudden anger.

"Don't make the mistake of confusing me with that naive lieutenant I told you about a few moments ago, Mr. Marsh. I've gained a lot of experience since Vietnam, both on the Air Staff and in the field. What's more, I spent three long years as a training wing commander. I know how the Air Force legal system works."

She straightened, her nostrils flaring. "Unless and until you have enough evidence to convince a staff judge advocate that charges should be preferred against me, I'm answerable only to those in my chain of command. Not to you."

Marsh fought to keep his face impassive. Dammit, how had he lost control of this interview?

"If you know the legal system," Barbara Lyles said, entering the conversation for the first time, "then you know that it'll be easier on all of us if you cooperate and answer our questions."

Colonel Endicott sent the agent a contemptuous glance. "Easier for you perhaps. Somehow I don't envision a murder investigation ever being 'easy' on the suspect."

Turning on her heel, she headed for the door. Marsh wasn't going to let her walk out without voicing the question that had brought him and Julia Endicott to this small windowless conference room.

"Colonel!"

When she swiveled back to face him, he went for the jugular. "Did you kill Captain Hunter?"

"No!" Her voice quavered with fury. "And I resent the hell out of the fact that you and General Titus could even think that I did."

"You haven't heard all the evidence against you," he said bluntly.

"I will," she promised fiercely. "I'll hear every word, read every scrap of misinformation you've gathered. You can count on that, Mr. Marsh. But first I'm going to talk to Claire."

The agent hesitated, then came to a swift decision. He wouldn't get any more out of her now. Not with her fire up and determination setting her face into tight, unyielding lines. Reaching into his suit coat, he pulled out a business card.

"Call me if you want to continue our interview later tonight, after you've spoken to Claire. Otherwise, we'll meet here tomorrow morning. Shall we say eight o'clock?"

He couched the question in polite terms, but they both knew it wasn't a request. For the first time color slashed across her cheeks. She took the card and swept out of the office without another word.

The next time, Marsh promised himself as he stared at the closed door, Colonel Endicott wouldn't be the one who terminated their interview.

"Whew!" Barbara pressed the stop button on the tape recorder. "She's going to be a tough one to break."

Shoving his hands in his pockets, he fingered the loose change. "I've broken tougher."

Julia made her way back to her office through the echoing halls. She felt disoriented, displaced, as though she'd last walked these corridors a lifetime ago.

Two staff officers rounded the corner and gave a respectful "Afternoon, ma'am."

She forced herself to respond, although her heart jackhammered so painfully in her chest she could hardly breathe. She had to call Claire. Surely, Claire, of all people, wouldn't . . . couldn't . . . believe that she'd killed Gabe Hunter.

Shoving open the door to the Public Affairs Directorate, she brushed past her secretary's desk. The small dark-haired woman rose and followed her into her office.

"Where on earth have you been? I've got a stack of calls for you, and your staff is standing by to get your chop on the final base-closure list release. Did you get the word the list passed the subcommittee by voice vote?"

Julia stared at her blankly. "What?"

"The base-closure list. It's out of subcommittee and on its way to the full Armed Services committee. The chairman has promised to get it to a floor vote before the Senate breaks for Christmas. Didn't you get the note we sent down to the vice chief's office?"

"No, I didn't get the note."

Her secretary clucked in exasperation. "Typical. We can bounce satellite beams off the moon, or whatever, but we can't seem to get one little message passed to the person who needs it in this zoo."

"It doesn't matter, Maria."

Desperate to call Claire, Julia didn't want to take the time to explain what was still unexplainable in her own mind. She wouldn't be able to handle Maria's shock and disbelief right now. She could barely handle her own.

Her stomach heaved as she realized she'd have to turn her duties and responsibilities over to the chief of media relations. In the director's absence she had no choice. General Titus had relieved her. Hamilton would have to shoulder the burdens of Air Force public affairs until their boss returned.

"I need to make a phone call," she told the secretary. "Ask Colonel Hamilton to stand by. I'd like to talk to him and to you after I make the call."

"Will do," the efficient Maria replied, heading for her desk.

Deep, still silence surrounded Julia when the heavy wooden door shut out the sounds of the busy outer office. Her gaze moved to the bank of windows, now painted black by the early winter dusk. She found it bitterly ironic that she'd walked out of this office buoyed by a bright sunlight rare for D.C. in December and come back to a darkness that mirrored the despair clutching her chest.

Her knees suddenly weak, she sank into the chair behind her desk. Do it now, she admonished herself. Do it now, before you lose your nerve completely.

Call Claire.

Her fingers shook as she pulled the Rolodex out of the credenza and set it beside her phone. One clear, polished nail slid over the index tabs until she found the one she was searching for. Lifting the receiver, she punched in the number of the woman who had once been her closest friend. The woman who had married Gabe Hunter just weeks before he disappeared.

"Hunter residence. May I help you?"

"Claire?"

A sharp, frozen stillness settled over the line.

"Claire, it's Julia."

She waited while the silence stretched endlessly. Her palm slick, Julia gripped the phone. Her throat felt raw as she forced out the words:

"I just heard about Gabe."

A strangled sound, half sob, half gasp, beat like a panicky moth at the walls of her heart.

"I need to talk to you."

"No." Claire's whisper barely carried over the phone. "I don't want to talk to you. Not now. Maybe not ever again."

"You have to."

"No."

"Dammit, you owe me that much." Julia cringed at the desperate note in her voice.

"Whatever I once owed you was buried beside the road to Long Binh!"

Closing her eyes against the pain that swept her, Julia let her head drop back against the chair.

"Oh, God!" Like brittle, over-stressed ice, Claire's voice cracked and splintered. "I'm sorry, Jules. I still can't . . . grasp it. After all these years. I didn't have any warning. They—they just showed up at my door. In uniform. Like the first time."

Like a woman old before her time, Julia wearily lifted her head. "We can't talk about this over the phone. I'll drive down. I can be there by . . . " She glanced at the clock on the wall. "By nine."

For a moment she thought Claire would refuse. But the ties forged two decades ago in the fires of war proved stronger than the specter now hanging between them.

"All right."

Carefully Julia replaced the receiver. She sat staring at the dark windows for a long, long time before she lifted the phone once more and buzzed Maria.

"Would you come in now? And bring Colonel Hamilton with you."

An agonizing hour later, Julia's breath frosted on the icy darkness as she fumbled the key into the ignition of her two-seater Mercedes. A promotion gift to herself when she'd made colonel, the sleek sports car usually gave her a sense of quiet joy. Tonight she felt only a choking mixture of despair, fear, and shame. The scene she'd just gone through with her secretary and her subordinate would stay burned in her mind for years to come.

Julia knew their stunned shock was only the first taste of what she could expect in the days ahead. As a public affairs officer she'd worked damage control for too many sordid scandals to hope something as sensational as her removal from office wouldn't spread at mach speed. Her stomach churned at the thought of walking through the halls of the Pentagon, of catching the sidelong glances, hearing the whispered comments.

She felt an overwhelming urge to run, to hide for a day, a week, forever. She wouldn't run, though, and she sure as hell wouldn't hide. She wouldn't give Gabe Hunter that final triumph.

Damn you, Gabe! Damn you to the hell you deserve!

Her hand shaking, Julia twisted the key. The Mercedes turned over with a muted, well-mannered growl. Gripping the wheel with both hands, she backed out of her reserved slot and joined the stream of commuter traffic heading south on I-95. It would take her a good two hours to reach the small town a few miles south of Richmond where Claire Hunter made her home. Julia needed the time, every minute of it, to get herself under control.

The bumper-to-bumper traffic crawled south, forming a river of red taillights in the inky darkness. A few flakes of snow danced in the golden sweep of the Mercedes' lights. The forecast predicted intermittent flurries tonight, Julia remembered. She caught herself making a mental note to leave for work earlier than usual tomorrow morning. Even the hint of bad weather always caused total chaos inside the beltway.

Her nails dug into the leather-wrapped steering wheel. She didn't have to leave early, she reminded herself savagely. She didn't have to get to the Pentagon by six to review the early bird clippings from the early morning editions. She didn't have to research the hot news items before she attended the secretary of the Air Force's staff meeting at eight.

She wouldn't be attending the secretary's staff meeting.

How had it come to this? she wondered bleakly. All the years of hard work? All the late hours and remote tours of duty? The early promotions, the service schools, the challenges and exhilaration of command? How had it all come down to this?

Relieved of all duties.

Stripped of her authority and responsibilities.

An officer whose past could very well destroy her future.

They'd never envisioned it would end this way, she and Claire. All those years ago when they'd shared so many dreams, so many hopes. Julia would be a general, the intelligence officer had predicted confidently. As for herself, well, she wasn't as sure that she wanted to make the Air Force a career.

Besides there was Gabe . . .

FOUR

October 31, 1971,
Tan Son Nhut Air Base

"He needs me, Jules."

Claire Simmons's soft voice barely carried over the liquid strains of the Fifth Dimension. The popular group's latest vocal poured from the speakers being rigged on the roof of the women's quarters in preparation for tonight's Halloween Bash. The lead singer's lament about Bill, her Bill, streamed through the fixed wooden slats over the screened windows and bounced off the plywood walls of Julia's eight-by-ten room.

She'd miss the revelry tonight, since she had the stick as the MACV public affairs duty officer. She didn't mind, though. Vietnam was still too new, too intense, for her to need partying to blunt its impact.

Besides, there was Gabe . . .

Dragging a brush through her shoulder-length bob, Julia glanced in the mirror at her friend. The brunette sat on the metal bunk, her back propped against the wall.

"He needs you, Claire? Gabe Hunter doesn't strike me as the kind of man who needs anyone."

"Yes, he does." Metal bedsprings squeaked as the other woman drew up her knees. "He just hasn't gotten around to realizing it yet."

"Watch it," Julia drawled. "You're even starting to sound like him."

Smiling, Claire raised her voice to be heard over the beat of the music. "You've only been in-country a little over three weeks. You haven't had time to get to know him. There's another man behind that cocky swagger and ridiculous mustache. A kind man."

At Julia's derisive snort, Claire's smile softened, deepened. Her face took on the luminous, Madonna-like beauty it often did when talking about Gabe.

"He's been kind to me," she said gently. "He saw how—how overwhelmed I was when I first arrived. You know, being one of just a few round-eyes on base. So many men hit on me, and Gabe sort of set himself up as my protector. Those careless kisses of his have kept the worst of the hounds away."

Those careless kisses, Julia thought indignantly, had staked Hunter's public claim to the lush, well-rounded intelligence officer.

"It started as a sort of a joke between us," Claire confessed, hugging her knees. "But now it's more. A lot more."

"Is it?"

"For me it is. For him . . . " Her shoulders lifted under her khaki T-shirt. "I've become a habit. I'm comfortable, and always there for him."

Julia tossed the brush down, as irritated by her friend's passive role as by Gabe Hunter's all-too-casual acceptance of that role. Planting both hands on her hips she glowered at Claire.

"This *is* the seventies, you know. Women don't have to be 'comfortable' anymore. Haven't you heard about the National Organization for Women? Or the Equal Rights Amendment?"

"I'm not about to burn my bra," Claire replied with a bubble of laughter. "As top-heavy as I am, I'd fall flat on my face without it."

"That's not what I meant, and you know it!"

Sighing, Claire rested her chin on her knees. "I know. I'm not stupid, Jules, but I know Gabe. He grew up the youngest of four brothers. His brothers all thought they had to toughen him, Detroit–style. He still feels he has to prove he's harder, and faster, and better than anyone else. He's just beginning to understand that he doesn't have to prove anything with me."

The love shimmering in her friend's brown eyes made Julia acutely uncomfortable. She had her own opinion of Gabe Hunter, one that hadn't changed in the weeks since he'd swept her up in his arms. In the face of Claire's tender feelings, though, she'd kept her opinion to herself these past weeks. Mentally biting her tongue, she rooted around in her metal wall locker for a pair of black socks.

The locker, the bed, and the pint-sized refrigerator she'd purchased, sight unseen, from the previous occupant of the room constituted the only furnishings in her quarters. She couldn't have crammed in anything else. She could barely turn around in the tight space as it was.

She hadn't been lucky enough to snag an air conditioner yet, but with the continuing draw-down of U.S. troops, Julia had hopes of buying one of the ancient hand-me-downs that passed from officer to officer with each rotation. In the meantime she relied on the fan perched atop the fridge to stir the humid air enough to let her sleep at night. As spartan as her quarters were, though, it didn't occur to her to complain. The wooden barracks buildings occupied by the women officers and air crews were palaces compared to the living conditions of the grunts in the field.

When Julia turned away from the locker, socks in hand, Claire took up her argument again.

"You'd like Gabe if you just let yourself get to know him."

"I don't have to like him. You do. That's all that matters."

Julia tugged on a sock, ignoring Claire's troubled expression. She knew the antagonism that crackled whenever she and Gabe got within a few yards of each other disturbed her friend. Despite Julia's growing closeness with the other woman, or perhaps because of it, she couldn't bring herself to unbend around Hunter.

Nor could she shake her inexplicable, irritating, annoying attraction to the man.

She'd tried to avoid him these past weeks. Certainly, she'd been busy enough. Like most other headquarters personnel, she worked twelve- to fourteen-hour days. Her job required her to draft responses to the continuous requests for information from the media of all nations and analyze their coverage of the war, line by line, broadcast minute by broadcast minute.

At first she'd been intimidated by the constant demands for information coming into her section in MACV's Public Information Division. She'd done her best to respond promptly, earning some points with the media still in-country. She wasn't entirely comfortable releasing battle statistics without authorization from her boss, but she was learning the ropes—fast!

For the first week or two she'd returned from work and flopped onto her bunk in total exhaustion, as drained by the muggy heat as by her demanding job. Only recently had she begun to venture out in the evenings. With coworkers she'd dined at both the USAF and the VNAF officers clubs on the base. A stringer for AP had invited her to dinner at the terrace restaurant of the Continental Palace, which so many of the journalists made their unofficial headquarters. A couple of times she'd joined the other women and their assorted companions gathered around the rickety picnic tables between the women's barracks buildings to share cold beer and hot war stories.

Despite Julia's long days at work and her best efforts to avoid him, Gabe Hunter kept invading her space. He'd strolled over that night at the officers club and accepted her coworkers' offer to share a table. Doubling up at the jam-packed club was a standard courtesy, but the brush of Hunter's thigh against hers raised goose bumps on her skin and destroyed the enjoyment of the Vietnamese chef's valiant attempt at a Mexican buffet.

A few days later, he'd stopped by her office at MACV to introduce a buddy who'd flown in her father's squadron at a previous base. Julia shared a cup of coffee with the aviator and gratefully added his reminiscences to her treasure house of memories. All through their conversation, however, she'd remained aware of Gabe Hunter sitting just outside the periphery of her vision, his black boot planted on an open desk drawer.

More than once she'd caught sight of him among the group gathered around the picnic table outside the women's barracks. She'd opted not to join the convivial group those nights, pleading fatigue or work or the need to write letters.

What she couldn't escape, though, was Claire's devotion to Hunter. Often, Julia knew, the intel

officer spent her nights at the hootch Hunter shared
with other fliers. The parties at the Zoo were the
best on Tan Son Nhut, or so knowledgeable sources
had informed her. Julia had declined several invi-
tations to experience them herself. She didn't
want to put herself within Hunter's reach in that
environment.

For the same reasons she'd agreed to pull duty
officer instead of attending tonight's Halloween
bash. She had no desire to see the slavish adoration
in Claire's face when Hunter condescended to
remember her presence. Nor did she care to watch
him casually pull Claire into his embrace while
joking with his buddies as if she didn't exist.

Irritated anew on her friend's behalf, Julia
reached for the dark blue slacks that, along with a
short-sleeve light blue cotton blouse, constituted
the USAF female utility uniform. She hadn't yet
reached the point of wearing green men's fatigues,
as most of the women did, Claire included.
Although the heat and humidity made the tucked-
in blue blouse uncomfortable, the "greenies" still
looked sloppy to her. She suspected that they'd
grow on her, though, with the coming of the hot
season.

She slipped the St. Christopher medal Claire had
given her inside the neckline of the blue shirt. Cool
and smooth, the silver medallion joined the dog tags
nestled in the cleft between her breasts, safely out of
sight. Uniform regulations prohibited the display

of any jewelry except a watch or an ID bracelet, although Julia had noticed that she appeared to be one of the few who adhered to rules. Many of the women wore earrings or gold chains even with their fatigues, while a surprising number of troops sported peace symbols or braided black power bracelets.

Her father, Julia thought as she grabbed her purse, would *not* have approved of the modern Air Force. But he hadn't lived to see the race riots that swept the country in '68, she reminded herself, or the emerging women's movement.

"I guess I'd better go help with the party decorations," Claire said, pushing herself off the bed. "You sure you can't get someone to cover for you a while tonight? I'm told the guys from Red Horse have come up with some really gruesome costumes."

"I can imagine. The combat engineers are nothing if not resourceful. I'll pass on this one, though. I've got the first draft of the monthly battle stats to pull together for public release tomorrow."

"Okay. See you, Jules."

With Claire's departure, Julia shoved her wallet, a compact, and a lipstick into her black leather purse, then checked the zippered pocket that held her father's Smith & Wesson.

Julia was one of the few of the rear-area support troops who carried a weapon. Most of the M-16s and service-issue sidearms remained under lock and key in metal storage containers at various duty sections to prevent loss or the occasional drunken duel. No wonder the grunts in the field had a host of names for headquarters personnel, Julia thought sardonically. The kindest of the nicknames included typewriter commandos, PX cowboys, and RATs— short for rear-area types, or rearies.

She'd been required to obtain special authorization to bring the weapon in-country. Doggedly she'd filed the repetitious forms. She'd been determined to carry her father's pistol back to his war. Its heavy weight felt familiar and comforting as she picked up her purse. Her father's silver oak leaf winked at her from the inside lining before she closed the flap. Slinging the purse over her shoulder, she left the room.

Without the cooling stream of air from the fan, her skin dewed with a now familiar, sticky dampness. By the time she'd taken a few steps along the upper balcony, her freshly washed hair had gone limp. Waving to the crowd in the patio below, Julia made her way to the stairs that led to the street. A five-minute hop-tac ride took her from the laughter and pre-party revelry to the grim realities of war as recapped by the monthly battle stats.

The war didn't stand down on Sunday, but the MACV staff went to reduced manning in most sections on Sunday evenings. Julia had worked a short shift that morning, gone back to the officers quarters to shower and grab a few hours of sleep, and would now cover the Public Information Directorate until eight a.m.

After the muggy heat outside, the air-conditioned chill of the headquarters raised goose bumps all over her body. Shivering, Julia took a brief situation report from the officer she was relieving, then checked the dailies—the teletyped reprints of articles from U.S. and international publications.

Julia thumbed through the stack of articles. Of late the media's focus was shifting more and more from Saigon to Paris and Hanoi. Given the pullout of U.S. combat troops and "Vietnamization" of the war, the shift was understandable from a newsman's perspective. As her friend from AP put it so succinctly, Asians killing Asians didn't play on the nightly news in Podunksville, USA.

From a participant's perspective, however, the war remained very real and very immediate. U.S. servicemen still went home in body bags. New troops still arrived in-country as replacements, scared and confused and determined not to be the last American GI killed in Vietnam.

Frowning over the thrust of the headlines, Julia made her way to the small, partitioned room that housed the MACV media relations branch. The duty NCO was already at his desk.

"How's it going, Sergeant Malinski?"

"Good, Lieutenant. Damn good. Four more hours, and I cross off another one."

The beefy public affairs specialist hooked a

thumb at the twelve-month calendar cascading down the wall behind his desk. A sea of red X's obliterated most of the days leading to November 11.

"I'm so short now, I can walk under the door instead of through it," the Army sergeant said smugly. "Ten days and a wake-up, then it's good-bye Vietnam, *adios* body counts, *sayanora* red-assed, left-wing liberals disguised as reporters and hello . . . "

Julia flashed him a warning look. She'd made it clear her first days on the job that she wouldn't allow the wholesale media bashing her predecessor had evidently permitted.

"Sorry," Malinski mumbled.

Slinging her purse over the back of a chair, she raked a hand through her limp hair. "Have we got the preliminary weekly stats?"

"We do, and you're not going to believe the numbers."

She stiffened. "Bad?"

"Good. Incredibly good." Malinski waved a typed sheet in a ham-like fist. "Five U.S. KIA's for this week. Only five! That's the lowest weekly toll in six years. If things don't heat up too much tonight, we'll hit a new monthly low, too."

Only five U.S. soldiers killed in action.

The dull ache Julia had carried in her heart for the past four years sharpened to a blade of pain. *Only* five families would have to deal with a devastating loss. *Only* five women would have to clutch a folded flag to their breast as they watched their husband or son lowered into a freshly dug grave.

Ignoring the lancing hurt, Julia forced herself to concentrate on her professional responsibilities. With a swift competency mastered in the past three weeks, she used the composite weekly statistics to draft the standard monthly report for release tomorrow afternoon. Her fingers flew over the keys of the blue IBM Selectric.

U.S. MILITARY CASUALTIES
MACV PUBLIC INFORMATION DIVISION
1 November 1971
U.S. military losses for the month of October 1971 include 108 killed and 694 wounded in action.
In accordance with President Nixon's Vietnamization policy, phased withdrawals of U.S. military personnel continue. U.S. troop strength dropped below 200,000 effective this date. This constitutes the lowest number of U.S. personnel in South Vietnam since December 1965.

Julia paused, staring at the date she'd just typed.

Vietnam had been just a word to her in 1965. A place where America had vowed to halt the spread of communism. Several of her father's peers had served as advisers in the distant country. They'd talked about guerilla-style tactics and a slowly escalating American commitment in men and equipment, but Julia had been too involved in her school activities and too caught up in the throes of teenage crushes to appreciate the snippets of conversation exchanged among her parents and their friends. Two years later Vietnam had claimed her father.

Now the Americans were pulling out. The war was over, or almost over, according to the statistics and the public policy statements emanating from the White House. Despite the numbers, despite the policy statements, though, men were still dying in Vietnam.

Julia's fingers curled over the keys. Dammit, she hadn't come over here to type numbers. Spinning around, she rapped out a quick order.

"Get me the names, ranks, and units of the five men killed in action this week. And any personal information you can find out about them."

The sergeant stared at her in surprise. "We don't include that kind of data in the monthly statistical summary, Lieutenant."

"This time we will. I want to make this release more human."

The NCO's brow creased. "The last guidance from the JUSPAO office at the embassy is to downplay the American role over here. You know, *de*personalize it."

"I know what the guidance is, Sergeant. Just get the information, will you?"

Her tone was mild enough, but the overweight public affairs specialist didn't miss the determination behind the request.

"Yes, ma'am. I'll see what Casualty Reporting can come up with."

With Malinski's absence, the partitioned room settled into a quiet broken only by the murmur of audiovisual specialists reviewing combat footage in the small theater across the hall and an occasional clatter from the bank of teletype machines. Swiftly, Julia completed the standard release, which included brief summaries of ground action and air strikes U.S. personnel had participated in during the month that would end in just a few hours. She'd update the draft with the final stats as reported by the four military services tomorrow.

Sergeant Malinski returned some time later with the bare facts he'd been able to glean from the Casual Reporting System: Name. Branch of service. Rank. Date of birth. Home of record. Next of kin. Number of dependents. Date of death.

Julia skimmed the information, then sent the reluctant sergeant upstairs to pump the G-1 duty officer for more details from personnel records.

In Malinski's absence, she pawed through the daily "activity" reports forwarded up the chain of command from the public affairs officers in the field. It took awhile, but finally she found the specific incidents that had resulted in the five deaths. With those reports in front of her, Julia began to sow the seeds of a story in the dry, unfertile ground of the monthly battle summary.

During the week of 31 October, U.S. forces in South Vietnam sustained the lowest casualty figures since Marines in full battle gear splashed ashore at DaNang in 1965.

Five U.S. servicemen died during this week. Two Army. Two Air Force. One Marine. The youngest was nineteen, the oldest, thirty-four.

They came from across America, these five men. From New Jersey. Alabama. Texas. South Dakota. California. Two were single, three married. One was the father of four.

Her fingers flew over the keys. In succinct phrases she emphasized the diversity these five men had brought to the common crucible of Vietnam.

"Hey, Endicott."

Julia jumped. Her fingers skidded on the keys, leaving a line of r's across the page. Still caught up in the intensity of her thoughts, she scowled at the unexpected and unwanted visitor.

"What are you doing here?"

Hunter strolled into her office, undaunted by her less than enthusiastic greeting. Glass clinked as he plopped a paper bag on top of the scattered papers and took possession of one end of her desk.

"Claire said you couldn't make the party tonight, so I decided to bring it to you."

"Thanks, but no thanks, Hunter. As you might have noticed, I'm on duty."

His mustache tipped. "I'm not."

Julia tilted her chair back, away from his dominating presence. Suddenly, the office that had seemed so empty just moments before felt crowded.

Too crowded.

If she swung her chair around, her knees would knock Hunter's. Unlike hers, his legs were bare. Bare and muscular and covered with the same gold fuzz that curled across the broad slopes of his pecs. Casually, Julia let her gaze drift down the gaudy orange and purple parrots decorating the Hawaiian shirt that hung unbuttoned over equally garish Bermuda shorts. He'd wrapped a string of love beads around one ankle, she noted. Blue rubber shower clogs completed the ensemble.

"Is that the best you could do for a costume?"

"Costume?" He assumed a wounded expression. "This shirt cost me ten bucks during my R&R in Hawaii."

"You got taken."

Laughter glinted in his blue eyes. "You didn't see the little *wahinie* who was selling it."

Julia wasn't buying his brand of rakish charm. Not this time. Folding her arms, she regarded him steadily.

"Just out of curiosity, did you take your R&R with this little *wahinie* before or after you staked your public claim to Claire?"

The lazy laughter didn't leave his face, but his

voice took on a mocking edge that scraped against Julia's nerves like fingernails on a chalkboard.

"Does it matter?"

"It matters," she snapped. "To me, anyway."

"It shouldn't, Endicott. I haven't made Claire any promises. I never make promises I can't keep."

Julia couldn't miss the warning . . . or the challenge. To her disgust, an insidious desire to rise to that challenge licked at her veins. God, she'd love to take him down a peg or two!

The only problem was, she suspected Gabe Hunter would take her down with him.

FIVE

"I trusted you."

Claire didn't try to contain the pain in her voice. She couldn't have even if she'd wanted to. She closed her eyes to the muted, soothing colors of her living room and saw only the blacks and browns and greens of a long-ago war. Swallowing the rawness in her throat, she lifted her lids and let her old friend glimpse the agony she'd caused.

"Damn you, Julia. I trusted you."

The woman opposite her flinched. In stark contrast to the wine-colored wingback chair, Julia's face appeared pale, almost bloodless. She leaned forward, every line in her body taut. "You loved Gabe, but you trusted me. Think about that."

This time it was Claire who winced. The words struck home. "I can't think about anything but my husband," she said bitterly. "And your betrayal."

"I didn't betray your trust or our friendship."

"Didn't you?"

"No."

The two women stared at each other for long, agonizing moments, unable to breach the chasm that had yawned between them.

Once they'd been closer than sisters, Claire recalled with another shaft of pain. Once they'd shared laughter and tears and precious CARE packages from home. How many times had she and Julia gathered in one or the other's tiny sweat box of a room to talk about the war, the events happening Stateside, the damned heat and humidity? How many evenings had they munched on stale crackers spread with processed cheese, washed down with a Mateus or Lancer's Vin Rose purchased for less than two dollars a bottle at the Class VI store?

Most evenings, Claire recalled with a clarity so sharp it cut like a razor through her searing hurt. Every evening that they weren't working and Gabe hadn't claimed her attention.

After Vietnam—after Gabe—the ties forged between her and Julia during those months had stretched but never broken. Julia's subsequent assignments had taken her all over the world. She'd spent a tour in Korea, and served on General Schwartzkopf's staff during Desert Storm. Across the years and the miles, she'd kept in touch, and Claire had cherished their friendship.

Now it lay like a living thing between them, mortally wounded. Dying before their eyes.

Claire gripped her hands together so tightly that

her wedding band cut into the skin at the base of her palm. She glanced down, her eyes glazed with unshed tears. The plain gold band glinted dully in the light from the lamps scattered around the living room.

Years ago, when she'd bought this house for herself and her son—Gabe's son—Claire had furnished this room around Davey's boyhood needs. Now, with David married and raising sons of his own, she'd filled it with the Queen Anne furnishings she loved. The room was all rich jewel tones, framed colonial prints, and rose-scented potpourri that balanced the sharp, woodsy tang of the pine fire that usually crackled in the brick fireplace.

The hearth stood empty tonight, though. As empty and cold as Claire's voice as she forced herself to admit the truth she'd kept locked inside her heart for more than two decades.

"I wasn't blind, Julia. Or stupid. I watched Gabe's fascination with you grow every day."

"I didn't encourage it. You know I didn't."

"No, you didn't," Claire said slowly, painfully. "That's what challenged him. He was determined to break through the barriers you kept erecting."

Julia didn't have to acknowledge what both women knew was true.

"Funny, I can see it all so clearly now. Why didn't I see it then? Why, Jules?"

She closed her eyes, wracked by her own

incredible stupidity. How could she have been so
naive? So damned trusting?

Gabe and Julia.

Fire and ice.

The determined predator and the stubborn prey.

Julia's low, strained voice barely penetrated the
mists swirling through Claire's mind. "You didn't
see it because you were so much in love."

"I was," she whispered. "I was."

Memories burst like starbursts on Claire's
closed lids.

The first time she'd met Gabe, when he'd
whisked her away from a major who'd offered her
a ride to the women's quarters, then insisted on a
detour to his own hootch.

Her silent joy at the casual mantle of protection
Gabe threw over her after that incident.

Julia's arrival in-country some months later.

The wild Halloween party when Gabe had disappeared for hours, then returned, his eyes burning
with a need that had almost frightened her in its
intensity. The long hours she spent at the Zoo that
night, the air heavy with the scent of the grass his
hootch-mate had smoked earlier, and her body convulsed with a passion she'd never experienced
before, or since.

And Christmas, that bittersweet Christmas
when . . .

Oh, God! Christmas!

Slowly, so slowly, she raised her lids and met the shimmering emerald intensity of Julia's gaze.

"What, Claire? What are you thinking?"

"I . . . I was just remembering Christmas Eve."

For the first time Julia couldn't meet her eyes. Her gaze dropped. Dark lashes swept her cheeks, hiding all thoughts, all emotion, from view.

Suddenly, the hurt that had lodged like a heavy weight just under Claire's heart for weeks splintered into a thousand needle-pointed shards. She hadn't believed the colonel who'd knocked on her door two weeks ago and informed her that Gabe's remains had been recovered. In the years since Vietnam, she'd experienced too many false hopes and too many heartbreaking disappointments to accept that he had finally been found. For days after the notification team had left, she'd struggled with the inescapable fact that Gabe was really dead.

Then, a week later, Special Agent Ted Marsh had come to see her. He'd shown her the irrefutable proof . . . and implicated Julia.

Stunned, Claire had refused to believe the evidence he presented. Even when he'd shown her the St. Christopher medal, she'd denied the staggering possibility that her best friend could have killed the man she'd loved more than life itself. Still reeling, she'd let the OSI agent convince her that she had to refrain from contacting the woman identified as the prime suspect in the case.

But now Julia had contacted her.

And now Claire understood the significance of that night long ago when both the North Vietnamese and the two people she loved had violated the fragile Christmas truce.

"It happened on Christmas Eve, didn't it?" Her voice hoarse, she forced out the words. "Whatever ended with Gabe's death first happened between the two of you on Christmas Eve. Didn't it?"

Her eyes bleak, Julia acknowledged what Claire now knew with soul-shattering certainty.

"Yes."

December 24, 1971,
Tan Son Nhut Air Base

"I don't like it."

First Lieutenant Claire Simmons frowned at the huge black and white sector map pinned to one wall of her duty area at the Infiltration Surveillance Center. A line of small white circles tracked from Tchepone in southern Laos, down along the eastern border of Cambodia, and into South Vietnam.

"What's not to like?" the grizzled technical sergeant who'd put in the long shift with her asked. "As usual, Charlie's using the cover of this so-called Christmas truce to move supplies south. As usual, we're going after him with everything we've got. The truck count's up. So are our kills."

"Yes, they are."

Claire's gaze remained fixed on the white circles.

Each circle represented enemy movement detected by seismic and acoustic sensors strung along the Ho Chi Minh trail. Dropped along known routes by fighter aircraft in strings of six to eight, the self-destructing sensors relayed signals to orbiting aircraft, which in turn transmitted it real time to the Infiltration Center.

Along with a cadre of other intelligence officers, Claire had spent more hours than she could count these past months analyzing the electronic data to identify enemy truck convoys. The results of their analyses were then fed to fighters and gunships tasked to take out the moving targets. It was grueling work, requiring intense concentration and careful coordination.

Only now, after this particularly long shift, did she have time to focus on the larger, composite picture. Trends over the past few weeks showed a disturbing increase in estimated enemy tonnage moved, truck-storage areas uncovered, and new roads hacked through the jungle. While everyone expected an offensive with the coming of the Lunar New Year at the end of January, Claire was beginning to have the uneasy feeling that the North was planning to mount a larger thrust than previously predicted.

"I don't like it," she repeated, eyeing the sector map. "I'm going over to the Tactical Air Control Center. I want to see what's going on."

As usual, the TACC hummed with activity. The pulsing nerve center for all allied air operations in the Vietnam theater, the center was manned around the clock by USAF and VNAF officers. Phones rang constantly. Radios crackled as pilots called in coordinates. Enlisted personnel grease-penciled call signs and flight data on large floor-to-ceiling Plexiglas panels.

Claire's boss had mandated that all of his subordinates spend at least four hours a month at the TACC. He wanted them to see and hear and experience the immediacy of the intelligence they provided. Claire usually spent far more time at the center, particularly when she knew Gabe was flying.

"What's up?" she asked the communications tech manning one of the radio consoles.

"Tango India Charlie," he reported succinctly.

TIC. Troops in contact. Some Christmas truce, she thought wearily.

"Where?"

"Thirty-five miles northwest of Saigon. We've pulled one of our Shadows from his box. He's en route now."

Claire's heart thumped. Gabe was flying tonight, training a VNAF crew in gunship operations over their designated operational "box." She'd planned to join him later, after he got down, at the Christmas party he and his hootch mates were throwing. Her gaze flew to the status board and locked on the grease-penciled call sign below the contact report.

Shadow seven-seven. Gabe's call sign.

The tech saw her sudden intense interest. "I can pull them up on the UHF. Want to listen in?"

Claire dragged her gaze from the status board and reached for an extra headset. Static cackled over the earphones as the radio operator searched for the right frequency. Then Gabe's voice leaped out at her, identifying himself to the forward air controller directing the air support.

". . . Dancer seven-four, this is Shadow seven-seven."

"This is Happy Dancer seven-four. Glad you're here, Shadow."

"What have you got, FAC?"

"Troops under attack by a reinforced company of NVA. They're about to overrun the base camp. We need more candlepower. How far out are you?"

"About ten minutes."

"Can you make it any faster? We need help fast."

"Roger that, FAC. We're going to METO power. Tell the good guys to hang in there."

Claire had spent enough time with Gabe and the other Shadow crew members to understand the risk he was taking. He was pushing the 119's reciprocating engines to their Maximum Except Take Off power. Keeping the engines at that power for a sustained period could tear them right off their mounts or blow their cylinders, but it would cut precious minutes off the time to target.

Her chest tight, she watched the sweep of the

second hand on the clock mounted above the status boards. Two minutes. Three. Four.

"Happy Dancer, this is Shadow seven-seven. We're approaching your coordinates. I've got Trong Son village and the river right below me. Where do you want us?"

"Follow the river to the northwest. I'm about twenty klicks up river and talking to the ground troops now."

"I can see the tracers," Gabe radioed a few seconds later. "Looks like things are pretty hot down there."

"Start dropping your flares, Shadow. Lots of 'em. I'll direct you into orbit when you get here."

"Roger that, FAC. Get ready for some sunshine."

With its night-observation sight, 1.5 million candlepower illuminator, and on-board supply of flares, the AC-119 Shadow put teeth in its motto, "Deny them the dark." Claire had flown aboard the gunship several times and seen it turn night into day. Her fists clenched, she waited for the dramatic illumination she knew would presage the gunship's direct combat role.

Moments later, the forward air controller gave a shout of glee. "Way to go, Shadow! It's like daylight down here. I can see the buttons on the fuckers' uniforms."

"We aim to please, FAC. Put us in orbit, and we'll give 'em a taste of the seven-six-two's."

"Roger, Shadow. Just keep your eyes open.

Charlie might have brought some anti-air with him."

"We'll find out soon enough."

Over the static of the radio, Claire detected the change in Gabe's voice. His words came out faster. Jerkier. Colored by the high that came with the nearness of death. So many of the fliers she'd come to know in Vietnam were like that. So many of the grunts and nurses, too. Adrenaline junkies, the docs called them. They had to pump pure bravado, had to get themselves up to face death every day the way they did. Some became addicted to the rush that came with the constant pressure and action. A growing number, Claire knew all too well from the statistics briefed at the weekly staff meetings, turned to drugs when the rush couldn't be sustained.

Her heart pounding, she waited while Gabe banked his plane to point the four side-mounted guns downward and put the aircraft in a tight orbit over the target. Then the FAC said the words every pilot waited to hear:

"You're cleared hot, Shadow."

"Merry Christmas, you bastards," Gabe growled into the mike. Seconds later, the 119's guns spat out a deafening, rapid-fire thunder.

The firefight was over in less than twenty minutes. The circling gunship rained down a hail of devastating fire on the attackers, then dropped more flares to allow the defenders to mount a

counterattack. The NVA withdrew into the jungle.
Gabe and his crew illuminated their retreat for the
F-4 fighters that swooped in with bombs and
napalm.

"Thanks, Shadow," the FAC radioed. "I'll get
with the good guys tomorrow morning and count
coup for your BDA."

Claire closed her eyes. The forward air controller
would spend his Christmas morning counting
bodies for the required Battle Damage Assessment.

"Roger that, FAC. Let's go home, guys. Time to
sing some carols."

Her hand shaking, Claire pulled off the headset
and handed it to the grinning radio tech.

"Helluva truce, huh, Lieutenant?"

She nodded, swiping her sweaty palms down the
sides of her green fatigue pants. "Would you call
me when Shadow seven-seven touches down?"

"Will do."

The call came a half hour later. By then Claire's
heart had stopped hammering and her lungs had
resumed their normal rhythm. Knowing Gabe would
have to conduct an extensive mission debrief, she
decided to work awhile yet.

The numbers bothered her.

Every intelligence data-collection source, both
active and passive, indicated that the North was
moving its regular troops and supplies south for
another offensive. MACV knew it was coming. The

South Vietnamese knew it was coming. Even the media anticipated it.

Just yesterday Julia had told Claire that a reporter for Reuters had quizzed the government spokesman about it at the daily media briefing. Dubbed the five o'clock follies by the press, the briefing constituted an exercise in hostility and frustration for all participants, according to Jules. This time, however, the session had been even more acerbic than usual. The South Vietnamese colonel who doled out the government's version of the war had denied the signs of the pending storm and warned the journalists against rumor-mongering. He'd flatly refused to confirm the information the newsmen could pick up from every bar girl and grunt coming in from the field.

Everyone anticipated the offensive, but Claire now worried that when it broke, the storm would prove more ferocious than anyone expected. The firefight Gabe had just participated in involved uniformed regulars operating in an area thought to be occupied only by VC. Just how many of the NVA regulars had slipped south? Claire wondered. How big an offensive did they intend to mount?

She dug through intelligence reports gathered from all sources for the past month. Caught up in the numbers, she nodded her thanks when another officer brought her a glass of eggnog, so heavily spiked with rum that the first sip set her throat on fire. Vaguely, she caught the strains of "White Christmas" over the armed forces radio.

When she finally glanced at her watch, it was after ten. With a startled exclamation she shoved photo recon pictures she'd been studying into their TOP SECRET jacket, then put the folder back in the safe. A quick spin of the lock secured the safe. With a hurried "Merry Christmas" she rushed out into the night.

Soft, balmy air surrounded her. With the end of the monsoon season up north, the humidity had dropped to less torturous levels during the day and the nights were almost pleasant. A large, bright moon hung low in the sky. Its glow puddled like liquid silver on tin roofs weighted down with sandbags.

The three-wheeled hop-tacs disappeared from the base at curfew, but Claire was able to hitch a ride across base with the exec to the commander of the combat support group. The captain was agonizingly homesick, she soon discovered. His jaw worked as he told Claire about last Christmas Eve. He and his wife had stayed up all night putting together their daughter's first two-wheeled bike, then slept right through the girl's squeals of joy the next morning.

"Forty-three days until DEROS," he said fiercely, gripping the wheel with white-knuckled fists. "Forty-two and a wake-up. God, I hate this place!"

DEROS. Date Eligible to Return from Overseas Service. The Holy Grail. The magic date.

Claire murmured something appropriate, secretly ashamed of the fact that she didn't feel the same wrenching homesickness or burning desire to see her overseas return date roll around. She loved her parents. She did! They were good people, God-fearing people. They'd cherished her and her younger sister all through their childhood. She just wasn't that anxious to go home to them.

Actually, they hadn't cherished her, Julia had declared during one of their late-night gab fests. They'd smothered her. Her parents' rigidly moral-istic strictures had left a permanent mark on Claire. Otherwise, she wouldn't feel so ashamed of her body, or constantly try to hide it under those baggy fatigues. Nor would she be so damned grateful to Gabe Hunter for every careless bit of affection he bestowed on her.

She was more than grateful to Gabe, Claire acknowledged with a small private smile as the jeep rattled through the darkened streets. Every time he looped an arm around her shoulders and staked his claim, she shivered with delight. Every time he unbuttoned her fatigue shirt and played with the heavy mounds of her breasts, she grew a little less embarrassed by her overripe body. And when they made love—sweet heaven above—when they made love, she ignored the crushing guilt wrought by twenty-two years of scripture reading and lost herself in his arms.

A thrill shimmied through Claire. She barely heard the exec's commentary about Christmases past.

Gabe would take her in his arms tonight. He'd still be high from his mission, and he'd drive into her again and again, until she lost every shred of pride or control and sobbed for release.

Sometimes he'd oblige her, teasing and tormenting her to a fever pitch before he pushed her over the edge. Sometimes he'd pull out and leave her writhing in an agony of need. He'd roll her over then, or have her take him in her mouth. He didn't want her too satisfied, he'd tell her with a glittering, heavy-lidded grin. He wanted her edgy and unfulfilled and thinking about him.

Only him.

As if she could ever think of anyone else!

A rat the size of a small dog scurried out of the *benjo* ditch beside the road, then froze in the glare from the jeep's headlights. Instinctively, the exec swerved to miss it, then swore and aimed right at the beast. Claire clutched the windshield frantically to keep from getting tossed out.

"Sorry," the captain ground out. He yanked the vehicle back onto the proper side of the street. "Christ, I hate this place!"

By the time the exec braked outside the single-story building known as the Zoo, anticipation coursed through Claire's veins like heated wine.

She clambered out of the jeep and hurried toward the entrance to the long, low building.

Sandbags reached almost to its roof, and, blessedly, air conditioners rattled and wheezed at two of the windows. Plywood covered the upper half of the window openings, turning day into constant night for the fliers who had to snatch the required hours of crew rest between their missions.

None of the occupants of the Zoo was resting tonight, though. A chorus of raucous male voices belted out an X-rated rendition of "Rudolph the Red-Nosed Reindeer" that made Claire's eyes widen and the exec break out in a grin. Chilled air, mildewed boots, and the sticky-sweet odor of grass greeted Claire when she pulled open the door.

"Hey, Simmons!"

A tall, gangly man with a shock of prematurely gray hair waved at her from one of the open doorways halfway down the jam-packed hall.

"Hey, Gator," she shouted, waving back.

" 'Bout time you got here, woman!"

Claire threaded her way through the crowd that spilled into the narrow hall. She recognized a good many of the men and most of the women, including the nurses from the medevac-staging facility. Although the nurses occupied quarters across base, closer to the flight line, the few American women on Tan Son Nhut pretty well knew each other by sight, if not by first name. Claire didn't see Julia among the scattering of females, though.

Darn it, Julia had promised to come to the Zoo tonight. She knew how much Claire wanted her and Gabe to get past the prickly antagonism that filled the air whenever the two of them were in the same general vicinity.

"Where's Gabe?" she asked breathlessly when she finally made it to his hootch mate's side.

"First things first." The lanky Floridian grinned and jerked a thumb at the doorjamb above her head. "That's real, live, honest-to-goodness mistletoe, compliments of Military Airlift Command. Pucker up, Lieutenant."

Ignoring Claire's protest, he swept an arm around her waist and pulled her against him. Her full breasts mashed into his chest. Half laughing, wholly embarrassed, she accepted the hearty kiss he planted on her mouth, then eased out of his hold.

"Gabe?" she demanded, raising her voice to be heard over the final chorus of "Rudolph."

"Last time I saw him, he was heading for the latrine. The beer's on ice in the urinal."

Nodding, Claire threaded her way through the crowd. She had almost reached the end of the hallway when a pure, clear soprano rose above the boisterous laughter. She stopped in her tracks, transfixed by the crystalline notes. Along with everyone else, she twisted around to listen to the strains of "Silent Night."

The singer was one of the nurses, she saw. A small fragile-looking girl with a pixie cut and huge, dark smudges under her eyes. She sang for herself at first. Then her head went back, her lids fluttered down, and she sang for them all.

After the second verse she began the first stanza again. The other party goers joined in, one by one. Their voices lifted and slowly carried them all to their separate worlds. For a few precious moments all was calm, all was bright.

When the last chorus died away, Claire turned to find Julia in the doorway of the latrine. Red flags rode high in her friend's cheeks, and her green eyes glittered with feverish intensity. Her normally smooth Dutchboy was a tangle of silvery gold, as though she'd raked both hands through the shoulder-length mane.

Concerned, Claire started forward. She'd taken only a few steps when she caught sight of Gabe standing just behind Julia. His mouth was twisted in a sardonic, mocking grin.

Claire's heart sank. Her hopes of making peace between her friend and her lover took a downward spiral.

They crashed and burned when Julia brushed by her with a muttered comment about oversexed sky jocks and just what they could do with their mistletoe.

SIX

"It was only a kiss," Julia got out, her voice ragged. "One kiss."

"Only a kiss," Claire echoed.

A fresh wave of pain rippled across her smooth, unlined face as she leaned back in her chair. Her dark lashes swept her cheeks. In the silence that followed, Julia could only watch her and ache for the hurt behind the closed eyes and thin, trembling mouth.

Physically, the years had been kind to Claire. Her hair was a lighter shade of toffee now, incorporating her scattered silver strands instead of trying to hide them. Her soft, wide-spaced brown eyes still dominated the perfect oval of her face. She was too thin, though. Far too thin.

With the birth of her son, Claire's breasts had ballooned so painfully that, finally, she'd resorted to reduction surgery. Julia had been there with her, caring for Davey during the day, holding Claire's hand at night while she wept with the pain and the loss. Gabe had loved the huge, plush mounds of her breasts, she'd sobbed. That much of her he'd genuinely loved.

As if in echo of that agonizing night, Claire moaned. "He loved me. In his way. I know he loved me."

Julia lifted a hand, let it drop. "He did. That Christmas. The singing. The—the mistletoe. The high of the mission. It was only a kiss."

A desperate need to believe flickered in Claire's eyes. Seeing it, Julia wanted to cry. This was how it had been in Vietnam. How it had been all the years since. Claire wanted to believe. Needed to believe. Then, as now, Julia would let her.

"It meant nothing, Claire," she whispered. "Nothing at all."

The other woman leaned forward, hands locked together in her lap. Her throat worked, as though she had to prime it before it would release the hoarse, inevitable question.

"And after Christmas? After the singing and the mistletoe?"

Julia searched for the words to frame her answer. What was left of her future, perhaps of her life, rode on the next few moments.

"What happened when you . . . When you . . . ?" Claire stopped abruptly, her face going paper white. "No! I don't want to know."

"Claire—"

"Don't tell me." She pushed out of her chair, swaying a little. "I don't want to hear any more."

Alarmed by her deathly pallor, Julia sprang up. "Listen to me. Whatever happened between Gabe and me had nothing to do with what he felt for you."

"No! I don't want to hear it!"

"You've got to. You have to know—"

"Don't you understand? The more I know, the more I'll have to tell them. The investigators. They're coming back, Julia. To talk to me. After I . . ." She wrapped her arms around her waist. "After I recover from the shock and have had time to remember more details. So don't tell me any more. Please, Julia! Please!"

"All right, Claire. Calm down. It's okay."

"No, it's not okay. We both know it's a hell of a long way from okay." Tears brimmed in her dark eyes. "But I can't handle any more."

"What do you want me to do?"

"Just leave, Jules. Now."

Feeling infinitely weary, Julia picked up her belted all-weather coat. "Maybe when the investigation is over, we can talk through this."

Claire put a hand over her eyes. "Maybe."

One kiss.

A single kiss.

How could it change three people's lives forever?

The question haunted Julia during the long drive

back to her town house in Alexandria, a few miles south of the Pentagon. The light snow that had fallen earlier had disintegrated into a wet, sloppy slush. Heavy sprays hit her windshield whenever another car whipped past, which wasn't often in the dark hours before dawn. Weary beyond words, she exited the interstate and drove through Old Towne's deserted, lamp-lit streets.

One kiss.

It had happened so long ago. In another life. Yet Julia was sure that if she closed her eyes and opened her numbed mind, she'd feel again the hard, hot pressure of Gabe's mouth on hers. Taste his greedy hunger. Lose herself in the press of his body pinning hers against the latrine wall.

Gabe Hunter kissed the same way he did everything else, Julia had discovered—with a single-minded passion that overwhelmed her initial protests and consumed her with its white-hot heat.

Aching at the memory, Julia turned into the alleyway behind the row of restored town houses on Queen Anne Street and lifted an arm to press the garage door opener attached to the visor. The garage yawned open. Like a sleek, well-trained thoroughbred, the Mercedes glided into its stall.

Unconscious, mechanical instincts pulled at Julia. Dimly, she understood that she should shut off the engine. Close the garage door. Gather her purse and go inside. She managed to twist the key in the ignition and turn off the headlights, but couldn't seem to find the strength or the will to move.

She knew what waited for her inside. Darkness. Elegant emptiness. A hungry, bad-tempered cat. More memories.

The automatic garage light went out, plunging her into blackness. With a small sigh Julia pressed the remote control once more. The overhead light came on again. The door rumbled downward.

Weariness and a numbing despair clawed at her as she slid out of the Mercedes and climbed the stairs. She couldn't believe she'd left this house only this morning, secure in her work and her busy life. Now she had neither. Only a past that wouldn't let go of her.

She punched in the security code without conscious thought and let herself into the tiled utility room adjoining the airy, high-ceilinged kitchen. Kicking off her black leather heels, Julia dropped her purse on the island that served as cooking center and gathering spot during the informal parties she often hosted, then peeled off the all-weather coat. She tossed the overcoat at one of the cane-backed chairs pulled up to the island, and missed. The silver eagles pinned to the epaulets clattered as they hit the floor tiles.

Immediately, Henry the Cat let her know his displeasure at her long absence. The disreputable-looking feline jumped onto the island counter. Holding his broken tail at a stiff, ninety-degree angle, he marched across the sea green tiles and let loose with one of the *yeowl*s that lifted the hairs on the back of Julia's neck.

"Okay, okay," she muttered. "I know you're hungry."

She reached into a cabinet under the island for the bag of cat food and poured the dry pellets into his dish. Henry's tail flicked once, disdainfully.

Heaving an irritated sigh, Julia went to the fridge and pulled out the container of sardines she'd opened last night. When she lifted the Saran Wrap, the stench almost made her gag.

She hated sardines, and she cordially disliked the animal she fed them to.

For the thousandth time she asked herself how in the hell she'd let this tiger-striped fiend into her life. So he'd prowled through the open door when her town house was undergoing the basement-to-rooftop repairs necessary to make it livable. So he'd moved into the renovated structure before she had. That didn't mean he had squatter's rights. She could have called animal control. She could have lured him into a box with a single sardine and whisked him off to the Humane Society. Instead, she'd ended up sharing her quarters with a wretched excuse for a pet and regretted it ever since.

Averting her head, she dumped the sardines on top of the dry food, stirred the mess together, then dropped the dish on the tiles.

"Go for it," she muttered.

Henry condescended to leap off the counter and plant his squat, muscled body in front of the dish. His bent tail flicked right, left, then right again. Julia had satisfied his immediate need. He had no further use for her.

Wearily she accepted her dismissal. Leaving the overcoat where it lay on the tiles, she yanked off the Velcro tab tie to her blouse and opened the top buttons. She felt as though she were suffocating. As though the air had been sucked out of her lungs, along with every ounce of her usual energy.

It was after two, she reminded herself. She'd been up since five that morning. No, yesterday morning. In that unbroken stretch of time, her once secure world had splintered like a sheet of glass hit with a hammer. In another few hours she'd have to shower and dress and meet Special Agent Marsh at the small conference room where he'd continue his probe into her past. She had until then to try to tape over the splinters and keep the glass from shattering completely.

It didn't occur to her to go upstairs and crawl into bed. She couldn't have slept even if she'd wanted to. Instead, she walked into the dining-living area that took up the rest of the floor. Her stockinged feet made no noise on the polished hardwood floors. As she crossed to the wet bar built into floor-to-ceiling bookshelves, the sharp, piney scent of the Douglas fir she'd decorated for

Christmas just a few days ago assaulted her senses.
Blindly, Julia reached for a stoppered decanter and
splashed its contents into a heavy cut-crystal
tumbler.

Lifting the glass, she took a long swallow.
Blended whiskey burned its way down her throat.
She choked and blinked away the tears that stung
her eyes. A wine and occasional margarita sipper,
Julia kept the potent liquor on hand for her guests.
Tonight she needed something stronger than wine.
Far stronger.

Glass in hand, she crossed to the white leather
sofa facing the marble-fronted fireplace. Sinking
into its buttery-soft depths, she propped her feet on
the brass bound Korean trunk that served as a
coffee table and stared at the shadowy pine tree in
the corner.

Her mouth twisted. How ironic, how bitingly,
bitterly ironic that Gabe had come back to haunt
her now, a few days before Christmas.

As Claire had guessed, the macabre dance
between her and Gabe had begun, really begun, on
Christmas Eve. In a latrine, yet. With one kiss under
that damned mistletoe.

Her hands tightened around the tumbler of
scotch resting on her stomach.

Until that kiss she'd believed that she could control the confused, contradictory emotions Gabe
Hunter roused in her. Until that Christmas Eve
she'd been able to deny his hold over her. Then

he'd trapped her against the wall, held that dry, withered twig over her head, and taken her mouth with his.

All right, she'd had too much to drink. And, yes, she'd been feeling homesick and lonely and Christmas Eve mopey, like everyone else that night. Still, she shouldn't have let him . . . devour her. She shouldn't have arched into him when he'd dropped the mistletoe and dug his hands into her bottom to cant her hips to his. Dammit, she shouldn't have gasped when her blood raced and heat streaked like molten fire into her lower belly.

He'd heard her gasp. Exulted in it! When he'd raised his head, his blue eyes had glittered with the knowledge that she wanted him every bit as much as he wanted her.

She'd shoved him away then. She'd possessed that much pride, at least. She'd shoved him aside and stalked out the latrine door, only to find Claire standing a few feet from the entrance.

Julia had stopped in her tracks, shocked by the raw jealousy that ripped through her at the thought of Gabe taking up with Claire where he'd left off with her. In that moment, with the soaring strains of "Silent Night" filling her ears, Julia had known that one taste wasn't enough. She wanted more. She craved more.

She couldn't deny the humiliating reality any longer. Not after that kiss. But she could damn well lock it away inside her.

Those first weeks of the new year, it was easy enough to maintain the distance she'd always put between herself and Gabe. Iron Man Endicott's rigid code of ethics had shaped her values and underscored her own concepts of right and wrong. She wasn't the kind of woman to engage in grunt and grope sessions with her best friend's lover, and she knew Gabe Hunter wasn't interested in anything else.

What was more, she didn't have time to dwell on Gabe's unrelenting hold over her. Her job heated up with the anticipation of another Tet offensive, as did everyone else's.

Julia's head dropped back against the leather. Strange how she could recall the events of that terrible spring with more clarity than the events of this morning.

January of 1972 passed in a strangely contradictory way, she remembered. While Julia prepared and released reports that detailed the decreasing number of U.S. personnel in-country, Claire fretted over the increasing evidence of enemy presence in the South.

North Vietnamese and Vietcong troops engaged in more and more attacks against military and civilian targets, mounting thirty-four separate strikes in one twenty-four-hour period. Infiltrators entered the U.S. air base at Bien Hoa, fifteen miles northeast of Saigon, and blew up a stockpile of small-arms ammunition. Eighteen Americans were injured when mortar rounds hit a fire-support base some twenty miles from the capital. All U.S. personnel were confined to their bases in anticipation of the long-awaited offensive.

Then, almost overnight, the escalating tension eased. Tet passed without the expected attack. President Nixon's visit to China took place amid much pomp. Hopes for peace soared once more. The order confining Americans to their bases was lifted, and in March Julia attended a dinner hosted by the CBS bureau chief at the Continental Palace Hotel's famed terrace restaurant.

She lifted her head and tried to wash away the memories with whiskey. They wouldn't wash. Coughing, she slammed the tumbler down on the table beside the sofa. Liquid splashed onto her hand and the table's burled wood surface.

"Dammit!"

A low, deep-throated rumble from the far side of the room warned her that she wasn't alone. Twisting around, she returned the cat's unblinking stare.

"What's the matter? Are you seeing ghosts, too?"

The cat's yellowish-green eyes didn't blink.

Julia had no idea what the animal's problem was. She and the creature coexisted in the same house, but on entirely separate planes. The tough, independent feline had long ago made it plain that Julia's sole value was as a source of sardines. He found his own companionship, which didn't include her.

Tonight, though, she wouldn't have minded a little companionship. Just a brush of fur against her leg. A warm, heavy weight in her lap. Maybe the feel of another living creature could help her exorcise the ghosts. She patted the cushion beside her.

"Here, cat. Come here."

In answer, Henry flicked his tail and marched out of the living room.

"Screw you," she muttered.

Too tired to get up and retrieve some napkins from the bar, she sopped up the spilled whiskey with her sleeve. Then she reached up with both hands and pulled out the pins that held her hair in place. The heavy mass cascaded down her shoulders and provided a measure of relief.

She'd have to exorcise her own ghosts. And she knew they had to be vanquished before she met with Special Agent Marsh again in a few hours.

Deliberately, she let her mind drift back once more. To March 1972. To the sudden, giddy relaxation of tension. To the invitation to dinner at the Continental.

She'd accepted that invitation with a grim determination. She intended to enjoy herself. She planned to revel in what sybaritic luxury Saigon still had to offer. The events of the preceding weeks had left her tired and wound tight and in no mood to listen to Claire's raptures about Gabe Hunter.

Julia wanted off the Tan Son Nhut compound.
She wanted to wear her sleeveless, mini-skirted,
white linen dress instead of a uniform for a change.
For one night, if it was possible, she wanted to
experience the Saigon of Somerset Maugham and
Graham Greene. Maugham had supposedly stayed
at the Continental. Greene had written about its terrace, where in bygone days French planters had
sipped cooling drinks on hot afternoons.

Julia couldn't know, of course, that she'd step
through the hotel's massive double doors and forge
the final link in the chain that would bind her to
Gabe Hunter forever.

SEVEN

March 16, 1972,
Saigon

Julia climbed out of the dented blue Citroën, relic of
the prewar era, and handed the taxi driver a wad of
piasters.

He counted the bills, then flashed her a black-
toothed grin. "You number one fine lady."

Even after five months in Vietnam, the black
teeth and gums that so many of the older men and
women displayed when they smiled could still
startle her. The discoloration came not from poor
dental hygiene, Julia had learned, but from
chewing betel leaves, which supposedly produced
some kind of a narcotic effect. The black stain aside,
the Vietnamese were a beautiful people in her
opinion, and so unfailingly polite, even in the midst
of war.

She returned the driver's smile, then steeled herself to walk the gantlet of beggars squatting on the
steps of the Continental Palace. She'd discovered
soon after her arrival in-country that she couldn't
answer the plea in every pair of dark eyes or fill

every thin, outstretched hand. Still, she couldn't bring herself to brush past the maimed Vietnamese soldiers in tattered uniform remnants or the gaunt women who'd lost fathers and husbands and sons.

Her supply of piasters gave out long before she reached the white-uniformed doorman perched on a stool at the top of the steps. Since the massive hotel doors remained open during daylight hours to allow air to circulate, his duties appeared to consist primarily of smiling at the guests coming in and keeping the beggars out. He greeted Julia graciously and ushered her inside.

The Continental's lobby was solidly Victorian, an island of shabby, faded elegance in an otherwise bustling city. Ceiling fans lazily stirred the hot air. Four clerks in white shirts and black ties scribbled in thick ledgers behind the tall reception desk. An elevator boy in a white coat with a red sash smiled shyly at Julia from his post beside the old-fashioned brass cage.

Bypassing the elevator, she made her way to the terrace. On her first visit to the Continental, Julia had expected a broad patio surrounded by lush bougainvillea and sweet-scented jasmine, open to the sun and the stars. Somewhat to her disappointment, she'd found the terrace tucked in a corner, right under the bulk of the hotel. Once the watering hole of the French elite, it now catered primarily to foreign correspondents and to the cadre of slender,

dark-haired women who in turn catered to the correspondents.

Most of the women wore traditional high-necked
ao dais in pastel silks over black trousers. A few
sported mini-skirts cut a good deal higher than
Julia's. In contrast, the scattering of female correspondents present wore baggy pants or divided
skirts and the ubiquitous, utilitarian bush jackets.
With its copious pockets that could carry everything from notebooks and extra film to a change of
underwear, the cream-colored linen jacket had
become a standard uniform for journalists covering
the war in Vietnam.

The number of media employees accredited in
Vietnam had declined from a high of more than six
hundred a few years ago to just a little over two
hundred. Many of those were local nationals—typ-
ists and interpreters. Consequently, Julia knew
most of the foreign correspondents present by sight
and many by first name. Some she might have
counted as her friends if they hadn't been on opposite sides of the grim statistics her office released
each month.

Snaring a glass of tepid green tea from a white-
jacketed waiter, she returned the greetings that
came at her from all sides and edged toward a
stubby, bald-headed figure on the far side of the
terrace.

"Hello, Arnie."

The UPI reporter greeted her with exaggerated

relief. "Endicott! Thank God! I thought I was going to have to listen to these network assholes expounding their theory of the thirty-minute war all night."

Julia took a sip of tea to hide her smile. A veteran correspondent, Arnie Townsend had slogged through Europe alongside the GI's during World War II and covered the Korean War for the now defunct *Atlanta News Journal*. Currently a reporter for UPI, he made no bones about his disgust over television's profound impact on the way the public was fed the news. In his opinion, which he offered to anyone who asked and a good many who didn't, the United States had degenerated from a nation of literate, reading thinkers to a population of armchair viewers whose exposure to the world outside their living rooms came through distorted pictures and oversimplified news summaries.

"What the hell are you drinking?" he demanded, peering suspiciously at her glass.

"Tea."

"Good God!"

Julia grinned at his aghast expression. "I can't handle alcohol in this heat."

She wasn't about to admit that she hadn't had either the time or the inclination for alcohol since Christmas Eve. Her mindless response to Gabe's kiss had left her shaken and determined not to lose control like that again.

"Well, I can't handle anything else in this heat,"

the reporter muttered. He emptied his glass in one long gulp and shoved it at a passing waiter. Rocking back on his heels, he favored her with a piercing stare from under gray, tufted brows.

"So what's this dumbshit policy MACV has just put out?"

"Which dumbshit policy are you referring to?"

His mouth twitched at her bland reply. "The one requiring colonel-level approval for reporters to hitch rides on military aircraft."

Julia fought to keep her expression neutral. She'd argued fiercely with her boss against the proposed policy. Relations between the military and the media were bad enough without exacerbating them further. Why not let correspondents hitch rides on transports or supply helicopters if there was space on the aircraft? Old hands like Arnie were going to get where they wanted to go, with or without the military's assistance.

Her boss had been burned once too often, though. He wasn't going to answer for another damned story about drug abuse among U.S. personnel. He couldn't restrict reporters' access to the troops in the field, but he sure as hell agreed with any proposed policy that made it more difficult for them to get there.

If reporters couldn't get to the troops, Julia had countered doggedly, they couldn't witness the day-to-day courage of the thousands of men and women who didn't take drugs. Her boss had curtly dismissed her from his office. He was too short to argue the issue. She wasn't short, however, and she didn't resent any members of the press who tried to chronicle the human aspect of the war, even if they questioned its legitimacy.

"Come see me," she told Arnie quietly. "I'll get you whatever authorization you need."

Townsend grunted. "That's what I like about you, Endicott. You don't buy this crap about the war being over any more than I do. There's still a story here."

"I think so, too."

The low comment came from just behind Julia. Turning, she searched for a name to go with the handsome face at her shoulder and came up blank. She couldn't recall ever meeting the smooth, sandy-haired man before.

Nor could Arnie, evidently. The correspondent blinked at the newcomer a couple of times, then asked bluntly, "Who the hell are you?"

"Dean Lassiter."

The newcomer held out his hand first to Arnie, then to Julia. His gaze skimmed down her legs at the mention of her rank, then returned to her face.

"Been in-country long, Lassiter?" Arnie asked in his direct way.

"I got here this morning."

"What's your background?"

Lassiter didn't appear to take offense at the grilling. "I graduated from the Columbia School of

Journalism a year ago, and I'm now free-lancing for the *Register*."

"London or San Francisco?"

He smiled. "Greenville, North Carolina."

Arnie grunted. "Greenville, huh? Well, we all had to start somewhere." While the older reporter shared a few succinct tips with Lassiter on ways to acclimate himself to the heat, the water, and the sorry excuse for an international telephone exchange that was the bane of the Saigon correspondents' existence, Julia studied Lassiter. He stood a head taller than the stubby Townsend and carried himself with an easy self-assurance that didn't quite fit his pristine bush jacket. He hadn't been tested yet. She suspected his spotless linen jacket and his self-confidence would both suffer the first time he had to dive for cover in a *benjo* ditch, as a number of reporters had.

He was anxious to acquire the patina of a war correspondent, she soon discovered. Very anxious. When Arnie drifted away in search of another drink, Lassiter zeroed in on her.

"I overheard what you said to Townsend about getting him authorization to travel aboard military aircraft. Can you do the same for me and my photographer?"

"It depends."

"On what?"

"On where you want to go and what you want to write about once you get there."

A corner of his mouth curled in a faint sneer. "What is this, Lieutenant? Your own personal form of censorship? You only help those who write the kind of story you want written?"

Julia slanted him a cool look. She'd been in-country too long and was too much her father's daughter to take any crap from this newcomer. In her opinion, he constituted the press corps' equivalent of a snot-nosed, still wet-behind-the-ears lieutenant.

"I don't know you, Lassiter. Even more important, I don't know the quality of your work. You haven't even been in Vietnam long enough to get your credentials approved. Come see me when you have."

"I will."

Setting her empty glass on a linen-draped table, Julia nodded and walked away.

To her considerable surprise, Dean Lassiter showed up at her office late the following afternoon with a photographer in tow and a freshly signed press-accreditation card. He dropped the card on her desk, along with the plastic-coated ID that gave members of the media access to the military PX's. The Italian-born photographer, as dark and tough-looking as the American was fair and smoothly handsome, prowled the office. Lassiter grabbed a chair from one of the sergeant's desks and planted himself in front of Julia's.

"Just out of curiosity," she asked idly, "how much did it cost to get your credentials reviewed and approved so quickly?"

He scooped up the forms and dropped them into his pocket with a careless shrug. "More than the price of dinner at a three-star restaurant in New York, but less than what I paid for my ticket over here."

"You paid your own way?"

"The *Register*'s budget didn't stretch to an on-scene war correspondent," he replied, grinning. "In fact, it'll barely stretch to cover the costs of sending my copy back over the wires."

Interesting, Julia thought. A Columbia grad who frequented Manhattan's three-star restaurants and paid his own way to the war. Lassiter was obviously one of that rare breed, a journalist with an independent source of income.

"The *Register*'s a mom-and-pop paper," he acknowledged. "Strictly weddings and funerals and the occasional visit from Aunt Helen, but it got me credentialed. That and the fact that I sold a few pieces while I was still in grad school." He patted his pocket. "These babies are my ticket to the *Times*."

"The *New York Times*?"

"The one and only."

"You don't believe in starting small, do you?"

"No, I don't. Last year they ran over six hundred lines written by stringers about the war. I figure this year, with so many of the freelancers going home, some of those lines could be mine."

Lassiter had obviously done his homework. The *New York Times* was the only major daily that still maintained a fully staffed Saigon bureau. If the neophyte didn't step on too many toes and managed, somehow, to avoid the fierce rivalry that affected so many of the journalists, he just might make the contacts he needed to feed his stories into the prestigious *Times.* The man was independently wealthy *and* ambitious.

"Are you paying for your photographer, too?" she asked curiously.

He nodded. "I'm inexperienced, Lieutenant, but not without intelligence. I know very well I can't write about an event if I see it only through the lens of a Nikon. Besides, I've heard that traveling alone can be a little dangerous in this part of the world."

Wealthy *and* ambitious *and* smart.

Julia tapped a pencil on her desk. "So what's your angle? What kind of stories do you think you can produce that the *Times* regulars aren't already filing? They're covering the political and economic fronts in almost as much depth as the military situation."

"I want to see the war through the eyes of the men who are still fighting it. I want to understand the pressure of fighting a war no one believes in anymore."

"Why? That kind of human-interest story isn't

going to sell to a hard-line news group like the *Times.*"

"I'll sell it," he predicted confidently. "Trust me, Lieutenant, I'll sell it."

Julia drummed the tip of the pencil on her desk, thinking hard. Although Lassiter probably didn't realize it, he couldn't have timed his arrival on the scene any better. He was in a position to record the closing chapter of the war, at least from the American combatant's perspective. Intelligence analysts were still predicting a spring offensive by the North as an attempt to secure territory and strengthen their bargaining position at the peace talks. The battle, when it came, could well be the last major operation involving U.S. forces.

Maybe Lassiter could sell his stories, using that angle. If he did, and if she helped him, she would at least have the satisfaction of knowing she had a small part in the final chronicle.

"So what do you say, Lieutenant? Will you help me get where I want to go?"

She tossed the pencil aside. "I'll tell you what. I'll introduce you to one of our pilots who flies night-interdiction missions. If you can convince him and his hootch mates that you can do justice to their story, maybe I can work you clearance to fly with them. After that we'll handle it on a case-by-case basis."

"Fair enough."

"Let me make a quick phone call."

It didn't occur to Julia to match Lassiter up with anyone else but Gabe Hunter. They were two of a kind. Each utterly confident of his own abilities. Each willing to take dangerous risks in his profession.

Nor did it occur to her that the presence of a reporter and a photographer wouldn't be enough to protect her from Gabe—or from herself.

She hung up the phone a few moments later and grabbed her purse. "Let's go."

For the next three hours Dean Lassiter and Remo D'Agustino experienced firsthand the living and working conditions of the AC-119 air crews. Julia experienced for the first time the full force of Gabriel Hunter's powerful personality.

Always before she'd seen him in something other than his natural element. Behind the wheel of a jeep the day she'd arrived in Vietnam. With his arm looped around Claire's shoulders as they perched side by side on the rickety picnic table. In a dizzying Hawaiian shirt. And once while Christmas carols filled the air and heat rushed through Julia's veins.

Today she caught her first real glimpse of the skilled, confident aviator behind his cocky exterior. He wore his green flight suit and checkered scarf in preparation for his flight that evening. It fit his compact, muscular body like a second skin. His tawny mustache didn't come anywhere close to regulation trim, nor did the hair that curled on the back of his neck, but he was every inch a combat pilot.

Julia stayed in the background, out of the line of sight, while Gabe and his hootch mate, Gator, described their missions in as much detail as they could without divulging classified information. Arms raised, hands in formation, they banked and angled their heavy gunships around in a tight circle. Throughout the maneuver they kept the target pinned in the center of the circle with deadly fire from their side-mounted cannon. While Lassiter scribbled notes and D'Agustino clicked off shots of the fliers, they described trucks blown up. Base areas destroyed. Roads secured. Terrain denied. Friendly troops supported. Enemy troops neutralized.

Finally, Gabe glanced at his watch. "We're doing our pre-planning for tonight's mission in about an hour. I think I can get you cleared if you want to ride along. You guys up for a little sky time?"

Lassiter answered for them both immediately. "We're up for it."

Julia scrambled to her feet, protesting. "Wait a minute. I've got to work them a set of aeronautical orders through PAO channels first."

"You'd better work fast," Gabe challenged. "We're wheels up and guns hot at sundown. Gator, you think you can round up a couple of flight suits and some gear for our friends here?"

The lanky Floridian gave a thumbs-up. "Sure, I'll fix them up."

Julia waited until the pilot had escorted the two men out of the room, then rounded on Gabe.

"I want this orientation flight to happen, too, Hunter, but I don't want to lose my job over it. If I can't get them clearance for tonight, don't push it, okay? They can fly tomorrow, or the day after."

"You can do it, Endicott."

"They just got their credentials this morning," she muttered, bending down for her purse. "It may not be as easy as—"

She straightened, and her breath shut off like a faucet.

Gabe crowded close to her. Too close. She could see the golden chest hairs glistening above the neck of his white T-shirt. Feel the energy that emanated from the body encased in its green flight suit. Her mouth twisted.

"What is this, Hunter? An encore? Are you going to shove me up against the wall again, like you did on Christmas Eve?"

"Are you going to pretend you don't want me to, like you did on Christmas Eve?"

"Go to hell."

"I probably will, sweet thing. Want to go there with me?"

His warm breath washed her cheek, tickled her ear. Julia refused to back away from him, knowing damn well that he'd only follow if she did.

"I don't want to go hell with you, or anywhere else, for that matter. What I want is for you to keep your distance. You might not value Claire's love, but I do."

One sun-bleached brow lifted. "Her love? Have you and Claire got something going that she hasn't told me about? Something besides girl talk?"

Julia's jaw dropped.

Hunter brushed a careless knuckle down her cheek. "Hey, it's okay by me. I wouldn't mind a little three-handed poker."

Outraged, she knocked his hand away. "You pig."

"You should see your face, Endicott." His rich, hearty laughter sent her temper soaring. "Relax, I know damn well you're not into group gropes with members of either sex. You're too much woman to share yourself with anyone . . . except me."

"Get this straight," she ground out through clenched teeth. "I'm too much woman for you, period. Now back off."

She saw at once she'd made a mistake. The glint in his eyes took on a sharp, predatory edge.

"You're wrong there, Julia. I can handle you. I'm probably the only one around these parts who can. You think you're all prissy prim and straight-lined, like your old man, but you're not. You're hot and headstrong and all female under that uniform you wear like a shield."

He stepped closer. This time Julia had to retreat. Retreat, or feel his chest brush the tips of her breasts. To her disgust and fury, her nipples tightened in anticipation of the contact.

"Why don't you take the uniform off, Julia? We've got time. Take it off, and we'll pick up where we left off Christmas Eve."

"Get out of my way."

He didn't move. Didn't touch her.

"I'll lock the door. Gator will keep your reporter friends busy. But you'll have to ask me for it this time. I'm not playing the heavy-handed bad guy again. Ask me nice, Julia, real nice, and I'll give you what we both know you want."

Her hand lashed out. The crack of her palm connecting with Hunter's cheek sounded like a pistol shot in the small room. Needles of fire raced through Julia's hand and up her arm as she shoved her way past him. Shaking with anger, she headed for the door.

It didn't help to find Gator standing right outside, a helmet dangling from one hand. His glance flicked from her to Gabe, and a sly, smug, disgustingly male expression settled over his features.

EIGHT

Julia's lids scraped like sandpaper against her dry eyes. With an effort she dragged herself from the past and discovered that a dull gray dawn had seeped around the edges of the drawn drapes of her living room. In the corner, the Christmas tree that had seemed so shadowy a few hours ago now had shape and substance.

God, was it just last weekend she'd put that tree up? Just three days since she'd made a party of the tree-trimming and invited a convivial group of friends to hang ornaments and sip hot, spiced wine? Now it seemed as though that impromptu party had happened in another life.

It had, she thought. She wasn't the same person who'd laughed and hung tinsel and chatted excitedly about the trip to London she'd promised herself as a Christmas–New Year's present. Nor was she the same officer who'd sailed out of her office to answer the vice chief's summons, smugly contemplating a future that included a possible promotion to brigadier general.

Her future now hung by a fine thread. Instead of looking forward to a holiday season crowded with parties, she was fighting for her life. Dammit, it was time she faced that fact. Time she kicked her self-protective instincts into overdrive.

Willing energy back into a body that wanted to curl up in a fetal position and refuse to move, she slid her feet off the Korean trunk. She was halfway upright before she realized that both of her legs had gone to sleep below the knees. Her ankles wobbled, and she landed awkwardly on the sofa once more, hands outflung on either side.

"Yeooooowr!"

She jumped half out of her skin as a bundle of tiger-striped fur exploded under her hand. The cat went straight up in the air, then came down with back arched and claws extended. Julia snatched her arm back just in time. Baleful yellow eyes glared at her from the far end of the sofa.

"Sorry," she muttered.

The crooked tail slashed left, right.

"It was an accident, okay?"

The beast sprang off the sofa and stalked away.

"Look, if you don't like it here, you can always leave, you know."

Unaccountably, the silly confrontation with her ungrateful boarder ignited Julia's small spark of energy. Flipping on the lights to dispel the lingering shadows in the living room and stairwell, she went upstairs to shower and change.

Two hours later, she reported to the colonel who would nominally serve as her boss during the period of the investigation.

Jerry Richards, chief of the Issues Group, had to feel as uncomfortable with the situation as Julia, but he was too much of a professional to show it. She didn't know what he'd been told, and didn't really care. The mere fact that she had to report to him at all ate at her pride like battery acid.

He indicated that she should use the desk of a major who was away on Christmas leave until other arrangements could be made. Julia's jaw locked. Overnight she'd gone from serving as deputy director of Public Affairs to borrowing someone else's desk.

None of the other four officers working in the cramped two-room suite appeared to have any clue to the reason for her unexpected appearance. It wouldn't take long for the word to spread, though. The halls of the Pentagon circulated rumors with greater speed and far more efficiency than they circulated air. By the time she walked back into the office after her meeting with Special Agent Marsh, their faces would hold the same closed, careful expression as Jerry Richards' now did.

Julia deposited her coat and hat at her borrowed

desk, then told Richards that she had an appointment to keep. Head high, she walked the short distance to the E-ring conference room.

The two OSI agents were already in place. They stood, not quite at attention, not quite at ease, and waited for her to walk around the conference table and take her seat. Julia wasn't ready to put herself in the hot seat yet, however. Placing her briefcase on the table, she laid out the rules of engagement she'd formulated during the drive in to the Pentagon.

"As you must have observed, I was stunned and probably a bit incoherent yesterday. I'm still in shock, but not quite as incoherent. Nor am I as willing to put myself at risk. Before we proceed any further, I want to understand exactly where we are in the judicial process."

Special Agent Marsh nodded, as though he approved of her stand.

Of course he'd approve, Julia thought cynically. He wouldn't want to jeopardize the case against her by keeping her in ignorance of her rights or the status of the investigation. Behind those shuttered gray eyes and carefully controlled exterior beat the heart of a cop who wanted to take down a killer.

"We're still collecting statements and evidence into the circumstances surrounding Captain Hunter's death," he informed her.

"Has an Article 32 investigating officer been appointed?"

"Not yet. The Staff Judge Advocate General wants to review your statement along with the other evidence before he makes a recommendation to your commander." Marsh didn't pull any punches. "In this instance an Article 32 may not be necessary."

Julia's stomach tightened. "I see."

Obviously, he though the evidence he'd collected would obviate the need for an investigation under Article 32 of the Uniform Code of Military Justice.

Comparable to a civilian grand jury, the Article 32 was considered a discovery or fact-finding process. Military commanders could use it as a means to gather and review evidence. Or, if the evidence presented by the trained investigators was so overwhelming, the commander could skip the added inquiry altogether and proceed directly to a trial by court-martial.

Trial by court-martial.

The words caught at Julia's throat. As a training wing commander, she'd preferred charges against personnel for infractions ranging from assault to drug dealing. She'd also served as a member of several courts-martial. Never, ever had she dreamed that she herself might one day stand accused before a panel of her peers.

She wasn't facing a court-martial yet, she reminded herself. No charges had been preferred, despite Marsh's insinuation that they might be imminent. She still had time to see what cards he held, then contact a lawyer if necessary.

"I want to read the autopsy report and the ballistics report you referred to yesterday," she told the investigator tightly.

"I've had copies made for you."

He'd anticipated her request. He was good. Too good. Julia had better remember that. She pulled out one of the straight chairs and sat. While Marsh extracted the reports she'd requested from a thick manila folder, Special Agent Lyles positioned her small tape recorder in the center of the table and inserted a fresh cassette.

At the sight of the recorder, a swift, hot rush of rancor raced through Julia. That innocuous machine offended her. She resented the need for it. Resented being forced to report to this windowless conference room. She even resented Special Agent Marsh's neat, smooth-shaven appearance.

As he had yesterday during their initial interview, he wore a civilian suit. Today it was a navy worsted with a discreet pine stripe. Not expensive, but it displayed his lean, muscled frame to advantage, she conceded. With his short, well-ordered mahogany hair and keen gray eyes, he looked sharp and clear-headed and in control. Obviously, he hadn't stayed awake all night as she had. He'd done his best to destroy her yesterday, then gone home to sleep the sleep of the unaccused.

"I've also made copies of the photographs of the evidence collected by the recovery team," he informed her. "You'll want to review them, too."

He placed several color photos encased in plastic protectors on top of the requested reports and slid the small stack across the table.

Hiding her trepidation at what she would see, Julia picked up the first eight-by-ten. It was a blow-up of the front and back sides of a silver St. Christopher medal. The thin chain attached to the medal had broken a few inches from its clasp. The skin at the back of her neck crawled as she remembered the exact moment the chain had snapped.

Hastily she set the first photo aside and picked up the second. It showed a Smith & Wesson .357 magnum blue-steel revolver with a rosewood grip. She didn't need to read the engraving on the name plate just below the cylinder. She knew what it said.

To Iron Man Endicott
From the Air Commandos at
Hurlburt Field, '66

Despite her best efforts, Julia's hand shook. The weapon had been a parting gift to her father from the cadre of special-operations instructors he'd commanded before his assignment to Vietnam. Eight months later, it had been recovered from the crash site and returned to her mother with the rest of Paul Endicott's personal effects—including the silver oak leaf pinned inside her purse. Her heart aching, Julia laid the print on top of the first.

"Is that the weapon you obtained special permission to carry to Vietnam with you?" Marsh asked.

"It . . ." She wet her dry lips. "It looks like the one I carried."

"You told me yesterday that the weapon was stolen from your room at the women's quarters. For the record, would you state the circumstances of that theft."

Julia pulled long-forgotten details out of her memory. "I often spent my days off helping Red Cross workers at the orphanage just off-base. I never took the weapon for fear one of the children might get hold of it."

If she closed her eyes, she could see again the small, lost army of dark-eyed children at the Ta Bi Tha orphanage. They had experienced more tragedy and violence in their young lives than Julia would ever know, and she hadn't wanted to add to it. To avoid any chance that an inquisitive child might delve into her purse and pull out the loaded weapon, she'd left the Smith & Wesson in her room.

"I'd spent the day at Ta Bi Tha and didn't notice my weapon was missing until the next morning, when I got ready for work."

"Do you recall approximately when the theft occurred?"

Although Marsh phrased the question in a neutral tone, Julia grasped the sinister implications behind it immediately. Her heart hammering, she gave the only answer she could.

"I recall exactly when the theft occurred. I spent my birthday, June tenth, at Ta Bi Tha. The next day I reported the gun missing to the military police on Tan Son Nhut."

The agent didn't say a word as he jotted the date down. He didn't have to. The knowledge that Gabe Hunter had turned up missing eighteen hours later burned in Julia's mind.

Her hand shaking, she picked up the final photograph. It displayed two bullets against an opaque white background. One was a shapeless blob. The other had been magnified many times over to show its distinctive tapered shape and crimped ring around the copper jacket.

"Ballistics theorize that the first round killed Captain Hunter. The second entered his body after he was already on the ground."

Julia looked up to find Marsh watching her intently. She had no idea what her face revealed at that moment. She could only hope it was as frozen as the rest of her.

"The second bullet most likely went in below the navel and spent itself in the soft internal organs," he continued. "If it had hit bone, it would've flattened on impact and lost its tapered shape."

She refused to think. Wouldn't allow herself to feel. She knew that there was worse yet to come.

Steeling herself, she opened the cover on the autopsy report. Its clinically detached language didn't soften its blow. Julia got halfway through the description of the remains and couldn't bring herself to finish. She'd have to read the report sometime, but for now all she could handle was the fact that Gabe had died from a bullet that entered his skull through the left anterior quadrant of his frontal cranial bone.

Beneath the autopsy was Claire's statement. Julia read it swiftly, cringing inside. The disjointed denials that there was anything, *anything!* between Lieutenant Endicott and Captain Hunter sounded too much like those of a woman who didn't want to admit the truth.

"Is there . . . ?" She cleared her throat. It felt as dry and sandpapery as her eyes had earlier.

"Would you like some water? Or coffee?"

Marsh's offer surprised her. She seized on it gratefully. "Coffee, please. Black."

"Same for me," his partner put in when he looked her way.

He went across the hall, returning a few minutes later with two steaming mugs. He handed her one and passed the other to the elegantly attired black woman. Someone had trained him well, Julia thought, sipping the hot liquid. A wife? He didn't wear a wedding ring, but a number of married men didn't.

Realizing that her thoughts were straying too far

afield, Julia reined them in. She took another sip, then set the mug aside.

"Is there anything else?" she asked.

"We have another statement."

"From . . . ?"

"Lieutenant Colonel James McMinn, United States Air Force retired. Do you remember him?"

She nodded slowly. "I knew him as Gator."

Until last night Julia hadn't thought of Gabe's hootch mate in years. She probably wouldn't have recognized him if she'd passed him on the street. She could picture his face in vivid detail now, though. During the long hours before dawn, she'd recalled a lot of details she'd tried so hard to forget.

Marsh lifted a typed sheet from the folder in front of him. "Captain McMinn was interviewed at his home in Florida by one of our agents. We got his statement over the fax right before we left to come over to the Pentagon. I'll have a copy made for you before we leave."

Unlike Claire's rambling, impassioned statement, Gator's was short, succinct, and damning.

Julia listened closely, her hands clasped on the table, as Marsh read the statement aloud. Then his eyes homed in on her face.

"It appears that Lieutenant Colonel McMinn has a different opinion of your relationship with Captain Hunter than the one you gave us yesterday, Colonel Endicott. You stated for the record that you weren't having an affair with Hunter. Colonel

McMinn states the opposite, based on his personal observations and the information Captain Hunter relayed to him."

"I can't answer for what Hunter told his hootch mate," Julia returned. "I think the legal term for that kind of secondhand information is hearsay. In my book, it falls under the heading of male bravado—"

"Whatever your relationship was with the deceased, Colonel McMinn describes it as passionate and volatile to the point of violence."

"Volatile, yes, I'll concede that. Violent . . ." Julia's nails dug into the palms of her hands. Deliberately she relaxed her grip. "I suppose that's how it must have appeared to Gator. He saw me slap Gabe—Captain Hunter. Once."

"According to McMinn, you rocked Hunter back on his heels."

"I gave it everything I had," she replied dryly.

Her answer earned a quick lift of Marsh's reddish brown brows. For an instant his mouth tipped toward a smile.

Could he be human after all? Julia needed to believe he was.

The smile died before it was born. "Would you tell us why you slapped Captain Hunter?"

She wanted to lie. The truth shamed her and only added to the evidence piling up against her. But she knew that her only chance of survival was to stick as close to the truth as possible.

"I had taken a reporter and photographer over to meet with him and some of his crew members. After the briefing, while the others were out of the room, Captain Hunter propositioned me. Crudely. And I slapped him."

Marsh didn't blink. "He propositioned you? To do what?"

"He invited me to have sex with him."

I'm sorry, Claire. So sorry. I can't deny it any longer.

"Did you?"

"No."

"You didn't have sex with him?"

"No."

"Was that the first time Captain Hunter propositioned you?"

"In so many words, yes."

"So he'd let you know before that he wanted to have sex with you?"

"Yes," she admitted slowly, reluctantly. "Several times."

Julia saw the speculation, quickly masked, in the gray eyes opposite her.

"What happened after you slapped Captain Hunter?"

She struggled to recall what had happened after her angry confrontation with Gabe. Those few moments in his room so overshadowed the rest of that day that she had to force herself to get past them.

"I think . . . No, I know. I told Captain Hunter

that he'd better not try to fly the journalists until I'd secured the okay through appropriate channels. Then I went back to my office and got on the phone to the MACV Special Projects Division. They worked approval for the flight with the deputy commander for Operations."

Marsh sent her a curious look. "Why didn't you just let Hunter press? Wouldn't it have been his neck on the line if he'd taken them up without proper authority?"

"Those men were my responsibility. I wasn't about to let two civilians fly aboard a gunship without proper authorization. Dean Lassiter and his photographer had just arrived in Vietnam the day before. They were too eager to consider the risks."

Marsh's partner stirred. Her black eyes widening, she entered the fray for the first time. "Dean Lassiter? Are you talking about the senior White House correspondent and political talk-show pundit? The man I keep hearing hailed as either the next network anchor or the next presidential candidate?"

"The same."

"I didn't realize Lassiter had spent time in Vietnam."

"He wasn't there long," Julia told her with a small, tight smile. "Just long enough to win a Pulitzer."

Her smile faded as she caught the quick look Special Agent Lyles exchanged with her partner.

Oh, smart, Endicott! Real smart! She'd just given them another person to add to their list of interviewees. Dean Lassiter, of all people. She knew what he could do with a story like this.

"So you got Lassiter and his photographer clearance to fly with Captain Hunter?" Marsh asked, moving the interview back on track.

"Yes, I did."

Vaguely, Julia remembered Gabe's mocking grin when she had shown up for the mission briefing with the aeronautical orders. She'd lingered at the briefing to hear the details of the mission. The Italian photographer's swarthy face had gone hard when he learned they were going after an armed convoy moving down the Ho Chi Minh Trail. Lassiter had scribbled furiously in his notebook.

He'd written a good story after that mission, Julia recalled. Stark and restrained, it nonetheless conveyed the essence of a gunship mission: hours of flying monotonous circles in the night sky punctuated by moments of sheer, adrenaline-spiked drama as they attacked a moving target. When the target fired back, as it had the night of Lassiter's first mission, the reporter's copy had gotten increasingly terse.

He didn't sell that story, to the *New York Times* or to anyone else. But he did sell the next one, to a major West Coast daily, and the one after that.

Within a week he'd established himself among the tightly knit journalistic community. With Gabe greasing the way for him, Lassiter and his photographer always managed to get to the action.

Gabe. Everything always came back to Gabe.

"When was your next contact with Captain Hunter?"

"Two weeks later," Julia answered slowly. "March thirtieth."

"Where?"

"At DaNang."

"What happened that day?"

She stared at him, thinking of all the answers she could give to that question. Finally she countered with one of her own. "How old are you, Mr. Marsh?"

He cocked his head. "Forty-two."

Forty-two. Four years younger than Julia herself.

"So you were . . . what, seventeen in 1972?"

"Something like that."

"Too young for Vietnam," she murmured, tracing a nail tip on the polished surface of the table. "Too young to know what happened that day."

"Tell me, Colonel."

She lifted her gaze to his. "On March thirtieth, Mr. Marsh, North Vietnam launched the largest offensive of the Vietnam conflict. Suddenly, the war we all thought was over blew up in our faces."

NINE

March 30,
DaNang Air Base

"That's China Beach."

The pilot's voice sounded thin and scratchy over the static crackling through Julia's headset.

"Always reminds me of the south Texas coastline, down around Padre Island," he commented.

She peered through the cockpit windshield at the glistening beach below. A soothing aqua sea edged a sweep of sand. The water deepened to emerald a few yards from shore, then to a breathtaking cobalt farther out, beyond the barrier reef.

"The USO shows are pretty good at the Beach Club, and you might actually get a cold beer if you hit the place early enough," the copilot shouted, leaning over the back of her seat. He'd given Julia his headset and his seat soon after takeoff from Tan Son Nhut and had to resort to bellowing over the roar of the C-130's four engines. "Too bad you're not coming up this way to indulge in a little in-country R&R."

The reminder of the reason behind her flight to

DaNang obliterated Julia's momentary pleasure in the serene sweep of sea and sand. She thumbed the transmit button. "Maybe next time."

"Yeah."

The pilot banked the cargo plane and brought it around on final approach. In the distance Julia could see the sprawling military complexes and hilltop fire bases that guarded the port of DaNang. The second largest city in the Republic of Vietnam, it looked immense from the air. Leveling the aircraft, the pilot coordinated his approach with the tower. Julia pulled off her headset and started to climb out of the seat.

The copilot motioned her back. "No, stay there. This old bird can put herself down without much help from either one of us."

He hung over her shoulder, pointing out various landmarks as they passed. Marble Mountain guarded the southern approach to the city. Steep, craggy Monkey Mountain loomed over it to the north. Crescent-shaped Half Moon Bay nestled between the two towering peaks.

As the C-130 swooped closer to the air base, the beauty of the bay gave way to the grim realities of war. Julia saw huge craters in the sand, remnants of Tet '68, and tumbled rubble in the outskirts of the city. Defoliants had denuded a clear zone all around the sprawling air base, which was guarded by tall sandbag and wire emplacements along its perimeter.

Julia had thought Tan Son Nhut a frenetic, busy airport, but from above DaNang Air Base looked even busier. Rows of concrete revetments marched down the length of the runway. Big-bellied cargo planes, needle-nosed fighters, recon birds, light observation craft, and whirring helicopters crowded the taxiways and parking aprons.

The 130 pilot put his heavy craft down with a breezy skill and a small thump, then reversed thrust. The four powerful turboprop engines whined in protest. The plane shuddered and gradually slowed. With the loss of the cooling airstream, the cockpit filled with suffocating heat and jet fuel fumes. By the time the plane pulled into its parking area, perspiration dampened Julia's green fatigue shirt and trickled down between her breasts. She pulled off the headset and climbed over the throttles.

"Thanks for the lift," she shouted over the whine of the dying engines.

The pilot gave her a thumbs-up. "Any time, Lieutenant. Nothing we trash haulers enjoy more than ferrying a pretty woman."

The copilot escorted her back to the cavernous belly, which was crammed with web-covered cargo pallets. Shouldering open the side hatch, he jumped the few feet to the concrete and held up a hand to help her down.

"Wish we could wait on you, Lieutenant. But

we're only going to be on the ground long enough to dump half our cargo and take on some fuel."

"I've got a ride lined up on another plane coming through this afternoon," she assured him.

"Good thing. DaNang isn't my favorite place to hang around after dark. Tough about your photographer friend, by the way. He was some unlucky dude."

Yes, he was, Julia thought grimly as she hitched a ride to base ops with one of the crew chiefs. Very unlucky.

D'Agustino had known the risks when he and Lassiter had followed Gabe north. Gabe had been sent to DaNang for a few weeks to augment its shorthanded AC-119 squadron. He'd warned the journalists that the base took in-coming fire almost every night. It was their decision to leave the relative safety of their hootch to capture the damage from last night's rocket attack on film—and D'Agustino's bad luck that a secondary explosion had ripped off his right arm just below the shoulder.

The MACV public affairs duty officer had received the casualty report within an hour of the incident and passed it to Julia's boss. He had yanked her out of sleep at four this morning with a phone call, furious with her for setting up the two newsmen with Gabe Hunter in the first place. In his words, she'd damn well better get her butt up to DaNang and pull that friggin' team out of there. He expected her to do whatever was necessary to minimize the brutally adverse stories he expected Lassiter to file as a result of the incident.

Julia made it to the Tan Son Nhut aerial port by five. With the help of a scheduler, she called DaNang and discovered that D'Agustino was being medevac'ed to a civilian hospital in Singapore, and would be shipped home from there. The same helpful sergeant put her on the first bird leaving for the northern base. The transporter assured her she wouldn't have any problem getting herself and Lassiter back, not with all the traffic going in and out of DaNang these days. Now she just had to convince Dean to return to Saigon with her.

With a quick smile of thanks for the lift to base ops, she shouldered her purse and climbed out of the truck. The 366th Wing's public affairs officer was waiting for her, alerted by a radio message relayed from the C-130. Short and stocky and intense behind his wire-rimmed glasses, the captain returned her salute, introduced himself as Chuck Dillon, and lifted his green fatigue baseball cap to wipe the sweat off his forehead.

"I'm sure glad to see you, Lieutenant. The old man's not real happy about the fact that a newsman almost bought the farm on his base last night. If you hadn't let us know you were coming up, we would've put this reporter on a plane out of here ourselves."

Julia walked with him to his jeep. "Do you know where Lassiter is now?"

"He's bunking down with Captain Hunter at the old Marine Corps compound on the other side of the base. It's too close to the perimeter for my comfort, but a lot of the guys prefer it."

"They prefer being close to the perimeter?"

The captain double-clutched, sending the vehicle off with a squeal of tires. "Most of the in-coming are aimed at the runways on this side of the base. They usually sail right over the old compound. Once in a while one falls short, though. Like last night."

Hot wind whipped Julia's face as the jeep zipped along the perimeter road. They rounded the end of the runway, then sped toward a wire-fenced complex of hootches. The Marines who'd originally built these shelters had dug in for war, Julia saw. Instead of the sandbags used elsewhere, they'd stacked sand-filled fifty-gallon drums in double rows around the lower half of the wooden structures. Thick plywood covered the window openings. With their tin roofs and lack of ventilation, the long, ungainly buildings no doubt sucked in heat like a sponge, but they'd protect the occupants from anything but a direct hit.

Assuming, she thought grimly, the occupants had sense enough to stay inside them during an attack. The captain returned a loose salute from the guard at the wire gates to the compound and drove through the rows of hootches.

Tall, feathery banyan trees dotted the complex and afforded some relief from the sun. Patches of scraggly grass grew between the hootches, providing a meager contrast to a landscape of military blacks and browns and grays. Finally, Dillon swung the jeep around a corner and screeched to a halt beside a white stucco house. Julia stared at the small, shuttered cottage in surprise.

"This used to belong to a plantation overseer or someone like that," Dillon explained. "When the French moved out, the Marine commander moved in. Our services squadron commander has it now. He's on R&R in Thailand, and invited Captain Hunter to bed down here in his absence."

Julia climbed out of the jeep, bemused by the contrast between the grim hootches and the neat white house. With its columned porch, blue shutters, and skirt of wavy banana plants, it resembled a plump white hen roosting amid a courtyard full of scraggly fighting cocks.

Trust Gabe to find this little gem, she thought sardonically. Then she noticed the bullet holes pockmarking the white plaster. Suddenly, the little house didn't seem quite so charming.

Dillon rapped on the door twice. Receiving no response, he pushed it open. Julia followed him inside and sagged in relief at the rush of fan-cooled air that wrapped around her. Blinded by her transition from glaring sunlight to the dim, shuttered interior, she didn't see Lassiter at first.

Gradually, her eyes adjusted to the gloom, and she made out the figure of the reporter sprawled on an uncomfortable-looking wrought iron sofa. One leg dragged the floor. The other was hooked over the metal sofa arm. His heavy breathing rumbled in the dim quiet, broken only by the whir of the oscillating fan. While the PAO went into the hut's other room to check it out, Julia prodded Lassiter's shoulder.

He jerked awake, his arms and legs flailing. She jumped back just in time to avoid a fist to the chest.

"Wh—what?" He swung upright, blinking furiously to clear his vision.

"Dean, it's me. Julia."

"Julia? What are you doing here?"

He struggled to his feet, and her stomach lurched at the ravages his stay in DaNang had left on his handsome face. Cheeks unshaven, eyes bloodshot, sandy hair standing straight up, he looked far different from the man who'd casually dropped his credentials on her desk. Even his cream-colored bush jacket had lost its pristine newness. It had been bloodied, just as Lassiter himself had.

"I'm sorry about Remo," Julia said quietly.

He shoved a hand through his disordered hair. "Yeah, me too. He was a hard man to get to know, but a damn fine photographer. So what are you doing here?"

Julia blinked, taken aback. From her brief association with the two men, she had understood that they tolerated rather than liked each other. Still, she'd expected Lassiter to display a little more remorse over the photographer's terrible injuries.

He caught her reaction and grimaced. "Look, I told D'Agustino not to go any closer. But he had to run those extra twenty yards. Had to get one more shot. The grunt he was shooting had sense enough to hit the dirt when things started popping, but Remo had to have one more—"

He broke off as Dillon came back into the room.

"Who are you?"

"Chuck Dillon, the wing PAO. I drove Lieutenant Endicott over here to pick you up."

Lassiter's red-rimmed gaze swung back to Julia. "Pick me up?"

"My orders are to make sure you get back to Tan Son Nhut."

"Hey, that's fine by me. I got what I wanted up here, anyway. I can't leave until I get a chance to talk to Hunter, though."

"Where is he?"

"I don't know." Lassiter dragged a palm across his whiskered chin. "We were up all night, or most of it. I collapsed on the couch while Gabe was still going over the details of the rocket attack with the deputy commander. I remember him shaking me a little while ago. Saying he'd be back shortly."

Julia glanced at her watch. It was almost eleven. "We've got a couple of hours before we have to be back at base ops. We can wait that long."

Captain Dillon pulled his fatigue hat out of his pocket and slapped it against his leg. "I can't, unfortunately. I've got to work the official release on last night's attack."

He pulled out a notepad, scribbled a number, and passed the scrap of paper to Julia. "Here's my office number. Call me if you need a ride back to the flight line. You'd better check in with ops periodically to verify the status of your bird."

Julia tucked it into her pocket. "I will. Thanks."

He left with a curt nod to Lassiter.

"What did you do to get on the wrong side of Dillon?" she asked curiously when the door had shut behind the captain.

"The guy's an ass. A delusional ass if he thinks I'm going to run my copy by him. Especially last night's."

"You've already written it?"

"I wanted to get my impressions down while they were still vivid."

With her boss's injunction to minimize, if possible, the adverse press that might result from D'Agustino's injuries in mind, Julia probed for details. "What happened last night, Dean?"

He scooped a spiral-bound notebook off the table beside the sofa. "Here, you can read it yourself while I clean up."

"You'll let me read your copy and not Dillon?"

"You, Endicott, are not an ass."

Notebook in hand, she looked around the room

for some place more comfortable to sit than the wrought iron sofa. She didn't have many options to choose from. The room's furnishings consisted of the sofa and one armchair, a side table, and a Formica-topped kitchen table with two plastic chairs. Behind the table was a counter that sported a chipped enamel sink and a two burner hot-plate. The kitchen, Julia assumed.

Light filtered in through the slats of closed shutters, illuminating dancing dust motes and tiny, flitting, white-winged insects. Frowning, Julia followed the flight path of one bug to a swarming mass burrowed in a decayed patch of the plywood wall. Termites. Hundreds, no, thousands of them. She'd never realized they could fly.

Grimacing, she retraced her steps and settled at the dusty kitchen table. She flipped through the scribbled pages for one dated March 29. Within the first few words she lost herself in Lassiter's sparse, compelling prose.

ROCKETS HIT DANANG

DaNang Air Base, South Vietnam, Mar. 29

A barrage of 107mm rockets rained down on the base last night, destroying an ammunition storage facility.

The attacks are a nightly occurence. Most residents believe these so-called nuisance attacks are primarily intended to keep DaNang's air crews and support personnel from getting any sleep. In that they succeed.

Lassiter went on to describe the small, isolated teams of spotters on Monkey Mountain. Their watch for fiery red contrails as rockets ignited and arced through the night sky. The radio alert from the spotters. The sirens that blasted the stillness of the night and sent DaNang's inhabitants scrambling for flak vests, helmets, and cover. The eerie, whistling sound of in-coming. The agonizing wait. The explosive detonation.

Then Lassiter's account segued from detached reporting to an achingly intimate portrait of a young maintenance tech, an adviser to one of the Vietnamese Air Force units. Sergeant Scott Forbes and his VNAF counterpart had come in from the field just hours before, intending to fly to Saigon in the morning to scrounge some badly needed parts. They'd bunked down in an empty hootch next to the storage facility. When the siren went off, they ducked for cover. Cringed at the sharp, whistling sound. Heard a thud. Waited long, tense minutes. Then they grinned at each other and crawled back into their bunks.

Moments later an explosion ripped the night apart. The storage facility nearby had blown. Flames engulfed their hootch. The sergeant stumbled out, blinded by smoke. Realizing his counterpart hadn't emerged, he threw his arm over his face and ran back in. He carried his friend to safety in his arms.

Her throat tight, Julia reread the stark tale of heroism that transcended duty, friendship that knew no uniform. Only on the second reading did she pick up the subtle shadings and unspoken questions. Why were men like Sergeant Forbes still dodging rockets? How long would these peace negotiations take? When would the killing stop and the long-anticipated peace begin?

Julia sat back in her chair, impressed by Lassiter's skill. He'd crafted a story that would sell to either the hawks or the doves. In one piece he extolled American bravery, and damned the need for it. He didn't need D'Agustino's pictures, she thought. His words would stir anyone to demand answers to the hidden questions.

She was reading through other stories in the notebook when Lassiter emerged from the other room. His eyes were still bloodshot and his face lined with fatigue, but he'd washed and shaved and tamed the spikes in his hair. He glanced from the notebook on the table to her face.

"What do you think?"

"I think the *Times* is going to snatch it up," she replied. "It's good, Dean. Better than good."

"Yeah, I think so, too."

She checked her watch, then put in a call to base ops. The sergeant who answered seemed distracted, but verified that her C-130 was still in-bound. She'd better make that one, he warned, for the afternoon thunderstorms would roll in soon after that and they were getting reports of some weird activity up north, along the DMZ.

"We can't wait much longer," she warned Lassiter.

They didn't have to.

Ten minutes later, Julia was in the hut's minuscule bathroom when she heard the front door open. She turned off the taps, wiped her hands on a much used khaki-colored towel, and walked through the bedroom. Gabe's voice carried to her clearly.

"Relax, Dean boy. No one saw anything, I'm telling you. No one but you and me."

Dean mumbled something under his breath.

"Remo had those cameras stuck to his face," Gabe tossed back. "This is strictly—"

He stopped abruptly as he caught sight of Julia in the doorway. A slow, wicked grin lifted his tawny mustache. Rocking back on his boot heels, he hooked his thumbs in the unzipped pockets of his green flight suit.

"Well, well, I almost didn't believe Dean when he told me that Goldilocks walked right into the big bad wolf's lair. Yet here you are in the flesh."

Julia strolled into the living area. "You've got your nursery rhymes all mixed up, Hunter. Red Riding Hood was the one who tangled with the wolf. As I recall, she left him in little pieces."

"I prefer my own version of the story."

"I'll bet you do. In any case, this Goldilocks is about to blow the wolf's lair. Lassiter and I are hopping a C-130 back to Tan Son Nhut."

"So I hear."

Dean turned on his heel and headed for the other room. "I'll get my gear."

Gabe folded his arms. He looked tired, Julia thought, but as cocky as ever.

"Why don't you stay awhile after we put Lassiter on that 130?" he suggested. "I've got this hut all to myself for another two nights."

Julia shook her head. "You don't ever give up, do you, Hunter?"

"No, sweet thing. I don't. I surely don't."

His reply was an affirmation—and a promise she couldn't mistake. The sheer gall of it took Julia's breath away. She was still fumbling for a snappy come-back when Lassiter strode back into the room.

"Have you got transportation?" he asked Hunter.

"Right outside."

The reporter reached under the sofa to pull out another bag. Julia winced as expensive camera lenses rattled and clacked together.

"Is that Remo's gear?"

"Yes. I promised I'd get it to him."

Dean dug into the bag and hefted a small black canister in one palm.

"The explosion that took Remo out shattered his lens, but I managed to salvage the film."

He would, Julia thought.

"These should be some pretty spectacular shots."

"Yes, they should. Let's get going."

An almost palpable tension gripped them the moment they walked into base ops. Tight-faced air crews huddled over weather printouts in the briefing room. Phones shrilled nonstop. The airfield-management specialist behind the counter waved a distracted hand, signaling them to wait while he took a call from the tower.

Frowning, Gabe hailed a two-man flight crew heading for the door, parachutes humped over their backs. "What's going on?"

"We're not sure," the pilot replied. "We've got all kinds of garbled reports coming in. All we know for certain is that Camp Carroll is taking heavy artillery and tanks are rolling across the DMZ."

"No shit? They're really sending tanks across the DMZ?"

The flier grinned. "No shit. Sounds like we'll have us a nice little turkey shoot this afternoon."

"Sounds like."

Gabe swung back to Julia and the reporter. "I've got to head over to the squadron. Get on that C-130, you hear me? Both of you."

Lassiter started to protest.

Gabe cut him off with an impatient chop of his hand. "I can't fly cover for you now, Dean boy, and I don't have time to set you up with anyone else."

"I'll manage."

"Look, this move across the DMZ is only a feint. Intel expects the real thrust to come across the Central Highlands. Get back to Saigon. Talk to Gator. He'll get you to the action."

Lassiter conceded grudgingly. Gabe tipped him a salute, then gave Julia a swift, rakish grin. "See you back at the ranch, Endicott."

He swung away, already thinking of his plane, his crew, his mission.

"Gabe . . ."

"What?"

She knew better than to jinx him by wishing him good luck. "See you back at the ranch."

His thumb went up, and he was out the door.

As the tense afternoon wore on, the scope of the activity along the DMZ some thirty miles north unfolded. Fuzzy and unclear at first, the picture gradually assumed frightening dimensions.

Contrary to Gabe's blithe assumption, the tank thrust wasn't a feint, but a precurser to a full-scale attack by three heavily armored divisions. The enemy quickly surrounded the forward fire bases. Every fighter at DaNang scrambled to provide air support to the defenders. Gunships roared down the runway and lifted into the sky. Cargo planes ferried emergency stocks of ammunition to the forward air strips. The Tactical Air Control Center in

Saigon diverted the C-130 that Julia was waiting for to Quang Tri City, which lay in the path of the attack.

Sometime around three that afternoon, thunderstorms rolled down off the mountains, blanketing the entire northern sector in a heavy cloud cover. Frustrated, the fighter crews were unable to assist the beleaguered ground troops because of the weather. Only the gunships were able to operate.

An AC-119 from DaNang answered a desperate call from the 8th Battalion of Vietnamese marines at Fire Base Holcomb. Flying dangerously low through shrouding fog and rain, the Stinger finally located the target via an infrared strobe and orbited for an hour and a half, firing on enemy positions. Another gunship braved intense ground fire to touch down at a forward base that was being over-run. It took on the two dozen surviving defenders and lifted off again with guns blazing. Only later would Julia learn that Gabe was at the controls, and that his aircraft had taken more than three-hundred hits from the murderous ground fire.

Stranded in DaNang, she and Dean Lassiter grabbed a meal at the officers mess. While he commandeered a phone to dictate his story to a copy taker, Julia offered her services to the harried PAO. Gratefully, Dillon accepted her help in responding to the demands for information coming at him from the media in and around DaNang. She was still manning the phones when an exultant Lassiter tracked her down a few hours later.

"They bought it!"

"Who?"

"The *Times*! They bought the rocket-attack piece. It's going to run in tomorrow's edition, without the pictures. They want another piece on today's action as well."

"Dean, that's wonderful!"

A trained journalist herself, Julia saw no incongruity in congratulating him for profiting from what might have been a horrific tragedy. Someone had to record mankind's tragedies as well as triumphs.

Some time after midnight, things quieted down enough for Dillon to shut down his operation. Exhausted, Julia opted to share the stucco house with Lassiter instead of driving to the Army complex, where the nurses were housed. She rousted the reporter from the bed and sent him grumbling to the couch, dragging his helmet and flak vest with him. Julia arranged the vest and helmet she'd scrounged for herself on the floor beside the bed, then sank on top of the blanket, fully clothed.

An hour later, the wail of a siren pierced the night. Jerked from sleep, Julia rolled off the narrow bed and into the flak vest in a clumsy, panicky movement. Cramming on the helmet, she yanked the mattress over her body.

From the other room came the sounds of Dean scrambling under the kitchen table. Eyes squeezed shut, she strained to hear the whistling that preceded impact. None came, nor did a deafening blast. The rockets must have passed over this side of the base. If they hit on the other, she couldn't hear it. Trembling, she lay in the dark for what seemed like hours.

"What in the hell are we doing here?" Dean's voice sounded thin and reedy in the dark.

Julia managed a shaky laugh. "I was just wondering the same thing."

Sure she'd never get to sleep again, she shoved the mattress back onto the bed and curled up. The second attack came a half hour later.

After the third, she decided to spend the rest of the night on the floor. She was still huddled under the mattress when a gray, watery dawn broke. Stiff and aching in every joint, she started to crawl out. To her surprise, she saw the floor beside her was covered with a light dusting of white.

She thought at first some plaster had cracked and fallen. Dragging a fingertip through the dust, she held it up to examine the particles. Belatedly, she realized the white film was actually thousands of tiny wings. Sometime during the night the termites munching their way through the rafters overhead had swarmed and shed their aerodynamic appendages.

"Yuck!"

She scrambled back, intending to push herself to her knees, only to find her way blocked by a solid, immovable body. She twisted around to find Gabe sitting on the floor beside the bed, his back to the wall and his eyes glinting in the pale light.

"Well, well, Goldilocks. Imagine Papa Bear's surprise when he got back to his hootch and found you in his bed."

"In case you haven't noticed," Julia responded dryly, "I'm under the bed, not in it."

She shoved the mattress aside and sat up, wincing at the pull of the heavy flak vest on her stiff shoulders. "How long have you been here?"

"A couple of hours."

He'd sat beside her for several hours? While she slept? The idea raised goose bumps on Julia's arms.

He read her thoughts exactly. "Don't worry, Endicott. I looked, but I didn't touch. Not with Lassiter in the next room."

His grin faded. For a fleeting moment the other Gabe surfaced, the one he rarely showed the world. Hard. Determined. Eyes glittering like the ruthless predator he was named for.

"We both know, though, that the time's coming when I will," he told her softly.

In that instant the tension between her and Hunter was stripped down to its most basic element. It swirled around her like a living, breathing thing. Julia fought the absurd urge to fold her arms across her chest in an age-old, protective gesture. She refused to give Gabe that satisfaction. Instead she pushed herself to her feet.

"I won't hold my breath, Hunter."

TEN

"Mr. Lassiter?"

"Yes?"

"May I speak with you for a few moments? Privately?"

Ted Marsh contained his impatience while the reporter slanted him an assessing glance. Obviously, Lassiter was weighing whether he should detach himself from his circle of friends to speak with someone who hadn't been invited to this white-tie affair at the opulent Willard Inter-Continental Hotel. Marsh didn't intend to leave until he'd spoken to his quarry.

He'd had to flash his ID for the tuxedoed doorman to get through the massive front doors. Then again for the concierge, who'd grudgingly confirmed that, yes, the vice president's reception for the media was underway in the downstairs ballroom. And finally for the security detail posted outside the entrance to the chandeliered hall.

Once inside, he'd picked Dean Lassiter out of the

milling crowd easily enough. Tall, gray-haired, and casually elegant in his tux, he held court in a brightly lit alcove. Marsh had waited a good ten minutes for a lull in the lively conversation before making his request.

He'd counted on Lassiter's curiosity as the means to separate him from the group that eddied around him. He wasn't disappointed. Excusing himself, the correspondent moved away from his cluster of friends and acquaintances.

"Do I know you?"

"No. I'm Special Agent Ted Marsh, with the Air Force Office of Special Investigation. I'd like to ask you a few questions about a case I have under review."

"Here?"

Lassiter managed to convey both surprise and a hint of irritation in the single, well-modulated syllable.

"No, not here. There's a small, private office outside the ballroom and down the hall to your left. Would you meet me there in, say, fifteen minutes?"

"This isn't a particularly convenient time or place. Why don't you call my office and schedule an appointment, Mr.—?"

"Marsh. Ted Marsh."

"Call my office, Ted. I can give you far more attention there than I can here."

"I've scheduled two appointments with you, Dean." Marsh pointedly adopted Lassiter's familiar form of address. "Your personal assistant canceled one yesterday because the White House called a press conference. The second got scrubbed this morning due to deadline pressure. When I checked back this afternoon, your assistant said you're leaving early tomorrow morning for a Christmas vacation in the Cayman Islands. After that, you're flying to Paris to cover the summit. I want to talk to you about the case I'm working, and our talk needs to happen before you get back to the States next month."

"What kind of case?"

"Murder."

Interest sparked in Lassiter's dark eyes. But he wasn't ready to jump yet.

Marsh gave him just enough to lure him out of the damned ballroom and into the private office.

"Captain Gabriel Hunter, 1972, Vietnam."

The reporter's face went blank with confusion. For several moments he didn't move. Glasses clinked. Laughter carried above the noise of the crowd. A second or two later, the sound of a finger tapping against a microphone jerked Lassiter out of his blank stare. His gaze focused, sharpened. Not enough to alert those around him to something unusual. Just enough to make the agent smile inwardly.

Ted Marsh had spent the last nineteen and a half years as an investigator. First as a military cop. Then, after slogging through night school to get his

bachelor's degree, as an officer assigned to the Air
Force OSI. He'd taken a host of courses in interrogation and interview techniques to hone his professional skills and fulfill requirements for the
master's degree he'd collected some years ago. In
the process he'd gained a reputation in military-
investigative circles as a skilled interrogator. He
knew how to read people.

Lassiter was hooked.

"Down the hall and to your left," Marsh
repeated. "I'll wait for you there."

Threading a path through the crowd, he left the
noise of the ballroom and made his way to the
small office. Too restless to sit, he leaned his hips
against the elegant desk that graced the anteroom.
One hand jiggled the loose change in his pants
pocket. Weariness tugged at the edges of his mind.

He'd put in a long day. Several long days. The
case had grabbed him, and he couldn't let go.

After his second interview with Colonel Endicott
yesterday morning, she'd decided to cease all further discussions with the OSI until she'd had time
to consult with an attorney. His hunting instincts at
full blood, Marsh had decided to use the delay to
follow up with Dean Lassiter. He didn't like having
to cool his heels while he waited for access to the
elusive, charismatic reporter. Nor did he like having to filter the remainder of his interviews with
Julia Endicott through a lawyer. He'd put up with

both, though. He'd put up with a good deal more than those minor inconveniences to work this one.

He hadn't had a case that intrigued him so much in years. A victim who'd been dead for more than two decades. A suspect who walked the corridors of power, with media connections that could prove highly embarrassing to the Air Force. No wonder Bob Pfligerman, chief of the OSI's Criminal Division, had detailed Marsh to work this one personally.

The coins in his pocket clinked as Ted recalled his first search of the computerized index to see what, if anything, the OSI had on Colonel Julia Endicott. Nothing. *Nada.* No flags had been raised during the extensive background-investigation update conducted every five years to recertify her security clearances. No references cited her as a witness or participant in other cases. She didn't even have a record of a parking or speeding ticket.

The squeaky-clean file might have impressed Marsh if he hadn't heard her anguished moan when he'd informed her that Captain Hunter's remains had been recovered. And watched her green eyes as she stared at the wall in the interview room, seeing images she carefully edited before sharing.

What had happened between her and Hunter? What was she hiding? Did she kill him?

His cop's mind weighed the possibility.

She had the means—her father's Smith & Wesson. She had the opportunity. From what he'd read in the past twenty-four hours about the Easter offensive launched by North Vietnam on March 30, 1972, intense fighting had broken out on three major fronts. Captain Hunter was just one more MIA in the battles that convulsed the country for months. Anyone with guts enough could've slipped away and ambushed him that night. Julia Endicott certainly fell into that category.

She had the means. She had the opportunity. Now Ted had to nail down the motive. Why would she kill Hunter? Why would anyone kill him?

He turned the question over and over in his mind. Granted, the cocky bastard probably had asked for it. If Julia Endicott's index had been pure as the driven snow, Gabriel Hunter's was another story. When Pfligerman first handed him the case, Ted had retrieved the aviator's file from the OSI's computerized archives.

In his considered opinion, Hunter epitomized the kind of warrior every commander wanted in his ranks during war—and hated to see walking in the front door during peace. Most men could channel and redirect the aggressive instincts they loosed during combat. Some couldn't. Hunter fell into the latter category.

He'd shipped over to Vietnam the first time as a brand-new lieutenant, right out of pilot training. He'd served through most of '67, when Vietnam was America's war, winning a string of air medals. After he returned to the States, Hunter's performance reports took on a zigzag pattern. He received top marks for initiative and leadership, and a career-damaging downgrade for "questionable" judgment in aerial maneuvers. In 1969 he paid a stiff fine as punishment for instigating a brawl that caused several thousand dollars in damage to the Ramstein AB officers club bar. He'd returned to Vietnam in July '71, was recommended for a Silver Star for bravery during the opening salvo of the Easter offensive. Then he disappeared.

His widow accepted his posthumous Silver Star. Seven years later, she concurred in the Air Force's recommendation to change his status from MIA to KIA. With her son and her best friend on either side of her, she'd attended a memorial service and said a final good-bye to her husband.

Ted wanted to get down and talk to Claire Hunter again. She'd been less than coherent during their first interview. Understandably so. She'd soon have to bury the husband she'd mourned so long ago.

Marsh guessed Colonel Endicott wouldn't sit beside the widow at this service, as she had the last. He'd heard the desperation behind Claire Hunter's insistence that her husband and then Lieutenant Endicott had shared only friendship. He knew damn well she wanted to convince herself as much as him.

Which brought him back full circle. What had happened between Hunter and Julia Endicott? Did she kill him? Maybe Lassiter would have the answer.

The journalist walked into the office twenty-five minutes later. "Sorry. I got dragged up to the podium. May I see your identification, please?"

Ted reached into his coat pocket and pulled out the worn leather card case that held his photo ID.

Lassiter skimmed it, handed it back, and folded his arms across his chest. "Now, what the hell is this about Gabe Hunter?"

"We have reason to believe he was murdered."

"By someone other than the VC, I take it, or you wouldn't be here. Who do you think murdered him, and why?"

"No one's been charged yet, but . . ."

Ted hesitated, aware that he was stretching regulations here. He shouldn't reveal the name of the suspect until her commander had preferred formal charges. He also knew he was taking a hell of a risk talking to a journalist about an ongoing investigation. He'd worked in this town too many years to go strictly by the book, however.

"We're currently questioning Colonel Julia Endicott about her knowledge of the circumstances surrounding Captain Hunter's death," he replied.

Lassiter's gaze sharpened. "So the rumors were more than just rumors."

"You know her, I understand."

"Of course. I'm a journalist, she works Air Force

public affairs. I haven't seen her in years, not since I switched to the White House beat, but I know her. You don't seriously think she murdered Gabe, do you?"

"Why is that such an implausibility?"

"Julia Endicott isn't the kind of person who would commit murder. But if she did, she's too damned smart to leave a trail that would prove it."

"We haven't proved anything yet," Ted replied. "We're still investigating."

"What have you got on her?"

He'd only bend the regulations so far. "Sufficient evidence to question Colonel Endicott."

Lassiter didn't like the reply. That much was obvious from the faint narrowing of his eyes. His reporter's instincts had been fully roused, though. He wanted as much of the story as he could uncover. Ted had a feeling he'd have his hands full keeping the initiative in this interview.

"I understand you first met Colonel Endicott in Vietnam. Is that correct?"

"Did she tell you that?"

"Yes."

"Have you verified it with other sources?"

"I haven't, but I could if necessary."

"So why are you wasting my time asking questions you obviously don't need answered? Let's cut to the chase, Marsh. Ask me the questions you do want answered."

"Fair enough. To your knowledge, did Julia

Endicott have sexual intercourse with Captain Gabriel Hunter in Vietnam?"

"So what if she did? That wouldn't prove she killed him."

"No, but it would establish a motive. She's admitted that Captain Hunter solicited her to have sex with him on several occasions, the latest of which was some time in March 1972. A short time later he married her best friend. Less than a month after that, Captain Hunter disappeared, presumably the victim of a VC ambush. Sexual jealousy has driven a good many people to commit murder."

"Julia wasn't jealous of anyone, much less the woman Gabe married . . . I forgot her name."

"Claire. Lieutenant Claire Simmons."

"Right, Claire. She was a real mouse, as I recall, but . . ."

"Yes?"

Lassiter's shoulders lifted under his perfectly tailored tux. "Extremely well endowed."

Ted hid his surprise. Small and slender, Claire Hunter didn't fit his definition of well-endowed. He filed that seeming inconsistency away for future examination.

"During our interview yesterday, Colonel Endicott indicated that she was with you in DaNang at the start of the 1972 Easter offensive."

Lassiter let out a long, slow breath. "I haven't thought about DaNang in years. Jesus, what a night! Two nights! I didn't sleep for forty-eight straight hours."

"Tell me about those forty-eight hours."

Lassiter's eyes took on the distant look that Marsh had noticed all too often in investigating this case. The reporter, like the other witnesses he'd interviewed, was remembering a time and a place the agent couldn't relate to.

"Julia arrived at DaNang on the morning of March thirtieth. Holy Thursday. We caught a hop out of there on Good Friday. I remember the date because Gabe remarked just before I left that it *was* good, damned good. He'd flown a hot mission the night before, the one he was later awarded the Silver Star for, and he'd . . ."

"Yes?"

His forehead creasing, Lassiter studied the tips of his shiny black leather shoes.

"He'd what?"

"Hell."

The muttered oath acted on Marsh like a whiff of raw steak on a dirt yard dog.

"You might as well tell me now," he said, his cop's sixth sense tingling. "If this case goes to trial, you could be subpoenaed as a witness."

Lassiter lifted his gaze. His eyes hard and agate black, he gave the answer Marsh had been waiting for.

"Despite his all-night mission, Gabe was flying high that morning. According to him, he'd gotten back to the hootch around dawn and found Julia in his bed. It was the best damn Friday he'd ever experienced."

"Let me make sure I have this straight. Captain Hunter implied that he'd spent the night, or what was left of it, in bed with Colonel Endicott?"

"He didn't imply it. He stated it."

Marsh stiffened. There it was. The final piece. Means. Opportunity. And now motive.

Hunter had bragged to his hootch mate *and* to Dean Lassiter about sleeping with Julia Endicott. One man's testimony might be written off as hearsay. A second man's could sway a jury, or, in this case, a duly constituted court-martial board. Marsh was so caught up in his racing thoughts that he almost missed Lassiter's next remark.

". . . until I saw them together that night at the Caravelle."

"I'm sorry. What did you say?"

The journalist flicked him an impatient glance. "I said that I didn't really believe Gabe had broken past Julia's prickly barriers until I saw them together that night at the Caravelle."

"What night was that?"

"The night before I left for Cambodia. That was . . . the thirteenth, I think."

"The thirteenth of May?"

"Right."

"What happened on that night to make you

believe that Captain Hunter and Lieutenant Endicott had engaged in sexual intercourse?"

His mouth curved. "Can't you bring yourself to put it in layman's terms, Marsh? Why don't you just ask me how I knew Hunter was fucking her?"

"For the same reason you don't use the term in your political commentaries," he returned, unruffled. "I'm working here, Lassiter, not trading bar stories."

"Point taken. All right, how did I know they were sleeping together? How could I not know? You could see the sexual tension between them. Smell it even. All the way across the crowded room."

"What room?"

"My room at the Caravelle. I was leaving for Cambodia the next morning, and I wanted to thank Gabe and Julia and the others who'd helped me. I threw a party of sorts. Everyone came, even the mouse . . . Claire. It started out small, but reporters were pouring back into Saigon since the war had heated up again. People kept showing up at the door. The place was wall-to-wall flesh, yet everyone there felt the heat that sizzled between Julia Endicott and Gabe Hunter." He smiled. "We all envied him, you know."

"No, I didn't."

"We envied Gabe, and lusted after Julia. Hell, the reporters used to talk about her at the bar, even the old Saigon hands with their pretty little Vietnamese mistresses. Julia stood out like a beacon. She had the kind of cool, hands-off looks that challenges men to do just the opposite, if you know what I mean?"

Ted knew exactly what Lassiter meant.

Even with all his years as an investigator, Marsh had slipped out of the impartial, impassive questioner's role more than once during his interviews with Julia Endicott. Her looks weren't what fascinated him, though. Well, not entirely. The intelligence in her eyes pulled at him far more than their fathomless emerald hue. He also admired her sheer guts in facing her inquisitors alone to this point. He'd almost regret closing this case.

Almost.

"Even Claire must have noticed the attraction," Lassiter continued. "I remember that she got a little green around the gills and left early. Julia and Gabe left later. When Hunter walked out the door with her, we all felt it, right where it hurt. He'd claimed the prize, and we got stuck with the leftovers. The party fell apart soon after that."

"Did you see Lieutenant Endicott again before you left Saigon?"

Lassiter shook himself out of his reverie. "No, not before I left. I saw her a few weeks later, when I made a swing back through Saigon on my way home."

"And Captain Hunter?"

"Gabe? The last time I saw Gabe Hunter was when he strolled out of my room at the Caravelle with Julia."

ELEVEN

May 13, 1972,
Saigon

Julia picked up her hairbrush and attacked her just washed hair. Dean Lassiter's invitation to a farewell bash at the Caravelle this evening couldn't have come at a better time.

She hadn't been out of uniform in a month and a half. She'd only left the base a half dozen times, mostly to make the Joint U.S. PAO briefings at the embassy. She couldn't remember when she'd felt so tired, or so grimly proud of the men and women she served with.

After weeks of intensive battle, South Vietnamese forces aided by massive U.S. air strikes had thrown back the enemy on every front. Fierce fighting still raged around An Loc, seventy miles north of Saigon. Government forces hadn't yet reclaimed Quang Tri City, which had fallen to the communists a few weeks ago, but they were close, so close.

What was more, President Nixon's decision to resume B-52 bombing of Hanoi and mine Haiphong harbor for the first time had, finally, brought the

North Vietnamese back to the Paris talks. After the most massive military campaign of the war, peace shimmered on the horizon.

Julia was in a mood to celebrate tonight. She wanted to forget the awful statistics she'd been gathering and releasing these past weeks. She wanted to wear civilian clothes and laugh and act like a woman instead of a lieutenant for a few hours.

She gave her hair a dozen vigorous strokes, noting that the pale blond ends now drifted past her shoulders. She'd have to get the thick mass cut soon, or start wearing it up with her uniform. She'd worry about that tomorrow, though. Tonight, the long, loose hairstyle Barbra Streisand had made so popular perfectly complemented her hip-hugging slacks and midriff-baring crocheted vest. In her considered opinion, she looked thoroughly with it.

Although . . .

She surveyed herself in the small mirror attached to the wall. The dog tags had to go. They didn't do a thing for the V-necked vest and low-cut hip-huggers. Slipping the embossed discs over her head, she dropped them into the side pocket of her purse. The St. Christopher medal Claire had given her brushed the slopes of her breasts. Its delicate silver chain was all the accessory she needed.

"Jules? Are you ready?"

"Almost," she called out. "Come on in."

Claire pushed open the door. "Wow, you look great!"

Julia stretched the truth a bit. "You do, too."

At least her friend had traded her baggy fatigues for civvies. Unfortunately, the shapeless trapeze dress was a chartreuse shade of yellow-green that gave her skin a sallow cast. The dark circles under her eyes didn't help, either. Like everyone else, Claire had worked fourteen- and sixteen-hour shifts, seven days a week, since the start of the offensive. Her rich fall of chestnut hair had a luster all its own, though, and her smile was genuine Claire.

"Hurry up, slowpoke. Gabe and his new hootch mate are waiting."

Julia's hand froze on the latch to her locker. "I thought Gabe had to fly tonight."

"His missions got scrubbed." Claire's smile wavered at the stubborn look on her friend's face. "Please, Jules. I haven't seen him in weeks. I—I need to be with him. Let's just go to the party at the Caravalle and relax and have fun together."

Julia hadn't seen Gabe Hunter in weeks, either, but she knew darn well she wouldn't relax in his company. Their hours together at DaNang had only intensified the confused melange of feelings the man roused in her. She hated his cocky arrogance, and admired his gritty courage. His patented, mocking grin irritated the hell out of her. The careless, affectionate smiles he bestowed on Claire had almost the same effect. Julia steadfastly refused to respond to his heavy-handed sexual innuendoes, and he refused to play the game by any rules but his own.

"Please, Jules."

"Okay, okay. Just let me dig out my platforms. I refuse to wear boots or granny shoes tonight."

She yanked open her locker, grimacing at the musty odor of mildew that had come with the start of the monsoon season and refused to go away. Rain poured down now at least twice a day, interspersed with bursts of hot, humid sunshine. Every piece of clothing Julia owned carried a rusty, disused scent. She'd long since abandoned panty hose because of the uncomfortable feminine itching their trapped heat caused.

Using a nail file, she scraped the green mold off her wooden-soled clogs, then slipped into the three-inch platforms. The wood felt damp and slick against her bare feet. She'd have to watch her step tonight. She'd almost forgotten how to walk in real heels. Grabbing her purse, she shooed Claire out the door.

"Okay, Simmons, let's go party."

Dark thunderclouds rumbled overhead as they made their way along the balcony to the wooden stairs. The first fat splatters hit the tin roof a few seconds later. Holding her tasseled knit bag over her head, Claire dashed from the entrance to the women's compound to a covered jeep. Laughing,

she tumbled into the front seat. Julia caught a flash
of Gabe's favorite purple parrot shirt as he leaned
over to give Claire a quick kiss.

Hard hands reached out to help Julia clamber
into the back. She landed with a whoosh beside a
grinning stranger.

"Endicott, this is Weems," Gabe tossed over his
shoulder. "Weems, be advised that Endicott carries
a loaded .357 with her at all times."

The newcomer grinned. "I'll remember that."

Gabe spun the wheel and cut away from the barracks, raising a wall of water from the runnel on the
side of the road. Claire shrieked as the rainwater
splashed over her legs, then laughed again and
clutched Gabe's arm. Deliberately, Julia turned her
attention to the man at her side.

Having arrived in-country all of three days ago,
Phil Weems was full of news that hadn't penetrated
her absorption with the war for the past month and
a half. Julia felt a sharp sense of disorientation as
she listened to his account of student takeovers of
administration buildings at Harvard and Cornell to
protest Gulf Oil's operations in Angola. Angola,
apparently, was the new campus cause célèbre.
Vietnam had taken a backseat.

Strange, she'd almost forgotten that another
world existed outside Vietnam. She hadn't forgotten the confusing sense of combating a war
in the midst of a continuing troop draw-down,
though. Like all replacements who'd arrived in

Vietnam in recent years, Phil Weems expected to turn around and head home within a few weeks. Julia didn't have the heart to tell him that the peace process seemed to have lasted longer than the war.

Gabe pulled up at the entrance to the ten-story Caravelle with a whine of tires on the slick road and a splash that added to the misery of the beggars hunched on the steps. With the fall of Quang Tri City in the north a few weeks ago, more than a quarter of a million refugees had fled south. The camps thrown up hastily throughout South Vietnam couldn't handle the flood of displaced persons. The few hours Julia hadn't worked at MACV these past weeks she'd spent at a Red Cross–operated orphanage a few miles outside Tan Son Nhut's north gate. The children wrung her heart, as did these quietly beseeching beggars.

Claire and Julia had both emptied their wallets of piasters by the time they made it into the crowded lobby. While Gabe and Phil Weems still negotiated with a gang of street boys to guard the jeep, the two women took the elevator to the sixth floor. As soon as the doors clanked open, they saw that Lassiter's party had spilled out of his room into the hallway. The rest of the doors on either side of the dim hall stood open, and the crowd flowed freely from room to room.

Claire opted to wait near the elevator for Gabe, but Julia spotted short, stubby Arnie Townsend, her friend from UPI, and joined him. Her determination to forget her military occupation for a few hours didn't survive the first five moments of conversation. Everyone there shared Julia's small, intense universe. Angola was two continents away. Vietnam was here and now.

Four hour later, she sat cross-legged on the floor amid a group of old Indochina hands. Her skin was dewed with damp from the humidity, and her hip-huggers dipped low in the back as she leaned forward to listen intently.

"It's all over now but the shouting," Reuters' bureau chief insisted. "Friendly forces are within five miles of An Loc. They'll retake it within a week. Quang Tri City might take a little longer, but I'm telling you, Highway 1 is one long stretch of smoldering tanks and trucks."

"The next big one's going to be in Cambodia," a thin, ginger-haired correspondent for the BBC predicted. "The guerrillas are almost knocking at the door to Lon Nol's palace."

"A chosen few among us will be there when he answers the knock," Lassiter put in smugly from behind.

A chorus of hoots and good-natured insults greeted this sally from the newest star in their midst. Dean had reason to act smug, Julia thought with a smile. He'd convinced a small-town, family-operated newspaper to provide him with a thin set of credentials. He'd paid his own way to a war everyone thought was over. A week after his arrival, he'd covered the first twenty-four hours of the '72 offensive through the eyes of the DaNang-based air crews when most of the press corps had been stuck in Saigon.

His stories had captured international interest. *Time* and *Newsweek* magazines were both courting him with tantalizing offers, and he'd even been approached by the broadcast bureau chiefs to do some on-scene reporting. Now he was heading for Phnom Penh with the wealth and interest of the prestige press behind him.

As icing on his cake, Dean had just received word that a respected senior editor considered his story about the rocket attack at DaNang worthy of nomination for a Pulitzer. As the editor had phrased it, the story movingly highlighted the tragic ambiguity of the war and stirred everyone who read it to press for a swifter conclusion.

Dean Lassiter was flying high, deservedly so. Julia had no doubt he was destined to soar higher yet.

He hunkered down beside her. "Have you seen Gabe?"

"No, I haven't."

"Damn, I need to talk to him. He promised to give me the names of some of his buddies flying for Air America in Cambodia."

"Look for Claire," Julia repeated casually. "When you find her, you'll find Hunter."

"She left over an hour ago. Said the noise and the heat were making her sick."

"Sick?" Julia scrambled up, remembering Claire's wan face and tired eyes. She must have really been feeling ill to leave the party. "She didn't go back to the base by herself, did she?"

"Gabe's friend, whatever his name is, had to go into crew rest and shared a taxi with her." Lassiter frowned, searching the room again. "Where the hell did Hunter go to?"

From the corner of one eye, Julia caught a glimpse of gaudy orange and purple parrots. Gabe's favorite party shirt drew her eye—and everyone else's in the room.

"There he is," she drawled.

Julia was too honest with herself to deny the frisson of electricity that lifted the fine hairs on her arms, and too intelligent to ascribe it to sexual attraction. Gabe Hunter didn't attract her. She disliked too much about him to feel attracted to him. He . . . affected her.

Dean promptly deserted her and made his way to Gabe's side. Julia drifted over to the impromptu bar that occupied the dresser, two nightstands, three straight chairs, and a plastic suitcase. Each guest, invited or otherwise, had contributed to the bar stock. She plucked a bottle of champagne from its nest in the ice-filled plastic suitcase. She had little knowledge of or experience with fine wines, but this one was good. Very good. Bubbles tickled her nostrils, and the pale gold liquid slid down her throat with seductive ease.

Intending to rejoin her group, she turned. A flash of purple drew her gaze. Gabe leaned against the far wall, Lassiter and another journalist close at hand. He didn't even pretend an interest in their conversation. His eyes stayed on Julia. Only Julia. On her face. The V-neck of her crocheted vest. The stretch of bare midriff above her low-slung hip-huggers.

Her stomach muscles contracted, low and swift and hard.

All right! Okay! He affected her. He affected Claire, too, and who knew how many other women on base and off. She was damned if she was going to hurt Claire or become part of Hunter's harem.

Her chin went up, and she gave him a slightly more refined version of his own mocking grin.

His mustache lifted in response, and his blue eyes glinted. He lifted his glass in a small private salute, then downed the contents in a single swallow. From the flush that darkened his tanned skin, Julia guessed it wasn't his first drink of the night.

Lassiter shifted, following his line of sight to where she stood. Belatedly, she realized that others in the room were watching the little byplay between her and Hunter as well. Disgusted with herself for giving them all a cheap show, she turned her back and joined the closest group. She'd managed to put

Hunter out of her mind completely when his voice rumbled at her ear.

"Ready to go? We'll have to hustle to beat the curfew."

She stiffened involuntarily. He hadn't touched her, hadn't done anything more than warm the tip of her ear with his breath. But that hot wash ... affected her. Dammit, it was time to end this silly cat-and-mouse game between them once and for all.

"Yes, I'm ready."

She deposited her glass on the dresser and retrieved her purse from the corner where she'd stashed it. She turned to wave a final farewell to Dean, forgetting about her three-inch platform heels. Gabe's hand encircled her upper arm and saved her from toppling over.

"Thanks," she muttered, pulling free.

The back of his hand brushed her breast before dropping to his side. "My pleasure, Goldilocks."

It was time to end it, Julia decided grimly. Past time.

She waited just inside the open doors to the lobby until Gabe reclaimed the jeep. The pelting rain had ceased, but a fine, warm drizzle hung over the street like a shimmering curtain.

With the approach of the eleven o'clock curfew, most of the beggars had disappeared. Street women who hadn't yet found an all-night trick cruised past the hotel, perched sideways on the backs of the scooters operated by their fathers or brothers or boyfriends. Gabe deflected a half dozen offers from eager salesmen while he finalized negotiations with the boys who'd guarded the jeep. One persistent entrepreneur put-putted alongside Gabe as he pulled up to the front entrance, lowering the price for the slender woman behind him several times.

"No, thanks," Gabe replied. "She's number one fine Honda girl, but I've got my own girl tonight."

Not hardly, Julia thought as she crossed the rain-slick pavement. The cowboy flicked a quick, dismissive glance her way.

"She no do for you what this one do. Ten dollars, okay?"

Gabe cut off the man's detailed description of the woman's varied services. "Not tonight."

"I give you special deal. Eight dollars."

Julia swung into the jeep and deposited her heavy purse between the seats to keep it from being snatched by one of the gangs of motorcycle thieves who roamed the streets. Gabe shifted into gear and cut into the traffic. The Honda swerved, then pulled up on the passenger side.

"Six dollars."

Julia's glance slid from the driver to the woman clinging to his waist. She wore black silk trousers and the finely embroidered silk *ao dai* favored by the upper classes. She was obviously a new refugee, Julia thought with a painful contraction of her heart. A former office worker, perhaps, or a college student. She had a bright, plastic smile fixed on her face, but her eyes looked right through the jeep. Black, hollowed, flat, they saw images Julia couldn't begin to imagine.

Her hand shaking, she fumbled for her wallet, then reached out to offer the girl a wad of dollars. The driver leaned back, snatched the bills from Julia's hand, and roared off. The girl's expression never altered.

Her brittle smile haunted Julia throughout the short ride to the base. She knew she wasn't to blame for the war that had ripped that girl's world apart. The seeds of the current conflict had been sown long before either one of them had been born. Yet that vacant stare indicted her and everyone else involved.

Hugging her arms, Julia sank down in the jeep's seat. The front gate went by in a blur. Buildings loomed in the mist, then dropped away as Gabe took the perimeter road to the USAF side of the base. Lost in her thoughts, she didn't realize that he'd slowed until he pulled the jeep to the side of the road and shoved it into neutral. A twist of the key silenced the engine.

Startled, Julia scanned the empty road ahead, bounded on the left by a high stucco wall topped by rolls of concertina wire. Low mounds of rubble stretched off to the right. She didn't recognize any of the landmarks.

"Where are we?"

"About a mile from the VNAF officers club, more or less."

The words were casual enough, but the faint slur in them brought Julia twisting around in her seat. He'd had more to drink than she'd realized.

"Why did you stop?"

In answer, he flicked the headlight switch and plunged them into drizzly darkness.

"Are you crazy?" she demanded, more nervous about their isolated location than his idiotic behavior. "In case you've forgotten, the VC lobbed some mortars over the perimeter fence just a few weeks ago."

"We're far enough away from the perimeter. We need to talk, Julia. We need to do more than talk."

"You're right about that, but I'm not holding any conversations with you here. Start the jeep, Hunter. This place makes me nervous."

He leaned toward her, his face shadowed. One hand tunneled through the hair at the back of her head.

"Good. I want you nervous and off balance and wide awake . . . unlike DaNang, sweet thing, when a whole houseful of termites couldn't rouse you."

"I'm awake, all right, and starting to get real pissed."

She tried to jerk her head away. His fingers tightened on the back of her neck, holding her in place.

"Pissed is a start, but I think we can do better."

Stiff-necked, Julia resisted his pull. "What about

that little speech at your hootch a few weeks ago?" she sneered. "I thought you weren't going to play the heavy-handed bad guy anymore."

"I wasn't." His mouth hovered inches from hers. She could smell the liquor on his breath and the damp heat of his body. "Then you came sashshaying out of your hootch in those fanny-huggers—"

"They're called hip-huggers," she ground out, putting her balled fists against his chest.

"You haven't seen them from behind, Goldilocks."

His lips brushed hers. Julia straightened her arms, or tried to.

"Gabe, stop it!"

"I don't think so."

His mouth came over hers with bruising force. Julia kept her arms stiff and her mouth closed. Disgust washed through her for placing herself in this ridiculous situation.

He lifted his head. A curled fist under her chin raised her face to his. His scent filled her nostrils, hot and musky.

Julia wasn't frightened. Not of Gabe. She knew him too well to be frightened of him. Besides, he was an officer and a . . . Well, an officer, anyway. He wore the same uniform she did. Was bound by the same code of ethics that bound her. Still, the glitter in his eyes made her uneasy.

"Listen to me," she said, wincing inwardly at the breathlessness in her voice. "You're right. We need to talk. We've got to end this silly head game we've been playing with each other. It's not fair to Claire, and it makes us both look like idiots."

"Don't kid yourself, Julia. This has nothing to do with Claire, and you know it. This is you and me and the way you get all wet whenever you think you've scored a few hits in our little contest."

Furious, she yanked her arm back. His hand clamped around her wrist in midair.

"Oh, no, babe. Not this time." With a quick twist he shoved her arm up behind her back. "This time we take it slow and sweet and nice."

He pressed her to the seat. Pinned by their combined weight, Julia couldn't move her arm even after his fingers unclamped her wrist. His hand splayed on her midriff, then slid up her sweat-slicked flesh.

She used her free hand to shove his away. His fingers tangled in the chain to her Saint Christopher medal. The delicate silver links dug into the back of her neck, then snapped.

Enraged and panting, she started to struggle in earnest.

"Julia?"

Claire rested her clammy forehead against the door of Julia's room. She'd conquered the sickness that had attacked her at Lassiter's party last night, but nausea had hit again just before dawn. Even now, a half hour later, the roiling in her stomach threatened to rise and choke her. She dragged in short, shallow breaths to force it down. Slowly the nausea subsided. Lifting a hand, she rapped on the door again.

"Julia? Are you there? Please, I need to talk to you."

She strained to hear over the sounds of the radio blaring from the room next door. The Red Cross counselor who occupied that cubicle was listening to the early morning news on the Armed Forces Radio Network while she got ready for work.

Claire rapped again. "Jules?"

The radio was cut off, and the door next to Julia's opened. Susie Johnson, a petite redhead who performed the grim service of verifying and relaying family emergency notifications to U.S. military personnel, stepped into the rainy dawn.

"Hi, Claire. Are you looking for Julia?"

"Yes."

"I think she's in the showers. I passed her going downstairs when I was coming up a little while ago."

"Thanks."

Tilting her head, Susie eyed Claire's face. "That must have been some party you two went to last night. You look almost as bad as Julia did."

Claire returned a noncommittal answer as she followed the redhead along the balcony and down the wooden stairs. With a cheerful wave Susie headed for the entrance to the women's compound.

Claire reached for the handle to the screened door of the latrines, then froze. The unmistakable scent of *kemchi* assaulted her nostrils and sent her stomach into convulsions. She rushed past the astonished *mamasan* who cleaned and ironed and cooked her personal meals on a hot plate in the cement-floored utility room. Falling to her knees, Claire lost the little she'd been able to force down in the past twenty-four hours.

The retching seemed to go on endlessly, one wave following another. When the heaving finally subsided, she clung to the stool and tried to stem the tears that streamed down her cheeks.

"Are you all right in there?"

Julia's voice sounded low and infinitely weary. Claire tried to reply, but the only sound that emerged from her raw throat was a moan. The door behind her opened.

"Claire! What's wrong?"

Her eyes blurred by tears, she saw only the aquamarine of Julia's silk kimono. She tried again to speak, but couldn't work any words past the sobs that suddenly racked her.

"I'll get you to the clinic." Julia reached for her wrists. "Come on, let me help you up."

"I . . . I don't need to go . . . to the clinic."

"Yes, you do. You're sick."

"I'm not . . . sick. I'm pregnant."

For long moments Julia didn't move, didn't speak. The awful silence spurred Claire's pride enough for her to swallow her sobs. Sliding her hands from her friend's loosened grasp, she swiped the back of her wrist across her eyes. "I know, I know. This is ... the seventies." She managed a watery laugh. "Any woman who gets herself pregnant is a fool. I didn't ... I mean, I used ... Gabe used a condom, but—"

"Don't!"

Claire winced at the harsh, stinging lash. Her heart twisting, she read the condemnation and disgust in the other woman's paper-white face. Oh, God! She'd counted on Julia to help her through this.

Some of her despair must have shown in her face. Julia closed her eyes and seemed to shudder. Then she sank to her knees in the tiny stall and held out her arms. Wimpering, Claire threw herself forward. Fresh tears soaked Julia's silk-clad shoulder.

"It's okay," she murmured.

"No, it's not! Oh, God, it's not! I'm too far along to get rid of it, even if I wanted to, and I don't, Jules, I don't! I couldn't live with myself. I couldn't ever go to Mass again."

"I know, I know."

"They'll ... They'll kick me out of the Air Force as soon as they find out, you know they will. If Gabe won't marry me, I'll have to go home to my parents. They—they won't ever let me or the baby live this down."

The hand stroking the back of her head stilled.

"You don't want to marry Gabe Hunter, Claire. You don't really know him."

"I do," she wailed. "I do!"

"You can't. He's got a mean side. He's—"

"He's never been mean to me, Jules. Never! Of all the men I've met, he's the only one who hasn't made me feel like a freak because of . . . of these . . . damned balloons!"

"Oh, Claire!"

She pulled back, her face ravaged by tears. "He doesn't want to get married. He told me that before we made love the first time. What am I going to do?"

Julia opened her mouth as if to speak, then closed it. Her throat worked for a few moments before she finally replied.

"He'll marry you."

TWELVE

Ted Marsh planted a foot on a desk drawer and tipped his chair back to catch the sunlight streaming in through his office windows. Located in one of the many World War II–era buildings on Bolling Air Force Base scheduled for demolition, this second-floor office commanded a view of the unused hangars across the street. The heating system worked sporadically in summer and rarely in winter, and the air conditioning refused to work at all, but the building's interior had been gutted a decade or so ago to provide outsize, comfortable offices with plenty of natural light—a rarity in federal structures.

Hands in his pockets, Marsh jingled his loose change and skimmed the time line Barbara Lyles had constructed on the dry board that took up one wall of his office.

A long blue line stretched horizontally across the board. Red X's and scribbled notes intersected it at periodic intervals. The entries clustered at the right end of the line were the ones that held Marsh's interest.

May 13: CS, JE, and GH attend party at Caravelle Hotel. CS leaves early. JE and GH depart together just before curfew.

May 15: CS and GH marry.

May 28: CS, now CH, returns to States, separates from AF under regulation requiring discharge of married women unless waive approved.

Jun 10: JE spends birthday at orphanage.

Jun 12: JE reports weapon missing. GH fails to show for mission pre-brief same afternoon.

Jun 13: Jeep checked out to GH found alongside road to Long Binh; GH declared MIA.

Eyes thoughtful, Marsh fingered the loose change in his pocket. "We're missing a piece of the puzzle."

Barbara took a step back, a red marker in her hand. Frowning, she scanned the board. "What's missing? We've reconstructed the dates, the events, and the players involved. We've got the body, or what's left of it. We've got the weapon. We've got the motive."

"I'm having second thoughts about the motive."

Barbara's brows lifted. "Since when?"

"Since I talked to Lassiter. He's right, Lyles. Julia Endicott doesn't possess a co-dependent or inse-cure bone in her body. I'm having trouble seeing her as a woman scorned and in a jealous rage."

"You don't think the colonel had plenty of rea-sons to be jealous? Hunter comes on to her for months. They may or may not have slept together on several occasions. They certainly shared a bedroom in DaNang. The heat between them peels the paint off the walls at Lassiter's party. Hunter leaves with her that night. Two days later, he marries her best friend, whom he's also been sleeping with all along. That would certainly work me into—"

"Why?"

"Why what?"

"If he was so hot to have sex with Julia, why did he marry Claire Simmons?"

"A man like Hunter might not consider the two mutually exclusive," Barbara drawled.

"We're missing something," Marsh insisted. "Why did he marry Claire at that particular point in time? She was due to ship back to the States in less than a month. He was supposed to DEROS in July. Wouldn't it have been more logical to wait and get married at home, with their families around them?"

"They were in the middle of a war. One of them, Hunter in particular, could have bought the farm any day."

"They'd made it through the war for ten months. Why not wait two more?"

Barbara tapped her chin with the marker. "Okay, how's this scenario? Claire knows she's leaving soon. Although she insists there wasn't anything going on between the man she loves and her best friend, she's heard rumors or sensed the attraction.

She gives Hunter an ultimatum. Forces him to choose once and for all."

"Maybe."

Marsh wasn't convinced. Although he wouldn't categorize Claire Hunter as a mouse, as Lassiter had, his instincts told him she wouldn't have issued any ultimatums to Hunter. She loved him too much to risk losing him that way. Despite the odds, Marsh mused, her love had prevailed. She'd married Hunter, given birth to his son, stayed true to his memory all these . . .

His chair hit the floor with a thump. "Have you still got the microfiche of Hunter's personnel records?"

"Yes, on my desk."

"Do they record his son's birth date?"

"I don't know. I suppose . . ." Barbara drew in a swift breath as she grasped the question behind his question. "Do you think Claire was pregnant? That's what got him to the altar?"

"It's a possibility. Can you track down the birth date?"

She tossed the red marker onto the tray attached to the dry board and dusted her hands. "Sure. If it's not in Hunter's personnel files, the Accounting and Finance Center should have it. Mrs. Hunter would have claimed survivor's benefits for the child during the years her husband was still listed as MIA."

"Check it out, will you? I want the information before I talk to Mrs. Hunter again."

"When is that?"

Ted reached for the phone. "This afternoon, if she's available. If not, I'll delay our meeting with Colonel Endicott and her lawyer until she is."

He punched in Claire Hunter's number, hoping she would answer. Marsh wanted out of the office. After two days of cooling his heels while Colonel Endicott consulted with an attorney, he wanted to get the case rolling again. His eyes narrowed on the dry board. He wanted to know what happened between May 13 and May 15, 1972.

"Yes, Mr. Marsh, I was pregnant with my son when I married Gabe."

Claire stood at the living room window, rubbing her hands over her sweater-clad arms. She felt as cold and as brittle as the ice coating the bare tree limbs in her wooded front yard. Like them, she wasn't sure how much more she could take without cracking.

Tomorrow she'd attend a second memorial service for her husband. This time the ceremony would be small and private, with only her and her son and Davey's wife in attendance. There'd be no honor guard, no bugler playing taps in a haunting tribute to a warrior who'd never returned from the battlefield. Tomorrow she'd say good-bye to Gabe for the second time.

Today she was burying the last of her dreams. All these years she'd clung to the belief that her husband had felt more than a careless affection for her. She felt strangely empty, almost weightless without it.

"My son doesn't know," she told the investigator standing quietly behind her. "I never told him. There wasn't any reason to."

"I don't see a reason to now. I just needed to understand why you and Captain Hunter decided to get married at that time, with so much going on in-country."

So much going on between Gabe and Julia, he meant. He was too polite to say so.

Claire stared sightlessly at the bare tree limbs. As if it had happened yesterday, she could remember every moment of the night Gabe had come pounding on her door and demanded to know why the hell he had to hear about her condition from Julia. His eyes shooting blue sparks, he'd instructed her to make whatever arrangements she wanted.

He'd relented when the tears that Claire couldn't seem to turn off started down her cheeks. Taking her in his arms, he'd given her the same assurances Julia had. It would be all right. Everything would work out.

Because she'd wanted to so desperately, Claire had believed him. During their three-day R&R in Hong Kong, he'd treated her like a real bride on a real honeymoon. Claire didn't need to pull the albums from the shelf in the living room to recall the vivid images of those brief, wonderful days. In her mind she could see Victoria Peak silhouetted clearly against an impossibly blue sky and hear the waves slapping against the sides of the junk that took them to a floating restaurant. In her heart she felt a whisper of the aching desire that had brought her into Gabe's arms each night. He loved her, she'd managed to convince herself. He needed her.

In the past few days she'd forced herself to face the truth. Gabe had married her to give their child a name, but the kind of love Claire wanted to give him wouldn't have held him. He craved excitement. He needed the adrenaline fix he got every time he took his plane up. He would've left her eventually for someone more exciting, more challenging.

Someone like Julia.

Claire's mouth curled down. Even now she couldn't face the truth. If she were honest, she'd admit that Gabe had left her for Julia while they were still in Vietnam. Swallowing her bitterness, she faced Ted Marsh.

"Why did you need to know the reason Gabe and I married? What possible difference could it make to your investigation?"

He chose his words carefully. "The evidence points to Colonel Endicott as the person who killed your husband. We need to understand what could have driven her to commit murder. It's possible that your marriage enraged her or made her jealous to the point of violence."

"That's absurd," Claire stated flatly. "Julia wasn't jealous. She's the one who told Gabe about the baby. She stood beside me at my wedding."

Marsh absorbed her statement without comment. Tucking his hands in his pockets, he strolled across the room to study the silver-framed photo on the mantel above the fireplace.

"Was this taken on your wedding day?"

Claire moved to stand beside him. "Yes."

She'd never liked the shot, but it was the only professional portrait taken at the hurried wedding. An Air Force photographer had snapped it just as Gabe slipped the ring on her finger. Claire was wearing the silly tent-like outfit they called a trapeze dress back then—not by choice, but because she couldn't get into her Air Force uniform. One of the women at the barracks had scrounged up a little round pillbox hat with a half veil. The dainty hat and veil looked ridiculous with the trapeze dress, but every bride needed a veil, she'd insisted.

Julia was in civvies, too. She'd donned the only dressy outfit she'd brought with her to Vietnam, and looked far more like a bride than Claire did. A simple length of white linen with a square neck and short cap sleeves, the sheath dress flattered her slender figure and set off her shoulder-length blond hair. She stood at Claire's left as her maid of honor, still and pale, her face lacking its usual lively animation.

Even Gabe appeared different. His sun-streaked tawny hair had been tamed into place, and he wore a starched and crisply ironed 1505 tan uniform instead of the green flight suit he normally lived in. He stood at Claire's right, his hand holding hers as he slid the ring he'd purchased that afternoon onto her finger.

Claire gazed at the picture as though seeing it for the first time. There she stood, between Julia and Gabe—where she'd always stood. The aching sense of betrayal that had been her constant companion since Julia's visit a few days ago sharpened to a long, pointed spike.

"May I borrow this for a few days?"

She pulled her gaze from the grainy color photo. "Why, Mr. Marsh?"

Stretching out a hand, he lifted down the silver-framed photo. "I'd like to make a copy of this, if you don't mind. It's the only photo I've seen that includes both Captain Hunter and Colonel Endicott."

The victim and the suspect.

Claire's hands curled around her upper arms again. For all her sense of betrayal, she couldn't bring herself to believe that Julia was the prime suspect in the investigation into Gabe's murder.

"I want it back after you make a copy," she told the agent.

"Of course."

She stood unmoving while he examined the faces in the photo. Then his gray eyes lifted to Claire's. "If Julia Endicott wasn't jealous, what reason could she have had to kill your husband?"

"I don't know."

A thick smothering fog had descended by the time Marsh drove through the brick gates of Bolling Air Force Base. He turned left, heading past the row of condemned buildings that awaited their fate. As he passed the office of the Air Force Chief of Chaplains, he grinned. He'd always found it ironic that the headquarters for the chaplains and the OSI were collocated on the same air patch. One group specialized in redeeming sinners, the other in making them burn for their crimes.

He pulled into his slot at OSI headquarters and let himself into the secured building. As always, one or two of the doors in the long, narrow hallway showed light through their frosted glass panes. Long days and late nights came with the so-called honor of being selected to work at OSI headquarters.

Flicking the light switch in his office, he tossed the rolled-up tube he'd carried in with him onto his desk and shrugged out of his overcoat. A knuckle to the throat loosened his tie. He yanked open the center desk drawer and pawed through it in search of a roll of Scotch tape. As always, the drawer's jumbled contents reminded him of his ex-wife.

Before she'd left him, Carlene had catalogued several thick volumes of complaints about his absorption with his work, his long hours, his frequent travels, and his irritating personal habits. His damned messy drawers headed her list in the last category.

Marsh finally found the roll of tape shoved far back in the drawer. Peeling off a couple of long strips, he unrolled the paper tube and stuck the poster-sized print to the wall. Two more pieces anchored the bottom edge.

Marsh assumed his thinking position—one foot on the bottom desk drawer, chair tipped back, hands in his pockets—and gave himself over to the urge that had driven him to stop at a commercial duplicating center just outside the base. He'd had several copies of the wedding picture made, and a blow-up of just Julia Endicott. Life-size and unsmiling, she gazed back at him from the wall.

Christ, she had been something then!

She was something now, Marsh admitted, but the hair and makeup styles of two decades ago flattered her fine-boned beauty more dramatically than today's softer styles. Her silvery blond mane fell in a smooth curve to her shoulders. A heavy smudge of dark green shadow on her lids emphasized her seductive eyes. The sculpted cheekbones hadn't changed over the years, or the full mouth, although

Marsh preferred the soft red color she used on her lips now to the pale pink that had been so popular then.

The drift of his thoughts brought him up short. Frowning, he chinked the coins in his pocket together—another annoying habit of his, as Carlene had acidly pointed out. The minutes stretched. A door slammed down the hall. The darkness showing through the windows deepened to an inky black.

"Did you kill him?"

The beautiful, still creature didn't reply.

"Did you, Julia?"

Marsh didn't know when the suspect had made the transition from Colonel Endicott to Julia in the private reaches of his mind, but he wasn't surprised that she had. He focused better with an image in front of him. He needed to personalize the subject. See him or her as someone capable of the emotions that drove a person to commit crimes. Get past the barriers of rank and personnel records that always complicated a military investigation.

The eagles on Julia Endicott's shoulders didn't intimidate Marsh. He'd investigated too many people over the years to get wrapped around the flagpole by the fact that she outranked him. Some agents who'd come up through the enlisted ranks, as Marsh had, couldn't make the leap from being trained to follow orders to questioning those who gave them. Not even the anonymity of civilian clothes could overcome that mental obstruction. Marsh had never had that problem.

Rank aside, something about this woman kept her just outside his reach. He still couldn't see into the mind behind those wide, clear eyes that fascinated him so.

"What happened, Julia? What happened between you and Gabe Hunter that could have turned you into a killer?"

He studied the unsmiling mouth. The firm chin. The long, slender neck above the square-shaped bodice of her white dress.

Suddenly his chair thumped against the floor. Yanking his hands out of his pockets, Marsh rose and planted his knuckles on his desk. Once more he followed the long, clean, *bare* line of her throat.

"Bingo!" he said softly.

THIRTEEN

"We need to talk about the Saint Christopher medal found with Captain Hunter's remains. I'd like to know exactly when and how you lost it."

Her face expressionless, Julia weighed her answer to Special Agent Marsh's question.

She was ready for it. She'd had eight days to prepare herself. Eight days before she resumed an interrogation interrupted first by her decision to consult an attorney and then by the long Christmas weekend. Eight days to remember, and to prepare herself for this question.

She now discovered that eight days weren't long enough. Moisture dampened her palms. Slowly, carefully, Julia laced her fingers together.

"I lost it the night I went to Dean Lassiter's party at the Caravelle."

"That was May thirteenth."

"Was it?"

She was stalling. She knew it. Ted Marsh knew it as well. His smoky eyes narrowed fractionally; then he pulled a small black notebook out of his pocket and made a show of flipping through the pages. Julia didn't fool herself. She didn't doubt that the OSI agent had every word in the notebook filed in his mind. He'd simply turned the tables on her by letting her nerves stretch thin while he thumbed through the notebook.

He looked different this morning, she thought, unable to pinpoint just why. He wore the same pin-stripe navy blue suit she'd seen him in before. Today he'd teamed it with a pale blue shirt and a patterned maroon tie. The silver threads in his dark mahogany hair showed clearly in the light, as did the faint white lines at the corners of his eyes. Out-wardly, he presented the same neat, no-nonsense image he had during their previous interviews.

The change was internal, Julia realized with a sudden clenching in her stomach. Although he kept his expression neutral and his voice emotionless, she sensed a keener, sharper edge to him.

Dampness sheened the back of her neck as well as her palms. Too late Julia wished she hadn't opted to wear her heavy wool Air Force sweater and dark blue uniform slacks this morning. Out-side, their warmth had helped combat the blast of arctic air that had swept into the District a few days ago and lingered like an uninvited guest. Inside the heated building, however, they added to her clammy, nervous tension. She wasn't about to pull the sweater off over her head now, though. Not with Marsh observing her so steadily.

"According to Dean Lassiter," he stated, flipping the damned notebook shut, "you attended a party he hosted at the Caravelle Hotel in downtown Saigon on the evening of May thirteenth, 1972. You arrived with Captain Hunter and Lieutenant Simmons around seven that evening. You left with Captain Hunter at approximately ten-thirty. Were you wearing the St. Christopher medal when you left?"

Before Julia could frame her answer, the young officer at her side pushed his wire-rimmed glasses higher on the bridge of his nose and intervened.

"Do you have a copy of Mr. Lassiter's statement? I'd like to—" He corrected himself immediately. "That is, Colonel Endicott should review it before she answers your questions."

Julia bit down on the inside of her lower lip. Deliberately, she reminded herself that Captain Brian O'Rourke came highly recommended by a friend who knew the personalities in the Washington Area Defense Counsel's office. In the days she'd worked with the lawyer, he'd impressed her with his quick grasp of the evidence. She just wished he didn't look young enough to be her son, or stumble every time he remembered that he was here to advise, not defend. She wasn't on trial . . . yet.

"Mr. Lassiter didn't make a formal statement,"

Marsh replied. "We spoke off the record the night
he left for a Christmas vacation and then for a trip
to Paris to cover the summit. He's prepared to provide a signed statement, however, should one be
necessary."

So Dean was out of town, Julia thought. That's
why he hadn't filed a story on Gabe's murder and
her supposed role in it. He would, though. If and
when this inquiry led to formal charges, he'd capi-
talize on his personal knowledge of the players
involved to turn out one of the brilliant, double-
edged pieces he did so well. In his inimitable style
he'd paint a vivid picture of a woman brought to
justice after so many years, and indict the system
that had taken so long to bring her there.

So far the story had captured little in the way of
public attention. The *Air Force Times* had run a picture of Gabe and a few lines about the ongoing
inquiry into the circumstances surrounding his
death. Several major dailies had called for confirmation of the rumor that Colonel Julia Endicott's
sudden transfer from the Air Force PAO office was
connected to this inquiry. The *Post* and the *Christian
Science Monitor* had both shown interest in the
story, but a crash of a commuter jet crammed with
people heading home for Christmas had overshadowed all other news.

When Gabe's remains had been buried last week,
the NBC affiliate in the town where Claire now

lived had sent a reporter and camera crew to interview the widow. She'd declined to appear on camera. She'd put herself and her son through the ordeal of a public memorial service once, she'd told Julia raggedly over the phone when she'd begged her not to come. She didn't want to go through another.

The possibility of the far more sensational ordeal of a trial had remained unspoken between them. Julia knew that her answer to Marsh's question might well decide whether that trial would take place.

"Yes," she said slowly, "I was wearing the medal when I left the hotel."

"You weren't wearing it when you posed for the Hunters' wedding picture two days later."

I'm sorry, Claire. He knows, or he's close to guessing. I have to tell him.

"What happened to the medal, Colonel Endicott? How did Captain Hunter gain possession of it?"

Drawing in a deep, steadying breath, she admitted what she'd never told anyone—except the lawyer she'd met for the first time a few days ago.

"Captain Hunter tore the medal from my neck when he raped me, or tried to. I'm not sure which."

Marsh didn't so much as blink. "You're not sure if you were raped, Colonel?"

"No, Mr. Marsh, I'm not."

In the periphery of her vision Julia caught a flash of red wool as Special Agent Lyles leaned forward.

She ignored the other agent, her entire being concentrated on Marsh.

"Tell me what happened, Colonel."

His voice was low, steady, seductive in its invitation to throw off the weight that had pressed down on her for so long. Julia could tell him. She'd managed to tell O'Rourke without losing her composure. But she couldn't watch him watching her while she did.

She shoved back her chair and rose. His dark brows slashing downward, Marsh started to get up as well.

"Keep your seat," she ordered with a sharp, unconscious note of command. "I'm not going anywhere. I just need to move."

Not wanting her sweaty palms to betray her nervousness, Julia folded her arms. Back stiff, she focused on one of the pen-and-ink sketches of various Air Force aircraft that decorated the conference walls.

"Captain Hunter and I left the Caravelle a half hour before curfew," she related, forcing the words through a tight throat. "His hootch mate had driven Claire back to the base earlier. I was preoccupied and didn't notice that Gabe took a different route once inside the gates to Tan Son Nhut. He stopped the jeep on a deserted stretch of road along the perimeter and attacked me."

"He sexually assaulted you?"

"He tried to."

"He didn't achieve penetration?"

She could do this, Julia told herself. She could tell him about that black, awful night.

"I don't know. A little, I think. I was struggling and he had to—had to . . ."

She stopped, breathing hard and fast through her mouth.

Dammit, she could do this! She had to do this! Sooner or later Marsh would find the record of her visit to the clinic in her medical file. He'd know then what she'd hidden for so many years.

She should have torn that entry out of her medical records years ago. She would have, if the corpsman who'd issued her the spermicidal jelly and penicillin tablets hadn't discreetly labeled the purpose of her visit as birth control. Now, Julia knew, the time and the date of that entry damned her.

Zero-four-five hours, May 13, 1972. Hours after she'd left the party at the Caravelle. Hours before she'd knelt beside a retching, sobbing, pregnant Claire.

Remembering too late that visit to the clinic, Julia had driven to the hospital at Bolling a few days ago, only to find that her medical records had been requested by the OSI for "review." She'd realized then that it was only a matter of time until Marsh concluded that she'd lied about engaging in sexual intercourse with her victim.

Now she had no choice but to relive the night she'd tried so hard to forget. Her fingers dug into the thick wool of her sweater. Unseeing, her eyes fixed on the ink sketch. Forcing herself to breathe more slowly, she finished her terse account.

"Hunter had to straddle the gear shift. He got my slacks down, but we were both at an awkward angle. When he—" She dragged her tongue across dry lips. "When he positioned himself for entry, I brought my knee up between his. Hard. There was some . . . degree of penetration . . . for a moment."

After all these years she could still feel rage and shame and disgust. The black-and-white sketch blurred. Her eyes burned with the tears she refused to shed. She hadn't cried on May thirteenth. She wouldn't cry now.

"Here."

She blinked rapidly at the sound of a deep voice at her shoulder.

Julia had accomplished many things in her life that gave her a sense of pride. The fact that her hand didn't shake as she reached for the glass Marsh held out would rank right at the top of her revised list. The water slid down her aching throat like an icy shock.

"Thank you."

He took the empty glass from her hand. "Can you go on?"

When she nodded, he set the glass on the small silver tray beside the water carafe. He hitched a leg on the corner of the table. His wide shoulders blocked the others from her sight. Julia could have been alone with him.

Somehow that made it easier. She wasn't telling the story to an audience. She couldn't see the damned tape recorder. There was only her and Marsh.

She drew in a steadying breath. "Technically, I don't know whether Captain Hunter raped me or I impaled myself when I kneed him. Personally, I don't care."

"I don't think a jury would, either. Why didn't you kill him right then?"

The question was so offhand that Julia could only marvel at the casual invitation for her to incriminate herself.

"I might have, if I'd been able to get to my gun. Unfortunately, Captain Hunter anticipated just such an eventuality and kept my purse out of my reach while he . . . recovered."

"What happened then?"

"Then we played out a cheap, tawdry parlor farce. I wasn't about to walk along the perimeter alone at that hour of the night. Hunter made some acid observation about women who ask for it and don't know how to handle it when they get it. Eventually, he drove me back to the barracks."

"Why didn't you report his assault?"

"I should have. I intended to. But by the time I got back to the barracks, I felt so damned *stupid*!"

For a moment Julia was back in her eight-by-ten

room, pacing the cramped floor, feeling not just stupid, but dirty and violated and angry and scared.

"That was before anyone had coined either the phrase or the concept of date rape," she got out, her throat tight. "I saw what had happened to one of the girls in my dorm at college who brought a rape charge against the football player she'd been dating. He beat the charge easily and strutted around campus. She carried the label of cock teaser until she transferred to another school."

Marsh didn't reply. He didn't have to. In his line of business, he knew as well as Julia that the accuser all too often became the accused in rape cases.

"I left the party voluntarily with Hunter," she said bitterly, condemning herself every bit as harshly as she knew others would have. "You said yourself everyone thought I was having an affair with Gabe. No one would have believed me if I charged him with rape, and I wasn't ready to put myself through that."

"What did you do?" he asked quietly.

Her mouth turned down in disgust. "I went to the clinic. The corpsman on duty issued me some spermicidal jelly and penicillin tablets. I had no idea how many women Gabe had slept with besides Claire, and I didn't want to take any chances."

He didn't speak for several moments, weighing all she'd told him.

"Let's talk about Claire. I understand why you didn't go to the authorities. But I'm not sure I understand why you didn't tell your best friend that the man she loved assaulted you."

"I tried. When I got out of the shower that morning, Claire was . . . She was there, in the latrine."

"Is that when she told you she was pregnant?"

Julia's hands dropped to her side. A sense of futility stole over her. She'd tried to protect Davey and Claire. She'd tried.

"How did you know?"

"We checked her son's birth date. Mrs. Hunter confirmed it when I spoke with her."

"When did you talk to her?"

"Last week. The day before her husband's remains were interred."

"You badgered Claire about her son's birth date the day before she buried her husband for the second time?" Her lip curled. "Nice line of work you're in, Marsh."

The sarcastic comment shattered the almost-truce brought about by his offer of the water.

"Someone's got to do it, Colonel," he replied softly, dangerously.

The skin across Julia's cheeks tightened. Without another word she returned to her seat. Marsh chose to remain standing. Pushing his hands into his pockets, he fingered his keys.

"Why didn't you tell me about this incident when I asked you if you'd had sex with Captain Hunter?"

"I didn't have sex with Captain Hunter. He raped me, or tried to."

"Don't play word games with me again, Colonel."

Marsh hadn't meant for the warning to come out so sharply. He cursed under his breath as he saw Barbara's head lift in surprise and a militant light come into Julia's eyes.

The young lawyer also took exception. "I object to both your tone and this line of questioning."

"This isn't a trial. I'm not required to observe the rules of court-martial etiquette."

"Nor is my client required to submit to intimidation."

The agent swung his gaze to Julia. "Are you intimidated, Colonel?"

"No, Mr. Marsh," she shot back, "I'm not."

He felt a tug of admiration for her flinty courage. Despite the weight of the evidence against her, Julia Endicott refused to bend.

"Let's get back to the original question. Why didn't you tell me about the rape?"

"Why? Because I knew when I did, I'd hand you the motive you've been looking for."

"So you shot Captain Hunter to avenge what he did to you on the night of May thirteenth?"

"I didn't shoot Captain Hunter."

"Some people wouldn't blame you. Some people might say the bastard deserved shooting."

"He did, Mr. Marsh. I didn't shoot him, however."

"Then who did?"

Her lids fluttered down, then lifted. He caught a glimpse of fear, quickly hidden.

"I don't know."

He was silent for several moments, absorbing all she'd told him. There was more to the story, he knew, a final confrontation between Julia Endicott and Gabe Hunter. When had it come? What had happened?

"How did you convince Captain Hunter to marry Lieutenant Simmons?"

The swift change in direction threw her off balance. "How did you know I convinced Gabe to marry Claire?"

"She said you talked to Hunter that morning, told him she was pregnant. Did he take much convincing, Colonel?"

For the first time the fight seemed to go out of her. Propping her elbows on the table, she put her face in her hands. Her breath soughed in, then out, the rasping sound magnified by the hollow of her palms.

"I'm sorry, Claire. I'm so sorry."

Marsh hardened himself against the low, agonized whisper. "Would you speak up, please?"

Slowly she lifted her head. Her eyes went to the tape recorder in the center of the table. "Does this have to be part of the official record?"

He didn't hesitate. "No. Turn the tape recorder off."

His partner gaped at him.

"Turn it off."

Barbara Lyles reached out a long, tapered nail and flicked off the recorder.

Julia gave a small, almost imperceptible sigh of relief. "I want to talk to you privately."

Captain O'Rourke protested. "I don't think that's a good idea, Colonel Endicott. As your attorney, I advise you not to speak off the record or continue this discussion without legal counsel."

"I understand, Captain. What I want to say has nothing to do with me or Captain Hunter's death."

The attorney slipped his glasses off and folded them into his pocket. "I'll wait outside with Special Agent Lyles."

Barbara took her dismissal with less grace than the captain. Shooting Marsh a look that promised a long, heated discussion later, she shut the door behind her.

The others' departure made the small conference room seem at once larger and more intimate. It also freed Marsh to study Julia Endicott with unrestrained male appreciation as she walked to the end of the table to pour herself more water from the silver carafe. Not many women could carry off that bulky sweater and pleated slacks the way the colonel did, he thought. The dark color contrasted with the silvery gilt of her hair, while the pants displayed the slim line of her hips and trim behind.

Slightly disconcerted to find himself contemplating a colonel's behind, Marsh shoved his hands in his pockets and jingled his loose change.

Julia sent him a frowning glance over one shoulder. "That's an annoying habit. Do you do it on purpose, to distract your suspects?"

Marsh pulled his hands out of his pocket, smiling ruefully. "No. I don't even realize I'm doing it. My ex-wife had it close to the top of her list of my least desirable traits, though."

Surprise tingled through Julia as she returned to her chair. As far as she could recall, that was the first time she'd ever seen Special Agent Ted Marsh smile. He looked almost human.

Careful, she warned herself. She couldn't afford to think of him as human. Only as the enemy.

"I meant what I said about this conversation, Mr. Marsh. It's strictly off the record. I don't want this to appear in a transcript. Anywhere. Claire's been hurt enough. She doesn't need a record turning up that says her husband had to be forced to marry her."

"Did you force him?"

"More or less. He might have offered to marry

Claire, eventually, on his own. I doubt it, but in any case, we didn't have time to wait for him to get around to it."

"Because Claire was going home in a month?"

"Because she could barely get into her fatigues by the time she told me she was pregnant. In those days pregnancy meant an automatic discharge whether you were married or not. Pregnancy in a war zone meant you were on the next plane out of Dodge. She couldn't face her family without a job or a husband or her pride. I couldn't let her."

"So you talked to Hunter."

"No, I didn't talk to him. I gave him an ultimatum. He'd marry Claire, or I'd bring charges against him for rape."

Marsh sat back and stretched out his legs. His hands went for his pockets, but he caught himself just in time and hooked his thumbs in the seams instead.

"I don't see Gabriel Hunter as a man who'd respond well to ultimatums."

"The results speak for themselves, Mr. Marsh."

Julia saw no reason to tell him, on or off the record, that she'd threatened to put a SuperVel 110 grain hollow-point bullet into Gabe Hunter's balls if he balked at marrying the mother of his child.

"Did you see him again after the wedding?"

"Are we still off the record?"

His shoulders stiffened. Not much. Just enough to make his relaxed posture in the chair a little less

casual. She knew as well as Marsh that any state-
ments she made now couldn't be used against her.
There were no witnesses to verify what she said.
No tape recorders to capture it.

Had she been the one conducting this interview,
she would've terminated it now and resumed in
front of witnesses. She waited, her heart thumping
erratically to see what Marsh would do.

"We're still off the record, Colonel."

She looked him straight in the eye. "I never saw
Gabe Hunter again."

"Not even when his wife left for the States?"

"I said good-bye to Claire at the women's
quarters."

"You didn't run into Hunter at the O Club?"

"I—I didn't feel particularly sociable for a while."

A long while, she remembered.

Julia didn't speak for a moment, fighting the
memory of the anger and disgust and sense of vio-
lation she'd carried with her for so many long
months. More than anything else, she hated Gabe
Hunter for shattering her confidence in herself.
Never again had she blithely assumed she could
control the direction and intensity of her relationship with a man.

"I didn't go to the O Club," she said after a
moment. "I didn't even go into Saigon. I almost
accepted Dean Lassiter's invitation to dinner the
night before he left for the States.... It was the
night before my birthday, too, and I was feeling

down. But I found out he'd also invited Gabe, and I didn't go."

"Your birthday's the eleventh of June," he murmured.

She looked at him in surprise, then flushed. Of course, he'd remembered her birthday. That was the day she'd spent at the orphanage. The day her father's Smith & Wesson was stolen from her room at the women's barracks.

He picked up where her thoughts had left off. "The same day Gabriel Hunter failed to report for his mission-planning brief."

"That's right."

"Eighteen hours later, his jeep was found on the road to Long Binh."

Julia leaned forward, the skin tight across her high cheekbones. "I didn't kill him, Marsh. I didn't get into a jeep and drive to Long Binh with him. I didn't ask him to stop by the side of the road, then pull out my weapon and put a bullet through his skull."

"If you didn't, who did? And why?"

"I don't know!"

A silence settled over the conference room, broken only by the tinkle of coins tumbling against one another.

FOURTEEN

The moment the door closed behind Colonel Endicott, her lawyer, Barbara Lyles, rounded on Marsh.

"What's this off-the-record crap? Since when does the OSI operate like a gumshoe detective agency in some B-grade movie?"

"The OSI doesn't," Marsh replied mildly, reaching for his overcoat. "I, however, do, occasionally. Let's get back to Bolling."

The irate agent splayed her hands over hips covered by a flaring, fire-engine red wool skirt. "We're not going anywhere until you tell me what went on here, Ted."

Since Barbara's statuesque, six-foot-one frame blocked the door, Marsh conceded her point. Special Agent Lyles carried herself with the grace and the style of a model. She'd also aced every one of the FBI academy's martial arts courses before she decided to forsake the hopelessly chauvinistic Bureau for—in her words—the marginally more progressive military. Marsh knew he wouldn't get out of the conference room until he smoothed her ruffled feathers.

"Why did you let up on her?" she demanded. "Telling us about that incident with Hunter strung her wire tight. If you'd applied a little more torque, she might have snapped. I couldn't believe you agreed to talk to her without a witness present."

"She wasn't going to say anything incriminating. Even under pressure Julia's too smart for that."

"Julia?" Barbara arched a penciled brow. "The chief investigator and the prime suspect are on a first-name basis now? You two must have had some chat."

"Cut me some slack, Lyles." Marsh tossed his overcoat back on a chair. "You know damn well I don't call her Julia to her face. You also know that once the dike breaks and a witness spills her deep, dark secrets, there's no plugging the leak again. If she'd told me anything *off* the record, eventually she would have repeated it *for* the record."

Still miffed, Barbara didn't abandon her militant stance. "So what did she tell you?"

Marsh gave her a brief encapsulation of the conversation, then scooped up his overcoat again.

"Let's go back to the office. I want to go through Julia's"—he shot Barbara a dark look—"Colonel Endicott's medical records again. I shouldn't have missed that visit to the clinic the night Hunter attacked her."

"*If* he attacked her."

Marsh cocked his head. "You think she's making the rape attempt up?"

"Possibly."

His partner draped the wool cloak that matched her red suit around her shoulders. When Barbara went undercover, she somehow managed to blend into any setting she inserted herself into. When she worked out of headquarters, she scornfully disdained the female equivalent of the navy blue pinstripe suit and indulged her more flamboyant tastes.

"Colonel Endicott's seen the physical evidence," she pointed out. "She's heard statements from several witnesses who were absolutely convinced she and Hunter had something hot going between them. Maybe she's trying to lessen the charge against her by building a case against him."

"Maybe."

Marsh reached for the door, surprised at his own doubts. A few days ago he'd stared at the blow-up of a young Julia Endicott and wondered if jealousy could drive her to murder a man. Just moments ago she'd given him the answer. Not jealousy but cold, deadly rage. Revenge for Hunter's attack on her.

For some reason the answer didn't afford Marsh the satisfaction he'd expected it to. Listening to Julia's terse account of what had happened to her on that deserted perimeter road, he hadn't experienced the gut-tightening sense of anticipation he sometimes did when a suspect teetered on the edge. Nor did he quite understand why he'd held his breath and willed her not to fall.

"We need to take another look at our time line as well," he said curtly, ushering Barbara out of the conference room. "We've got a few more dates to add. The visit to the clinic the morning after Lassiter's party. David Hunter's birth date some five months after his father's death. And I want to—"

"Special Agent Marsh?"

He wheeled around to face a tall, trim major.

"I'm glad I caught you before you left. General Titus would like to see you."

A disgruntled Barbara Lyles waited in the outer office while Marsh entered the inner sanctum. The vice chief didn't waste time on pleasantries or preliminaries. Waving the agent to one of the uncomfortable Ethiopian chairs in front of his desk, he got right to the point.

"What's the status of your investigation into this Captain Hunter's death?"

Marsh didn't hesitate. Given the high profile of the suspect, he'd been providing daily progress reports to his boss. Colonel Pfligerman in turn briefed his boss, the OSI commander, who kept the top Air Force leadership apprised. In this case, though, the front office interest went deeper than usual. In the past weeks Marsh had learned a great deal about Colonel Julia Endicott, including the rumor that the vice chief had hand-selected her as the deputy chief of Public Affairs and was grooming her for future promotion to general officer.

Despite the rumors, General Titus hadn't hesitated to take the painful step of removing his protégé from office. He'd also maintained a necessary distance from the investigation to ensure a lack of command influence. Something must have occurred to get him involved at this point, Marsh guessed.

"My investigation is still in progress," he replied succinctly. "We've assembled the evidence, collected statements from witnesses, and have just finished interviewing Colonel Endicott."

Frosty blue eyes pinned Marsh to the hard, hand-carved chair. "Did she do it?"

He knew better than to remind the general that a court-martial board would decide the answer to that question. The vice chief wanted his opinion as a trained investigator.

"A few days ago, I would have said yes. Today . . ."

"Today what?" Titus snapped.

"Today, Colonel Endicott gave me additional information that I want to check out."

Briefly, he summarized Julia's account of the night of May 13, 1972. The assault had occurred more than twenty years ago on the other side of the world . . . if it had occurred at all. Yet the idea of a young Julia Endicott pinned to the seat of a jeep, fighting off an attack by another Air Force officer, squared the vice chief's jaw.

"The bastard," he muttered.

His rigid posture easing, General Titus rubbed the back of his neck. "How close are you to wrapping up your end of this case?"

"I need another week, maybe two. I want to review the transcripts of our interviews with Colonel Endicott and, if necessary, get a written statement from Dean Lassiter when he returns from Europe."

The vice chief grimaced. "He'll be back next Friday. In fact, he's flying home after the summit with the president aboard Air Force One. The National Security adviser called a while ago to give us a heads-up, and to suggest we might want to proceed quickly with this case."

"Why? Is Lassiter hinting that he might splash this case across the front pages?"

"No. Just the opposite, in fact. He promised that he wouldn't run with it unless or until we prefer charges. In his considered opinion," the general said dryly, "it's not hard news until then."

That was fine with Marsh. He didn't need to spend more hours countering erroneous statements published by the media than working his investigation, as usually happened with high-viz cases.

"I don't understand, sir. Why the pressure to move on the investigation then?"

"It seems there's a cabinet-level delegation leaving for Ho Chi Minh City next month to negotiate a new trade agreement. The White House doesn't want a twenty-year-old murder to hit the front pages and raise haunting memories of the war just when we're sitting down to talk trade with our old enemies."

Personally, Marsh didn't particularly give a rat's ass about trade concessions for the Vietnamese government. Professionally, he understood the political ramifications of what was, until a few moments ago, strictly a military matter. He'd been in the business too long to rush an investigation, though, particularly a murder investigation. He'd take whatever time he needed.

"Keep me posted," the general said in dismissal.

"Yes, sir."

A cold, smoggy haze hid the sun as Marsh and his partner drove through D.C.'s deserted streets. The light traffic constituted one of the few benefits of working the week between Christmas and New Year's. So many federal workers were on leave that the drive across the Fourteenth Street Bridge, through the Waterfront district, and over the Douglass Bridge to Bolling Air Force Base took only fifteen minutes instead of its usual, teeth-grinding forty.

In his office, Marsh shed his overcoat and tossed it negligently over a chair. His suit coat and tie followed a few seconds later.

"Okay, Lyles, you update the time line. I'll look through the medical records. Then we'll review the transcripts of the interviews page by page, line by line."

Barbara twisted off the cap of the red dry-board marker. "I still don't see the significance of this visit to the clinic. The colonel might have been using a diaphragm all along and simply needed a refill."

"In the middle of the night?"

"Maybe she and Hunter planned a marathon session. Maybe they intended to continue in her room what they started in the jeep, only the colonel didn't have any supplies."

Marsh pulled the fat, green-jacketed medical file from the stack of documents they'd collected on Colonel Julia K. Endicott. Dropping the file on his cluttered desk, he settled into his favorite position. The office chair groaned in protest as he pushed it onto its back legs.

"Tell me something, Lyles. Would you indulge in an all-night marathon with a man whose sexual activities worried you so much that you had to take penicillin tablets first?"

Struck, Barbara stood poised with the red marker halfway to the white board. "No," she replied slowly. "I'm not that stupid. Neither is Colonel Endicott."

Her gaze drifted to the life-size image taped to the opposite wall. She studied a younger Julia for several long moments.

"You tell me something," she challenged, turning back to her partner. "If the colonel didn't kill Hunter, who in the hell did? And why?"

The chair legs slammed the floor. His mouth grim, Marsh reached for the medical file.

"I don't know, but we've got the long New Year's weekend to try to figure it out."

"You're kidding, right?"

"Get to work, Lyles."

"Who?" Julia demanded of the disinterested cat. "Dammit, who? Why?"

The tom ignored her. Sprawled indolently in the white leather armchair that matched her sofa, he didn't even twitch his bent tail.

"I suggest you start showing a little more interest in this case," Julia huffed. "Who's going to dump those disgusting sardines into your dish if I spend the next fifteen or twenty years in Fort Leavenworth?"

Black gums curled back in a huge, lazy yawn. Henry planted his paws against the chair's padded arm and levered himself into a more comfortable position. Julia winced as eight needle-pointed claws sank into expensive white leather. She'd long ago given up trying to keep the cat and his claws off the furniture, but she couldn't bring herself to watch while he added a new set of punctures.

Stuffing her hands into the sleeves of her baggy Washington Redskins sweatshirt, she walked to the bow-fronted windows. On any other day the view of Alexandria's cobblestone streets and wrought iron street lamps would have given her a tiny thrill of pleasure. People had trod those streets for centuries. Both generals Washington and Lee had been pew holders at Christ Church, only a few blocks away. Gadsby's Tavern, a short walk from her front door, still served the raisin-stuffed, rum-soaked bread pudding that had delighted colonial epicureans. From the moment she'd purchased the narrow, crumbling four-story house that eventually became her home, Julia had loved being a part of that history.

She'd spent far more of her savings than she should have renovating the town house, but she'd always judged the money well spent. Ruthlessly, she'd ordered the subcontractor to take out interior walls and install tall, thermal-paned windows that echoed a colonial theme on the exterior and allowed light to flood the interior. The resulting airy, high-ceilinged rooms decorated in shades of white and sand were her refuge from the putrid greens and muddy browns of the Pentagon.

Today, however, neither the view outside nor the comfortable serenity inside soothed Julia. She felt edgy and restless and anything but serene. She dreaded the thought of going to work tomorrow. The major whose desk she'd been occupying would return, and her pride cringed at the idea of ousting the man from his own desk.

She dreaded even more the long, empty day and night ahead. She'd canceled out of the New Year's Eve party she'd planned to attend, as well as the brunch at a Georgetown bistro a friend had set up for New Year's day. Julia didn't want to socialize or field her acquaintances' sideways looks. What she wanted was the answer to the question she kept asking herself over and over.

Who? Who could have taken her weapon from her room and used it to kill Gabe?

Just about anyone, she was forced to acknowledge. The slatted doors in the women's quarters were certainly flimsy enough. Many had warped so badly from the humidity that they wouldn't close, much less lock.

Strange, Julia mused. She'd never worried about theft on Tan Son Nhut. Off base, she'd stayed constantly wary of the legions of pickpockets who swarmed the streets and the motorcycle cowboys who'd snatch a purse off a shoulder or a watch off a wrist as they zipped by. Within the air base's confines, though, the tough Vietnamese military police meted out summary justice for all infractions. The local national employees feared them almost as much as the VC.

Consequently, Julia had been shocked to discover her father's weapon gone when she readied for work. She'd spent so many long, draining hours at the orphanage the day before, then fallen into her bed exhausted. She hadn't even noticed the theft until the following morning.

Eighteen hours later, Gabe Hunter had been declared missing in action.

Julia had never connected the two events until she'd walked into the vice chief's office twelve days ago. Now she couldn't get them out of her mind.

"Who?" she muttered again, scowling at the empty streets. "Dammit, why?"

Whirling, she strode to the bookshelves built around the fireplace. The thick gray athletic socks she'd pulled on to combat the chill snaking through the hallways made no sound on the hardwood floors. Folding her legs, Julia sank down and started pulling out the memorabilia that filled the cabinet beneath the stereo unit. With every transfer she'd promised herself she'd sort through the assortment of albums and scrapbooks and manila folders stuffed with pictures as soon as she got to her new home. At every new assignment she'd barely had time to hang a few pictures before her job absorbed her.

She found the album she sought at the back of the cabinet. She fingered the cracked cover, her heart thumping. She hadn't opened it in years. Hadn't added anything to it since early spring, 1972. Hadn't wanted to remember. Her fingers trembled as she lifted the lid.

The pages had yellowed, and the small square snapshots harked back to an era of Kodak Instamatics. Julia swallowed at the shots of a teary-eyed, younger version of herself hugging her mother good-bye at the airport. For the first time since her mother's death five years ago, Julia didn't experience a pang of loss. She felt only a brief, shaming moment of relief that Mary Elizabeth Endicott hadn't lived to see her daughter accused of murder.

Biting down on her lower lip, she turned the page. Pictures taken during her two-day wait at Travis Air Force Base just outside San Francisco filled the next few pages. She'd used the lay-over to explore the city. The soaring, fog-shrouded spans of the Golden Gate Bridge made her throat tighten. So many troops had departed from Travis for Vietnam. So many had left more than their hearts in the city by the bay. They, like Julia, had left their innocence.

A few more pages brought her to a land of patchwork paddies and purple mountains, of bright red pagodas and armed camps surrounded by guard towers and rolls of concertina wire. Julia smoothed the wrinkles from the plastic covering the photos. There they were, she and Claire, in fatigues and silly grins, standing side by side at the entrance to the women's compound. A few shots of MACV headquarters followed, taken during Julia's first week at work. Then a more somber, tired-looking Claire sitting cross-legged on Julia's cot, a wineglass in one hand and a Ritz cracker spread with processed cheese in the other.

When she lifted the album to take a closer look, a brown envelope slid out. Edging a nail under the flap to loosen it, Julia withdrew a handful of black-and-white stills. Her stomach lurched, then a white-hot rage swept through her veins.

She stared down at Gabe Hunter's laughing face in loathing. She'd destroyed the few snapshots that included Gabe before she'd left Vietnam. Somehow, she'd missed these copies of the shots taken the first day she'd introduced Lassiter and his photographer to Hunter.

"Damn you!"

Grabbing the edges of the photos, she'd torn them almost in half before reason cut through her fury. Breathing hard, she dropped the black-and-white stills to the floor beside her. She'd study them later, when she could look at them without feeling this murderous rage. Maybe they would give her some clue as to what and who and why.

Her breathing slowed as she paged through the rest of the album. At the back of the book she discovered a stash of folded newspaper clippings.

During her year in Vietnam her duties had required her to read and analyze thousands of stories. Some had shocked Julia with their biased view of a war everyone wanted to end. Some had infuriated her with their restrained treatment of an enemy who committed far more atrocities than the Americans pilloried in the same paper. A few had portrayed the war as she knew it. Those she'd saved.

Dean Lassiter's account of the rocket attack at DaNang was among them. Julia unfolded the yellowed clipping and read again a tale of heroism above and beyond the call of duty and a friendship that transcended fear.

The story of the young maintenance tech carrying his wounded VNAF counterpart to safety moved her, as it had so many years ago. Dean's unvarnished prose captured a moment when men in uniform had still been heroes to her, and Gabe Hunter had still occupied a secret place in her heart.

How stupid, how incredibly young and stupid she'd been then.

Sighing, she refolded the clipping. The DaNang story had won Dean his Pulitzer a year after he'd returned to the States, but his famous Men's Room interview had launched his career as a political analyst. Julia sorted through the clippings and unfolded another, longer one.

It showed a disgruntled ambassador-at-large and a hollow-eyed Dean Lassiter framed against a door to a men's room. Dean's flight had landed at Yakota Air Base in Japan to refuel just moments after the diplomat's plane had touched down. The reporter had cornered the ambassador in the air terminal's men's room. Their interview had begun over the urinal and finished in the hall outside.

Tired and irate, the president's special adviser had let slip that the White House planned to accelerate U.S. troop withdrawals in South Vietnam even more. Although he hadn't said so in so many words, the ambassador certainly implied that the troop withdrawals were geared more to the upcoming presidential election in the States than the still far from stable military situation in South Vietnam.

Lassiter had sold that piece to UPI and AP, and seen it plastered on the front page of every major daily. Julia had gasped when she'd read it over the teletype, then silently applauded Dean for articulating what so many of the troops felt. The peace process had dragged on too long. The war was still claiming too many lives. Reelection politics be damned, it was time to end it.

Julia had started to refold the article when the date line at the bottom of the page snagged her gaze.

June 12. That couldn't be right. Dean had left Saigon the morning after her birthday. That would've put him in Yakota on June 11.

Wouldn't it?

She stared at the date. She'd never paid attention to it before. She'd never had reason to. Shrugging, she folded the clipping and slid it back into the article.

Two hours later, she'd returned the albums to their cabinet and was trying to force herself to open a can of sardines for the impatient cat. She reached

into the kitchen cupboard and retrieved a tin, then
stared at the label without seeing it. As it had for
the past two hours, her mind kept returning to the
date at the bottom of the Men's Room article.

When had Lassiter really left Saigon?

Julia gave herself a mental shake. Come on, Endicott, she admonished silently. Get a grip here. The
flights to and from Vietnam crossed the international date line. That no doubt explained the date
discrepancy.

Didn't it?

Tossing the can of sardines onto the counter, she
ignored Henry's disgusted expression and walked
back into the living room. Brow furrowed, she
searched among the crowded bookshelves for her
world atlas. She'd bought it years ago, before the
USSR fell apart, but national boundaries didn't
interest her right now. She fanned the pages once,
twice, looking for Asia. To her intense disappointment, the continental map didn't show the international date line. She fanned the pages again.

"Come on, come on. You've got to be here."

Finally, she thought to consult the table of
contents. There it was, on page one, a map of the
world showing the international date line smack in
the middle of the Pacific Ocean. Lassiter's plane
wouldn't have crossed it until after it left Japan—
which meant the reporter had left Saigon a day
later than he'd originally intended.

Okay. She had her answer. So what? Why did

this one little piece of information tug at her mind, like the half-remembered lyrics to an old, old song? What difference did the date make?

The question she couldn't answer still echoed in her head.

If she hadn't kill Gabe, who had?

It could have been anyone, she reminded herself. Even . . . even Lassiter!

Dropping the atlas, Julia walked to the sofa on legs that suddenly felt a little shaky. She sank into the cushions, telling herself she was crazy even to entertain such a absurd notion. Dean and Gabe had been buddies. Pals. Two opportunists who worked the system to their own advantage. Why would . . . ? Why . . . ?

The idea was so ridiculous she couldn't even articulate it in her own mind.

And couldn't get it out.

She tucked her knees under her, thinking back to the first meeting between the two men. She remembered their instant rapport. Lassiter's trip to DaNang. The rocket attack. Julia's flight up-country. A snowfall of termite wings.

A long-forgotten snippet of conversation drifted through the haze of her memories. She heard a faint echo of Gabe's voice, telling Dean not to worry. Assuring him that no one had seen anything. No one but him . . . and Dean.

Her heart thumping, she stared unseeingly at the thin sunlight filtering through the windows. Some time later, she reached for the phone. She needed to do some research. Most libraries would be closed for the New Year's holiday, but Julia knew at least one she could get into.

FIFTEEN

Shivering from a combination of nervous excitement and the biting January cold, Julia pushed open the glass doors to the Air Force History Office. A smile lit her face as she caught sight of the slender, silver-haired man who walked forward to greet her.

"Thanks for coming out on a holiday to let me in, Jonas. I really appreciate this."

"I'm glad I can be of assistance, Miss Julia," he replied in his soft, rhythmic Virginia cadence. "I've got the computer up and running for you."

The glass doors swished shut behind them, encasing them in the silence of a deserted workplace. Courteously, the civil service employee helped Julia out of her down-filled jacket. She hadn't taken the time to change her jeans and Redskins sweatshirt. In sharp contrast to her informal attire, Dr. Jonas Moreton wore the crisp white shirt, black tie, and gray wool cardigan with the leather patches at the elbows that had become his trademark throughout the Air Force.

Julia had met the historian fifteen years ago, during her first assignment at the Pentagon. During that exciting tour she'd spent some months working with the senior civilian who collected and catalogued Air Force art. Julia had researched the artists and subjects of the artwork, which captured every phase of military flight. Her research had brought her in frequent contact with the Air Force Historian's office, located on Bolling AFB across the Potomac from the Pentagon—and with Dr. Jonas Moreton, head of its research division.

Dr. Moreton had been only too pleased to take Julia under his wing and introduce her to the incredible treasure house of archives. Their acquaintance had deepened during the months that followed. Upon her return to Washington a few years ago as a colonel, it had ripened into a rich, mutually rewarding friendship.

Julia made it a point to invite the widowed Jonas to the social functions she hosted, which he always declined. He in turn invited her to private showings at the Smithsonian and the Library of Congress, which she always enjoyed immensely. More than once she'd tried to palm Henry the cat off on the widower. Those attempts had produced the only tense moments in their long friendship.

Jonas had been the first to call her with his support when word spread that she was under investigation. She knew he'd be the last to desert her.

"I won't be long," she promised, heading for the terminal.

"Take what time you need. I have plenty to occupy me."

Pulling the yellowed copy of Dean Lassiter's men's room interview out of her purse, she laid it beside the computer and started clicking keys. Within moments she had accessed the Air University Library catalogue.

Julia's top-level security clearance had been pulled the same day she'd been relieved of her duties. She didn't need entry to AU's extensive collection of classified documents, however. She was confident that she'd find what she needed in the unclassified files. The library contained more than two million items, including military documents, monographs, oral histories, maps and charts, regulations and— she clicked a button on the screen—an index of periodicals. Swiftly, she typed in a string of key search words.

1972.

U.S. ambassador-at-large, Vietnam.

Yakota Air Base.

Seconds later, a list of entries painted down the screen. One by one Julia opened the articles, skimmed their content, and printed out those that contained information about the ambassador's trip. Borrowing a highlighter from Jonas, she underlined dates and locations. Then she entered Lassiter's name into the search function. Within a remarkably short space of time, she'd reconstructed the two separate itineraries.

The special ambassador had flown from Travis to Alaska, then across the Pacific to Japan. He'd spent less than an hour on the ground at Yakota before continuing his flight to Saigon.

Dean Lassiter had flown in the opposite direction, from Saigon to Yakota to San Francisco. When his plane landed in the States, he'd done a gritty story on the shock the Vietnam returnees experienced when they were greeted at the airport and warned to change out of their uniforms before venturing downtown. Julia printed out his article about soldiers coming home to a country that scorned their service and added it to her stack.

Swiveling away from the computer, she cross-checked the two itineraries with intense concentration. Her initial assumption still held. For Dean Lassiter's path to have crossed that of the special ambassador's, he had to have left Saigon a day later than he'd intended.

Why?

What had delayed him?

She still didn't have an answer to those questions, but with each passing moment they didn't seem quite as startling. Her hands trembling, Julia folded the stack of printed articles and stuffed them into the brown manila envelope Jonas handed her.

"I have an invitation to a private showing at the Mary Pickford Theater tomorrow evening," he told her as they walked to the front door. "Would you care to attend with me?"

"No, thank you. I can't."

He searched her face, then held out a thin, wrinkled hand. "You mustn't let this unpleasantness tear you apart, Julia."

She managed a shaky smile. "You're probably the only person I know who would categorize a murder charge as unpleasantness."

He ignored her feeble attempt at humor. "The pain will pass, Julia. If history hasn't taught us anything else, it's shown that all things pass eventually."

"I didn't kill him. He deserved it, but I didn't."

Julia hadn't meant to say it. She'd sworn not to burden her friends and family with the desperate protestations of innocence that seemed to pour out of every accused criminal.

"I believe you," he said simply. "I've believed in you since the first time you came into my office, all eager and enthusiastic about preserving the Air Force's heritage. I always shall."

His unconditional acceptance pierced the wall Julia had built around herself in the past few weeks as nothing else could have. Tears stung her eyes. Embarrassed, she squeezed Jonas's hand gently, then stepped into the sharp, biting cold.

The wind off the Potomac knifed through her as she hurried to her car. Frost sparkled on the windows of her sleek gray Mercedes. Huddling in the driver's seat, Julia switched on the defroster and debated what to do with the articles she'd just retrieved.

She should give them to her lawyer tomorrow, she supposed. Captain O'Rourke would pass them to the OSI to check out the seeming discrepancy. She drummed her fingers on the steering wheel, impatient now for the workday she'd dreaded only a few hours ago to arrive.

Maybe she could expedite the process a little. Digging through her wallet, Julia extracted the card Marsh had given her the day of their first interview. She punched in the number, which, as she'd anticipated, rang at a central switchboard. After verifying that a senior NCO was pulling duty at OSI headquarters, she shifted the car into gear and drove the few blocks to the building that housed the headquarters of the Air Force Office of Special Investigations.

Her breath frosting, she climbed the few steps to the front doors. They were locked, but the phone mounted beside them brought a uniformed senior master sergeant to the door.

"Yes, ma'am?"

Julia flipped her wallet open to display her ID. "I'm Colonel Endicott. I have an envelope for Special Agent Marsh."

"Sure. Just a minute."

She returned her wallet to her purse and was digging for a pen to scribble a note to Marsh when the NCO stepped aside to usher her inside.

"His office is upstairs. I'll escort you."

"Mr. Marsh is at work?"

"Has been all weekend."

Julia followed the sergeant up a flight of stairs and down a long carpeted hall. Her fingers clutched the envelope as the NCO stopped before an open door.

"You've got a visitor," he announced, stepping aside.

Marsh glanced up, his eyes widening in surprise when he caught sight of Julia. Hastily, he shoved his chair back and rose.

She felt a dart of satisfaction at having caught the imperturbable Ted Marsh off guard. From her personal experience with the man, she suspected it didn't happen very often.

Thanking the sergeant for his escort, she strolled into the cluttered office. If the OSI agent had access to a secretary or a file clerk, he obviously didn't make use of their talents. He'd stacked folders and files on every level surface, including the two visitors chairs beside the door. An empty pizza carton sat atop the small table between the chairs, adding a pepperoni tang to the faint, spicy scent that emanated from the crumpled Taco Bell sack on the corner of his desk.

"The sergeant wasn't kidding?" she asked. "You really have been here all weekend?"

He raked a hand through his disordered hair. "Most of it."

For the first time Julia saw him in something other than his usual suit and tie. The thin January sunlight streaming through the windows behind him picked up the mahogany tint to his rumpled hair and the swell of muscle under his blue, open-necked oxford shirt. A light dusting of the same reddish-brown hair curled on his forearms under his rolled-up shirtsleeves. Like Julia, Marsh wore jeans. Unlike hers, his rode low on his hips and hugged trim, muscular thighs.

"Why are you here, Colonel?"

Remembering her mission with a small start, she stepped forward to hand him the envelope. "I wanted to drop this off for you. Since you were in your office, I decided to—"

She stopped in her tracks, her jaw sagging as she spotted the grainy blown-up color photo that had been hidden by the open door. She barely heard Marsh's muttered curse as her breath whooshed out.

Stunned, she stared up at herself. It took a moment to place the dress and the makeup and the hard, unsmiling look in her eyes.

"Wh—where did you get that picture?"

"From Claire Hunter."

Surprise gave way to hurt, then to swift, searing anger. "What is this, Marsh?" she sneered. "The latest addition to your own private rogues' gallery? Or is this your sick idea of a pin-up?"

Red singed the tips of his ears. "Neither. A photo

helps me remember that the suspect in my case is a living, breathing human."

Julia flinched. Although she'd accepted that she was, in fact, a suspect in a murder investigation, hearing it stated aloud still stung.

"I'm sorry if the picture offends you, Colonel. I didn't intend it as an insult, or an invasion of your privacy."

The sincerity of his apology defused some of her anger. She fought to bring the rest under control. For a woman who prided herself on her cool, calm approach to issues and problems, she'd ridden an unfamiliar emotional roller coaster lately. When would she regain control of her emotions and her life?

When this ended, she promised fiercely—if it ever ended—she'd reclaim her life. She'd walk away from the shambles of her career. She'd lie on a beach somewhere for weeks. Maybe months. Then she'd put her past behind her and start building a new one.

"Is that what you wanted to give me?" Marsh asked.

"What?"

He nodded at the envelope clutched in her fist. "You said you stopped by to drop something off. Is that it?"

"Yes."

She handed him the clippings, lingering just inside the door while he slid out the articles. She should leave. She had no business discussing the investigation in her attorney's absence. Yet Julia couldn't bring herself to walk out the door without seeing Marsh's reaction to the discrepancy in the dates. Her pulse skipped a beat or two as he unfolded the top article.

"That's a copy of an interview Dean Lassiter did the day he left Saigon. He cornered President Nixon's special ambassador to Vietnam in the men's room during a stopover at Yakota."

Marsh scanned the article, his dark brows creasing.

"The content doesn't matter," she said. "Look at the date on the bottom of the page."

He held the article up higher to the light. His frown deepened, then his gaze slashed to a dry board on the opposite wall. Julia's throat constricted as she interpreted the data on the board.

There they were. Her. Claire. Gabe. The cataclysmic events that had changed their lives had been reduced to a few initials, some cryptic notes.

"Let me make sure I understand this," Marsh said, planting himself in front of the board. "Dean Lassiter invited you to dinner the night before he left Saigon. You almost accepted. It was the night before your birthday, and you were feeling down. Is that correct?"

"Yes."

Julia edged past his desk and stood next to him.

The hair on the back of her neck tingled as she stared at the dates.

"Lassiter leaves the next afternoon, the eleventh," Marsh murmured, almost to himself. "Hunter flies a mission that night. The following night, he fails to show for his mission brief."

"What if Dean didn't leave on the eleventh?" Julia asked softly. "What if he left on the twelfth?"

His eyes fixed on the board, Marsh didn't reply.

"Look at the other articles," she urged. "I've highlighted the dates. Dean's flight from Saigon touched down in Yakota just minutes before the ambassador's. On the twelfth, Marsh. The twelfth!"

He thumbed through the stack of articles, then lifted his head. He stood so close to her, Julia could see the bristly shadows on his chin and cheeks— and the doubt in his steel gray eyes.

"All right. Let's assume for a moment Lassiter left Saigon a day later than he'd planned. How does that tie him to Captain Hunter's disappearance?"

She'd asked herself the same question repeatedly during the drive from her town house to Bolling. Hearing it from another person, Julia realized how desperately she'd been clutching at straws.

"I don't know how," she admitted. "I haven't been able to get beyond this mix-up in the dates— and something Gabe said to Dean at DaNang."

Marsh flicked her a quick look. "What?"

Julia offered the vague, half-remembered comment. It was all she had. "Gabe implied that something happened, something only the two of them knew about. I didn't catch what it was, and didn't really think about it at the time. There was so much going on."

Marsh let out a slow breath. "I'll check it out."

The quiet promise gave her more hope than it should have.

"Thank you." She hitched her purse strap up her shoulder. "Well, I'd better let you get back to work."

"Colonel . . ."

"Yes?"

"I was just getting ready to close up shop. Do you want to grab a sandwich and a cup of coffee somewhere? We could talk this out a little more."

Marsh could have kicked himself when he saw the blank astonishment in her eyes. She wasn't any more surprised at the offer than he was. He was trying to think of a way to retract it without making himself look like a total ass when she giggled. There was no other word for it. The colonel giggled.

Her laughter caught Marsh completely unprepared. The rippling, girlish sound took the mental image he'd formed of Julia Endicott, broke it down, and rearranged it. The result took his breath away. How in the hell had he ever thought the younger version of this woman more seductive than the one who now grinned at him?

"You ought to see your face," she told him, her green eyes dancing. "When you realized that you'd just invited your chief suspect to dinner, you looked like you swallowed your pepperoni pizza whole."

"Well . . ."

Her grin faded. "Don't worry. I won't embarrass you by taking you up on your rash invitation. I know what people might say if they saw us having coffee together."

Marsh felt the loss of her laughter like a blow.

"I've never particularly worried about what others might say." Snagging his sheepskin jacket from the back of his chair, he shrugged it on. "A friend of mine owns a place not too far from here. Joey Pastore serves up the best Italian subs you'll taste in this lifetime. Are you hungry?"

She blinked at the question, as though the idea of nourishment hadn't entered her conscious thought process in weeks. From the hollows under her cheeks, Marsh guessed it hadn't.

"Yes, as a matter of fact, I am."

He cut the office lights and ushered her out. "Good. Me, too."

"You're going to eat a sub after downing a pepperoni pizza?"

"I'll work it off later."

She was more than hungry, Marsh discovered twenty minutes later. She was starved.

Not for food, though. She barely touched the

thick, crusty roll heaped with meatballs, green peppers, fried onions, and Joey Pastore's famous marinara sauce. Her coffee cooled in its cup. Instead of food, Marsh discovered, the colonel craved someone to talk to.

"I can't discuss the investigation with anyone," she admitted in response to his subtle probe. "Certainly not with Claire. It hurts her too much. Nor with the man I've always turned to for career advice and planning. General Titus will be my accuser, if it comes to that."

They both knew it could well come to that.

"What about your friends?" Marsh asked.

What about a lover? was what he wanted to ask. Someone close enough to calm her fears and share the black reaches of the night. The detailed background brief he'd put together on Julia Endicott showed that several men had entered her life in the years since Vietnam, but none had stayed very long. Had Gabe Hunter made her afraid to trust herself or other men?

"I won't talk about the case to my friends," she replied with a lift of one shoulder. "I don't want to put them in the awkward position of pretending they believe me."

Marsh couldn't say much for her friends. He and Barbara Lyles knew the weight of the evidence against this woman, but few others did.

Resolutely, he pushed aside the thought of what his partner's reaction would be when she found out about this little off-the-record session with the suspect. As he'd told Julia earlier, he'd never particularly worried about what others might say. He'd been a cop too long to ignore his instincts. More and more those instincts were doubting that Julia Endicott had killed her lover.

"You're doing it again," she commented with a small smile.

"What?"

"That thing with the coins."

Sheepishly, Marsh pulled his hands from his pockets. "Sorry. I forget how annoying the noise can be."

"Actually, I'm starting to get used to it." Surprised, Julia realized the truth of that statement. She was getting used to more than just the irritating little clink of coins. She was starting to get used to this strange, symbiotic relationship she and Marsh shared.

Smart, Endicott. Real smart.

Disconcerted, she reached for her jacket. "I'd better get going. The cat who condescends to share my town house tends to get downright nasty if he misses his meals."

"Take him the rest of your sub," Marsh suggested.

"Onions and peppers? I don't think so."

"Trust me, he'll love it."

"Do you have a cat?"

"No."

"Do you want one?"

Laughing at her hopeful expression, he shook his head and reached for his sheepskin jacket. She rooted around in her purse, then extracted her wallet.

"This one's on me, Julia," he said easily, tossing some bills on the table.

She dropped her billfold back into her purse with a smile and a murmured thank-you. They were halfway to the door before either of them realized he'd called her by name instead of rank.

Sixteen

Marsh spent the next three days reviewing the transcript of his interviews with Julia. He also read every story Dean Lassiter had sold to various print media during his months in Vietnam and Cambodia. He wanted to understand the mind of the man he would interview again on Friday.

No student of journalistic art, Marsh nevertheless quickly grasped Lassiter's skill. The correspondent painted vivid, startling pictures with a minimum of words. Just as skillfully he buried his cutting political commentary in the drama and pathos of the events he described. Although Marsh dissected each of the articles Julia had given him, he kept returning again and again to the story that had won the Pulitzer.

He picked it up a final time Friday afternoon, an hour before his scheduled interview with the correspondent. Planting a foot on an open desk drawer, he pushed his chair back and read it once more.

The story absorbed him, as it had every time he'd

read it. So did the setting. They'd all been together in DaNang—Lassiter, Hunter, Julia. Not the night of the attack but the next.

Had the seeds of Hunter's murder been sown then? Or had they already germinated and started to show green? Was there any significance to the fact that the journalist had left Saigon the same day Hunter failed to show for his mission and not the day before, as he'd planned?

Frustration ate at Marsh as he tossed the article onto his overflowing desktop. He was running out of reasons to delay finalizing the investigation. His boss had started to get nervous about the White House interest in the case. Although General Titus hadn't applied any direct pressure, the OSI commander felt it.

Just yesterday Pfligerman had reviewed the status of the investigation and pointed out that evidence still pointed to Julia Endicott as the prime suspect in Captain Hunter's death. She had the means, the opportunity, and certainly the motive.

Marsh didn't need his boss to interpret the facts in the case. He carried them in his mind constantly, and felt their weight every time his eyes drifted to the photo of Julia still taped to his wall. He knew how easily a good trial lawyer could weave them into a picture of guilt.

Lieutenant Endicott had been having an affair with her best friend's lover. She'd left the party at the Caravelle with Hunter. She'd had sex with him that night, either voluntarily or otherwise. He'd married her friend two days later. Jealousy and rage had come together sometime before June 12, and she'd shot Hunter on a deserted stretch of road a few miles north of Saigon and buried him in a shallow grave. She was tall enough, and strong enough, for the physical effort required. She'd disposed of the murder weapon, then reported it stolen to cover her tracks.

Unless this interview with Lassiter turned up a new lead, Marsh didn't have anywhere else to go with his inquiry into the circumstances surrounding Captain Hunter's death. He'd have to finalize his report and turn the results over to the court-martial convening authority.

Involuntarily, his gaze returned to the woman who'd come to dominate his thoughts. Fighting an insane urge to apologize to the silent, unsmiling Julia, Marsh linked his hands behind his head. He was still staring at the photo of his only suspect when Barbara Lyles appeared at his door some time later.

"Ready to go?"

The chair legs *thunked* on the floor. "I'm ready."

Lassiter's assistant had balked at scheduling an appointment the day of her boss's return from the European summit. Mr. Lassiter would have to work up his notes from the flight back with the president, she'd protested, and tape a session for the political talk show he hosted. This time Marsh hadn't taken any crap. Mr. Lassiter could either see him today or be served a written subpoena to testify at a trial in the next few weeks. Consequently, the reporter's assistant was less than gracious when the two agents walked into the outer office.

"You'll have to wait," she told them curtly, a phone jammed to her ear. "Mr. Lassiter's still down at the studio."

Barbara's chunky gold bracelets banged as she shrugged out of her coat and folded it neatly across her arm. Cool and regal as ever, she took one of the leather armchairs.

Too restless to sit, Marsh examined the signed photos that decorated one entire wall. He counted six presidents, two queens, and a half dozen prime ministers, all either being interviewed or shaking hands with Dean Lassiter. He'd moved on to counting the lesser mortals when the celebrity himself opened the door and strolled in. Scrubbing pancake makeup from his forehead with a white towel, he apologized for the delay.

"Sorry. The show airs in an hour, and we needed to bleed another seven and a half minutes from the tape."

"No problem."

The two agents followed the reporter into the inner office. More grip-and-grin photos covered the dark green walls, as well as a dizzying array of framed awards and citations. Ignoring the gallery, Marsh introduced his partner.

"This is Special Agent Lyles, Mr. Lassiter. She's working with me on the investigation into Captain Gabriel Hunter's death."

Lassiter tossed his towel aside and took the ID Barbara held out. After returning her credentials, he gestured the two agents to the upholstered chairs grouped around a low coffee table.

Barbara dug the small tape recorder out of her purse and placed it on the table. "You don't mind if we record this, do you?" she inquired politely.

He waved an impatient hand. "I've been on tape often enough. What's this all about, Marsh? I told you everything I knew about Julia Endicott and Gabe Hunter the last time we talked."

"Since our last discussion, some questions have been raised concerning your whereabouts at the time of Captain Hunter's disappearance."

"*My* whereabouts?"

Astonishment slackened Lassiter's facial muscles. For a moment he bore little resemblance to the smooth, sharp-witted political commentator who appeared on national television every Friday night. He recovered swiftly, however. His eyes shooting black lasers, he threw a sharp demand at Marsh.

"Why in the hell are questions being raised about me?"

The agent pulled a small notebook out of his suit pocket. He didn't need to refer to his notes of their

previous conversation. He'd reviewed them a
dozen times in the past few days. He just wanted to
let Lassiter feel the heat for the time it took to
thumb through the pages.

"You mentioned stopping by Lieutenant Endicott's room to invite her to dinner the night before
you returned to the States. She confirmed that
invitation."

"And?"

"She also confirmed the date of that invitation as
June tenth, 1972. It happened to be her birthday."

Lassiter's impatience mounted. "So it was her
birthday. What has that to do with me?"

"I'm just fixing the dates. Did you leave Saigon
for the States the day after you stopped by Lieutenant Endicott's room?"

"Yes."

"Then why does your interview with the ambassador-at-large to Vietnam place you at Yakota Air
Base on the twelfth?"

"The Men's Room interview?"

Frowning, Lassiter took the photocopied article
Marsh handed him. He skimmed the print, then
focused on the date at the bottom of the page.
Refolding the article, he returned it. His eyes held
Marsh's.

"I left Tan Son Nhut the morning of the eleventh
aboard a Pan American contract flight. The plane
developed engine trouble and put down in Manila.
We were on the ground for sixteen or eighteen

hours before they got the problem fixed. The plane then continued to Yakota—where I shared a urinal with the ambassador-at-large."

Swiftly, Marsh calculated his chances of verifying that a flight flown more than two decades ago by a now defunct airline had experienced an engine problem after leaving Saigon. He estimated that the odds ranged from highly improbable to completely impossible.

"I appreciate that Julia Endicott is feeling desperate right now," Lassiter said curtly. "My sources tell me the evidence against her is overwhelming. But I don't appreciate wild accusations, even those made by an obviously distraught woman."

"Colonel Endicott hasn't made any accusations," Marsh replied calmly. "She has, however, remembered a brief conversation between you and Captain Hunter at DaNang, where he mentions something that only the two of you knew about."

"Like what?"

"I was hoping you could tell me that, Mr. Lassiter."

"Well, I don't have any idea what conversation Julia's alluding to." His voice sharpened. "I've held off doing anything with this story because she helped me out all those years ago, but you'd better warn her that the kid gloves come off if she tries to implicate me in her sordid little tale. I'm not going to be scooped on a story in which I figure as a player."

"This is a murder investigation, Mr. Lassiter, not a grab for headlines."

"Then I suggest you get on with your investigation." He rose abruptly. "If you have no further questions for me, I'll have to ask you to excuse me. I've got an appointment with the Secretary of Defense in a half hour."

Marsh had a lot of questions, but none that made any difference to the investigation if he couldn't place the reporter in Saigon the morning Captain Hunter disappeared. Frustrated, he grabbed his coat and followed Barbara out of Lassiter's office. The assistant smirked at their abrupt departure.

"Nice guy," Barbara drawled as they waited for the elevator. "Given a choice between our friendly correspondent and the colonel, I'd much rather pin the murder rap on him."

"That makes two of us."

As Marsh had suspected, tracing Lassiter's flight became an exercise in futility. The records maintained by the Saigon office of PanAm had disappeared when the communists overran the city in 1975. The airline's corporate records had gone up in flames in a warehouse fire a few years after it went out of business. Every phone call led down a blind alley. Every computer inquiry came back negative.

They searched the rest of Friday afternoon and most of Saturday. Barbara finally gave up around dusk. Promising to come in Sunday afternoon to

help work on the final report, she left Marsh with
the remains of a cold roast beef sandwich, an even
colder mug of coffee, and the bitter acknowledgment that there were no more leads to follow.

He had to wrap up the investigation. The realization dripped like acid in his stomach as he stood at
the window of his office, staring at Bolling's dark,
deserted streets. The coins in his pocket chinked
and jangled. Behind him his computer hummed
quietly.

Pfligerman wanted a summary of the investigation to take with him to the inspector general's staff
meeting Monday morning. The White House had
asked for a status report. Marsh could only guess
what knife-edged remarks Lassiter had dropped to
the Secretary of Defense during their appointment
last night. The wolves would be nipping at Julia's
heels come Monday afternoon.

Dammit!

Dragging his hands out of his pockets, he
returned to his desk. The green computer screen
glowed. The cursor blinked patiently, waiting for
him to fill in the final paragraphs. He curled his fingers over the keys, then cursed again.

He was missing something. He *had* to be missing
something. She hadn't killed him.

He didn't bother to ask himself when he'd
reached that conclusion. He could pinpoint the
exact moment. When Julia Endicott had stood at the
door to his office and shed her icy reserve. He could

still hear her musical laughter. Still see the smile in her green eyes. At that moment Marsh had known instinctively that she was no killer.

He had also developed the mother of all hard-ons, but no one needed to know that but him. He'd been a cop long enough to understand the uncomfortable phenomenon. Given a suspect as beautiful and intriguing as Julia, he could have expected the vivid mental images that had kept him wide awake and sweating the past few nights. She'd become part of his psyche. He'd extracted intimate physical details about her body from her medical records. He'd been given a glimpse of her darkest secrets. He'd burrowed into her mind, and she into his.

Marsh could understand and dismiss his physical response to the suspect. What he couldn't dismiss was his growing conviction that she hadn't killed Gabriel Hunter.

He had to be missing something!

Tight-jawed, he searched among the scattered files and folders on his desk for the one containing Lassiter's articles. His chair groaned in protest as he angled it back. Resting the open file on his stomach, he glanced up at the photo taped to the wall.

"Hell of a way to spend a Saturday night, isn't it, Julia?"

"Some way to spend a Saturday night, isn't it, cat?"

As usual, Henry the cat ignored the woman he

allowed to serve him. Holding his tail at a stiff angle, he gobbled down his dinner.

Julia propped an elbow on the counter and rested her chin in one hand. The whole kitchen stank of sardines. For once she didn't let the nauseating odor drive her away. She craved companionship, and Henry was the closest thing to it in her life right now—except for Marsh.

"Pretty sick, huh? The only person I really feel comfortable talking to about this nightmare is the one who dragged me into it."

If Henry agreed with her assessment, he didn't bother to show it. Sighing, Julia traced a pattern in the tile with the tip of one nail.

"That's not strictly true, of course. Marsh didn't drag me into this mess. I have to give Gabe Hunter full credit for that."

Saying Gabe's name aloud left a bitter taste in her mouth, as though she'd downed coffee dregs. Julia swallowed once or twice to clear the taste, then realized what she was doing.

Good grief! When had she become so pathetic? How had she let herself reach the state of whining to a cat who couldn't care less about a man who'd been dead for more than two decades? She straightened and caught a glimpse of her reflection in the dark, shiny oven panel.

Was that really her? That sad-looking creature in the baggy sweats, with no makeup and her hair pulled back in a sloppy ponytail? She stared at her pale face for long moments, then lifted her chin. She hadn't let Gabe Hunter destroy her in Vietnam. She was damned if she'd let him do it now.

"Sorry, cat, you'll have to dine alone tonight."

Henry didn't glance up as Julia swept out of the kitchen.

She took the stairs to the third floor with a determined burst of energy. A quick flip of a switch flooded her tall-ceilinged bedroom with subdued lighting. The master suite ran the length of the town house, with bow windows that overlooked the street at one end and a mirrored dressing area at the other. Like those in the rest of her home, the walls and furnishings in her bedroom had been done in the clean, soothing whites and beiges she loved.

The sweats came off and dropped to the floor of her walk-in closet. So did her cotton Jockey briefs. In their place she pulled on a silk teddy, a fuzzy ice blue sweater, and a pair of white wool slacks. Warm trouser socks and supple, cream-colored leather boots would do for the short trek to her favorite restaurant. A few quick strokes with a brush restored the sheen to her hair, and a whisk of blush put a little color in her cheeks.

"Better," she decided, assessing her image in the mirror above her dressing table. "Not great, but definitely better."

Henry the cat lay sprawled in boneless indolence on the white leather sofa when Julia came back downstairs. Not even his tail twitched when she bid him good night and let herself out the front door. Locking it behind her, she headed down the lighted cobblestone walk to Duke Street, two short blocks away. With each step icy January air bladed into her lungs.

She welcomed its knife-edged bite. Her body's tingling response to the cold revived her spirits and reaffirmed her decision to go out. She'd locked herself away from her friends, even from Jonas, for too long. If this case went to a trial by court-martial, she faced some tough days ahead. She'd darned well better start coping with that possibility instead of letting it drive her into a self-destructive, unhealthy isolation.

Still, she couldn't help a cowardly sigh of relief when she walked into her favorite bistro and saw no one she recognized among the noisy, laughing patrons. A tray of cold boiled shrimp and some casual conversation at the stand-up bar would be more than enough to satisfy her.

The Saturday night crowd stood shoulder to shoulder in the waiting area and two deep at the bar. When Julia finally wedged into a vacant spot at one of the circular, chest-high tables, the convivial group around it welcomed her. Within moments she'd been drawn into their lively discussion of the Skins' abysmal performance in the National Conference play-offs. Sipping a perfectly chilled chardonnay and munching on shrimp, Julia almost managed to forget the specter hanging over her.

It came rushing back when she returned from a trip to the ladies' room to find another glass of chardonnay waiting at her place. She hadn't ordered it and didn't really want it, but the temptation to get a little high, maybe even silly tugged at her. She hadn't laughed in weeks, she realized—except in Ted Marsh's office when he had surprised both himself and her with his rash invitation to dinner.

At the thought of Marsh, the muscles low in her belly suddenly contracted. Startled, Julia identified the sexual pull for what it was—a lonely woman's attraction to a man she'd shared a part of herself with, a part she'd never shared with anyone else.

She'd gone beyond pathetic, she realized in disgust. She teetered on the edge of pitiful. Her hand shot out and grasped the wineglass. She downed its contents in a few hasty swallows, then turned a brilliant smile on the tweed-jacketed man next to her.

"Have you been to the Charlie Chaplin festival at the Pickford Theater?"

He blinked in surprise. "Er, no."

"I've heard they're showing the original, uncut edition of *The Tramp*."

"Really?" His mouth relaxed into a smile. "I've always wanted to see that. Uh, maybe we could see it together sometime."

"Maybe."

He didn't have Marsh's keen gray eyes or lean, rangy build, but he'd do, Julia decided. For an hour or two of conversation and companionship, he'd do.

She couldn't even manage a few hours. Her head began to throb a short while later. The heat and the noise pulsed with an almost palpable beat. With a mumbled good-bye to her new acquaintance, Julia grabbed her purse and her coat and shouldered her way to the door.

Outside, she leaned a hand against an iron lamp post. Dizzy and breathing hard, she pulled cold air into her lungs.

"You okay, lady?"

She squinted through blurry eyes at the tourist who'd stopped beside her. Even so late in the evening, he sported a camera around his neck and clutched a walking map of Old Town in his fist. A woman hovered at his shoulder, wary and concerned and pinch-faced from the cold.

Julia pushed herself upright. "I'm fine. Thank you. The heat inside got to me, that's all."

He looked doubtful but relieved. "You sure?"

"Yes. Thanks."

Blinking to clear her vision, Julia walked to the corner, then turned off Duke Street onto Fairfax. Her boot heels slipped on the uneven cobblestones. Swaying, she nearly fell. She caught herself in time and started counting doorways in an effort to keep focused. What was wrong with her? She hadn't drunk enough for it to affect her so strongly.

She had just passed the twelfth door when a sense of being followed penetrated her woozy mind. She threw a quick look over her shoulder at the headlights slicing the night behind her. The vehicle crawled along Fairfax Street. Why was it moving so slowly?

Suddenly frightened, Julia searched the sidewalk ahead for someone to attach herself to. A couple strolled hand in hand not ten yards in front of her. Breathing hard, she propelled herself forward and joined the two men.

She felt a little foolish when the car behind her turned at the corner and headed north, but her escorts insisted on walking her to her town house. They waited patiently on the sidewalk while she mounted the stairs and unlocked her front door. Thanking them again, Julia went inside.

The moment she closed the heavy oak panel, the heat in the house brought on another wave of dizziness. She leaned against the door and waited for the swirling, light-headed sensation to pass.

But instead of passing, her dizziness grew worse. Clammy and disoriented, Julia groped for the stair railing. As she pulled herself up the short flight of stairs, her stomach lurched with the sickening realization that she'd been drugged.

SEVENTEEN

Ted Marsh rubbed the back of his neck. He was tired, hungry, and ready to call the night a total bust.

The deep silence of the deserted headquarters building dragged at him like a heavy weight. If he'd had any sense, he would've unplugged the damned computer hours ago and gone home. He needed to grab a hot shower, a cold beer, and about ten hours of sleep so he could bring a fresh mind to the case tomorrow. Instead, a sense of time running out kept him at his desk.

His gaze drifted again to the photo of Julia. Her face haunted his waking hours now as well as his dreams.

Expelling a long, whistling breath, Ted picked up Lassiter's Pulitzer prize–winning piece. Of all the articles Julia had printed out for him, this one packed the most punch. It also put the three major players in his case together at DaNang. He read the piece again, searching for some understanding of the tenuous relationship between Julia, Hunter, and Lassiter.

Halfway through the story, Ted realized that at least two additional participants in the drama had been present in DaNang. Minor participants, true, but players nevertheless. He was stretching, really stretching, but he jotted down the name of the young Air Force sergeant whose story Lassiter told in such compelling prose, then searched for the name of the Italian photographer.

Julia had mentioned him in one of their sessions, Ted recalled. Remi or Reno or something like that. He shuffled through the stacks of files on his desk. One slipped off the edge and spilled its contents to the floor. He was on his knees reaching for an elusive sheet of paper when a shrill buzz shattered the quiet.

He jerked upright and whacked his head on the open center drawer. Red stars cartwheeled across his vision as he groped for the telephone receiver.

"Yeah?"

His snarl produced a moment of startled silence. Then a woman asked hesitantly, "Special Agent Marsh?"

"Yes?"

"This is operator seventy-three at the Bolling Central Switchboard. I know we're not supposed to put after-hours calls through to anyone except the OSI duty officer, but I've got a woman on the line who's asking for you. She sounds pretty bad."

"Put her through."

After a short interval the operator came on again. "Go ahead, ma'am. He's on the line. Ma'am?"

A low moan came across the line. The sound lifted the hairs on the back of Marsh's neck.

"Who is this?" he rapped out.

"Ju-ul . . ." The slurred syllable trailed off into nothingness.

"Julia? Is that you? What's the matter? Where are you?"

She smacked her lips a few times. "Ho . . . me."

"Christ, what's the matter? Are you hurt? Do you need me to call 911?"

"I . . . need . . . you. Plzzz."

A dozen different possibilities flashed through Marsh's mind. She could be drunk. She could be high. She could be hurt or just alone and frightened and as desperate as Lassiter had implied.

"Plzzz," she begged. "No one . . . else. Just . . . you."

He knew her address. He knew more about Julia Endicott than her doctor, her lawyer, or anyone else in her life right now. He grabbed his jacket from the back of his chair.

"I'll be there in ten minutes."

It took him twenty.

He'd underestimated the Saturday night traffic on the Woodrow Wilson Bridge. Even this late in the evening, cars had backed up on both I-95 and

I-295 south as they waited to feed together onto the bridge.

Cursing viciously at the logjam, Ted grabbed his mobile phone and punched in Julia's number. The phone rang endlessly at her end. His heart in his throat, he redialed. He'd just decided to call 911 when the ringing ceased. A loud clatter rattled his eardrum. She'd dropped the receiver.

"Julia? Julia, this is Ted. Talk to me."

"Ted?" She sounded distant, tired, disinterested.

"I'm on my way. Talk to me. Tell me what happened."

"I think . . . something in my . . . drink. I feel so . . . sick."

Christ! Something in her drink! What the hell had she taken? Alcohol and drugs could make a fatal combination when mixed.

"All right. It's all right. Just keep talking to me, okay? Keep talking."

He kept her on the line, murmuring encouragement when she stumbled and tripped over her words, demanding an answer when her voice drifted off. Sweat rolled down the side of his neck and soaked his shirt collar. His hand felt slick on the plastic phone casing.

Lassiter's caustic comment kept echoing in his head. She was a distraught woman, a desperate suspect facing a murder charge.

"Talk to me, Julia," he ordered fiercely. "Tell me what you put in your drink."

"I . . . didn't. Someone . . . else."

The cop in him grasped the significance of her words instantly. His mind leaped from the image of a drunken, desperate woman to a possible target. He forced his response through a tight throat.

"Talk to me, Julia. Who put something in your drink?"

"I want . . . to go to sleep and . . . never wake up."

"No! Don't kid yourself, Endicott. You're too strong to give up. Talk to me, dammit!"

The traffic finally inched forward enough for him to wedge his Camaro onto the access lane. Ignoring angry honks and lifted fingers, he cut across five lanes of vehicles on the bridge and hit the high-occupancy lane. Eyes narrowed, he squinted against the glare of headlights and watched for the exit to Alexandria.

He took the exit ramp on two wheels. The Camaro sped along the shoulder and passed a slow-moving truck. Ted hadn't spent all that much time in Old Town, but the gridlike layout helped him locate Julia's street with just one wrong turn. Tires screeching, phone still plastered to his ear, he pulled up in front of a row of stately restored town houses.

"I'm right outside, Julia. Open the door."

She mumbled a low, indistinct response.

He dropped the phone, shoved open the car door, and sprinted up the short flight of stairs to her front door. Leaning on the bell, he waited impatiently for her to answer. He had just measured the bow windows as a possible means of entry when the lock *snicked* open.

He shoved the door back and inadvertently knocked Julia sideways. She staggered a few steps, then crumpled. Ted caught her just before she hit the hardwood floor and scooped her into his arms. Kicking the door shut behind him, he carried her up a half flight of stairs to a dimly lit living room. When he tried standing her on her feet, she collapsed against his arm, moaning. He took her chin in one hand and brought her face around to his. Her heavy-lidded eyes and slack jaw put a knot in his chest.

"Wake up, Julia. Come on. Tell me what happened."

"I . . . some wine. I'm so . . . dizzy."

"Wine? What else?"

Her lids lifted. "I . . . don't . . . know."

Her unfocused gaze kicked Ted in the gut. Her pupils had dilated until only a thin rim of green showed around the centers.

"All right." Steadying her with an arm around her shoulder, he searched for a coat or blanket to keep her warm. "Let's get you to an emergency room."

She shook her head, as if trying to clear it, and clung to him with both hands. "I . . . can't."

"Yes, you can. Come on."

"No! I can't." She sagged against his hold. "I

can't have this ... on my ... record, too! Please ...
No!"

Her frantic pleading sent a shaft of relief through
him. She wasn't as stoned as he'd thought. She
retained enough sense to realize that a drug incident would only add to the damage already done
to her career.

Ted hesitated, torn between her safety and the
need to protect what was left of her reputation. She
clutched his sheepskin jacket with both hands. Her
eyes held confusion and panic, but for a moment at
least they'd lost the terrible emptiness.

"I didn't take anything. Only wine. Someone
else ... Help me. Please!"

He gentled his hold and his voice. "All right, let's
get you into the shower. Then you're going to walk
until you crash."

She could hardly make it to the stairs, much less
up them. Ted caught her in his arms again and fumbled for a light switch to illuminate the stairs and
the hallway. Her head lolled on his shoulder as she
mumbled disjointedly.

He located her bedroom by a short process of
elimination. It was one of only two rooms on the
top floor of the town house. The smaller obviously
served as a combination office and guest room.
The larger contained a huge bedroom, a dressing area, and the scraggliest cat Ted had ever seen.
Half orange, half mottled gray, and all ugly, it lay
sprawled across the king-size bed. At their entrance

it lifted its head and gave the intruders a slitted, sleepy assessment. Then it rolled to its feet and departed the scene. Ted couldn't blame the thing. What happened next wouldn't be pretty or pleasant to watch.

Depositing Julia on the bed, he made a quick sweep of the dressing area. She claimed someone had slipped something into her drink. Ted believed her, but he was too much an investigator not to search for hard evidence to either support or refute her claim.

His quick search turned up no pill bottles. No powders. No syringes. He hadn't seen any paraphernalia downstairs, either. He strode back to the bed, not sure whether he was more relieved or worried. If Julia hadn't gotten herself stoned, who the hell had, and why? His mouth grim, he understood that those questions would have to wait until she was well enough to answer them.

Peeling off her fuzzy blue sweater and slacks, he pulled her to her feet. She moaned a protest and dragged against his hold.

"Come on, Julia. Let's get you into the shower."

More than once during their interviews Ted had glimpsed the steel at Julia's core. He now saw evidence that even steel could bend and twist if enough pressure was applied.

He left on her white silk teddy and pinned her against the shower wall with a splayed hand.

Closing his ears to her shrieking protest, he held her under the cold stream. She fought him for a while, but her movements were too uncoordinated and jerky to have any effect. At last she slumped against the wall and slowly, bonelessly, slid to the tiles.

When Ted cut off the water and dragged her up, her nipples had puckered and peaked against the silk. She had small breasts, he noted, small and proud and as finely shaped as the rest of her slender body. Her tight, curved bottom lived up to every one of his late-night fantasies, he admitted grimly as he toweled her down. Bundling her into the socks and baggy sweats he'd found on the floor of her closet, he began what became the pattern for the rest of the night.

"Hold onto me, Julia. That's it. Now move, lady. Move."

They walked the length of the long bedroom, turned, walked it again. He murmured encouragement to her. She responded at times, resisted him at others. When her strength faltered, he held her in his arms and rocked her and smoothed a palm over her damp hair until she was rested. Then he pulled her up and started the process again.

His voice grew hoarse. Hers gave out completely. Around three, he made her take another shower, not quite as frigid this time. Her lids drooped when he checked her pupils.

"Come on, Julia. Let's get you moving again."

She wanted to fight him. He could see the resistance in her shadowed eyes. But she gritted her teeth and put one stockinged foot in front of the other.

Two hours later, her pupils enlarged and contracted more normally in the light, and her mumbled words finally made a tired sort of sense. Ted decided it was safe to let her sleep. When he tried to ease her down onto the bed, however, she wrapped her arms around his neck.

"Please," she whispered. "Please, just—just hold me a little while longer."

Ted braced his arms on the bed, his muscles quivering. "I'll be right here. I won't leave you."

"Yes, you will. You'll have to. Just hold me until you do."

She only wanted comfort, he told himself. Comfort and warmth.

Comfort and warmth were all he intended to give—until she curled into his side and buried her face in his neck. Gradually, her breath warmed a deep patch just below his chin. Slowly, the heat inched down his neck. With every rise and fall of her chest, Ted felt her confusion and fear ease.

Downstairs, a mantel clock bonged the hour. A faint wash of light hit the bedroom shutters as a car drove by. Julia moved in his arms. Just enough to straighten her bent legs against his own. A few moments more. That's all he'd allow himself. Then he—

"Why do you have my picture in your office?"

The whisper drifted to him on the stillness. Ted weighed a dozen different responses and could find only one that came close to the truth.

"I talk to you. Ask you questions."

She was silent for so long he thought she might have eased into sleep.

"Do I answer?"

He curled a knuckle under her chin and raised her face. When he saw the need in her eyes, his instincts shouted at him to lie, or at least deny the truth. For once he ignored his instincts.

"All the time."

Her eyes were shadowed pools of green behind a fringe of dark lashes.

"I feel it, too," she said softly. "A strange sort of bond. You're the only one I can talk to."

They stood at the rim of a precipice. One step would send them over the edge. Ted sensed it with every nerve in his body. Julia showed it in her eyes. His common sense shouted at him to draw back. Now, before he went over and took her with him— or she took him.

"We're bound together, aren't we?" she asked. "For a while?"

"For a while."

Afterward, he could never say for sure whether she first took the step, or he did. All he knew was that their kiss started slow and grew hungry.

Her lips fit against his perfectly, as though her

mouth had been shaped for his. Ted told himself to savor the only taste he was likely to have of this woman, but he soon discovered she wanted more than a taste.

Her mouth opened under his. Their tongues met, matched, mated. Suddenly, a kiss wasn't enough for either of them. Ted slid his hands under her sweatshirt and molded the long, slender line of her waist. She started when his hand found her breast, then arched to his touch. Their bodies fused at knee and thigh and belly.

His breath rasped in his throat when he finally lifted his head. Hers came in swift little pants. Dragging his eyes from her swollen lips, he brushed her still damp hair from her forehead.

"I didn't mean for . . ."

She caught his hand, her fingers digging into his wrist. Her eyes burned into his.

"Didn't you? You haven't thought about touching me or kissing me when you look at my picture?"

"I've thought about it."

"So have I."

The fierceness left her face, and he saw only the want that remained.

"Please, I need you to touch me and kiss me. I need to know I'm real, not just a picture taped to your wall. I need to know you're real."

He understood. The desire to explore the dark tie that bound them pulsed into a driving urgency. He wanted to taste her heat and ignite the passion he'd sensed behind her cool facade. It wasn't enough any longer for him to get inside her head. In the most literal sense, he wanted inside her being.

A thousand ethical considerations held him back. The feel of her body under his drove him on. His blood thundering in his ears, he managed a crooked smile.

"We'll regret this tomorrow."

She glanced over her shoulder at the bow-shaped windows. The shutters still showed white against the darkness beyond. Twisting back, she framed his face in her palms.

"We've got a little time until tomorrow. Not much, but enough to make the regret worthwhile."

Groaning, he buried his other hand in her hair and held her steady for his kiss. She gave a sob of relief or triumph. Ted took his time, drinking in her taste, absorbing the feel of her mouth and hair and skin. She wrapped her arms around his neck and pulled him closer.

They shed their clothes in a few, swift twists and turns. Ted didn't try to turn the undressing into erotic foreplay. He'd gone beyond that point, and Julia didn't appear to want it. Her hands were hot on his body, stroking his shoulders and his back and his hips. Her fingers curled around his erection and brought him to hard, aching readiness.

Her skin was slick and smooth under his palms. He bent, shaped a breast, then teased a turgid nipple with his lips and teeth. She tasted the way he'd imagined Julia would—milky and hot and intoxicating.

When he raised his head, Ted gave a fleeting thought to the colonel he'd carefully observed from across a conference table and to the young lieutenant whose picture he'd contemplated for so many hours. Those women were cool, unsmiling, in control. Neither came close to the one he now held. Flushed, her eyes liquid with a heat that fired his own, she wrapped her legs around his calves and brought him against her pelvis. He anchored her head with both hands, resisting. His breath harsh and ragged, he made a last attempt at sanity.

"Julia. Sweetheart. I don't have any protection for you."

Her eyes widened, then she gave a small, helpless laugh. "At this point in my life I don't have anything left to lose."

Ted's jaw tightened at the reminder of the court-martial that awaited her next week. She grasped his shoulders, as if afraid that he intended to pull away.

"I can't . . . I won't worry about the future right now. Love me. Just love me. For a little while."

Her soft, whispered plea shattered the last of his control. He kneed her legs apart. Using his hands and mouth, he primed her for his entry. Gasping, she writhed under him, and in the process, did her share of priming as well.

He entered her with a fierce lunge. She matched him thrust for thrust. Each took what the other offered, and each held back a small, unreachable part of themselves. A low, hoarse moan rose in her throat as she convulsed around him and then Ted held nothing back.

Julia woke to a sense of peace she hadn't experienced in weeks. She lay unmoving for a few moments, trying to decide what had caused it.

Probably the sunlight streaming through the slanted shutters. Or the sound of the TV downstairs that told her Ted Marsh was still here. Her mind-shattering climaxes last night, certainly.

She recalled their first explosive joining in vivid detail, but had only hazy memories of the second. She'd felt so languid, so achingly exhausted that she hadn't quite believed Ted could coax her body to another release.

He'd done more than just satisfy her physical needs, though. He'd given her the validation she'd needed so desperately. She knew now she was more than just a photo or the subject of an investigation to him. He'd acknowledged that she was a woman, an individual apart from what was happening to her . . . at least for a little while. He'd worked the awful emptiness from her mind as well as the sickness from her body.

At the memory of being drugged, her sense of peace shattered. Throwing the covers aside, she pushed herself out of bed. She'd have to face Ted sooner or later and talk about last night. She might as well get it out of the way.

She took a quick shower, grimacing at her fragmented memories of the icy wet-downs she'd been subjected to last night. Toweling off, she pulled on a red sweater and a pair of jeans. She didn't waste time on makeup. A brush and a red barrette clipped at the back of her neck took care of her hair.

Her soft-soled moccasins made no noise on the stairs. The football play-offs underway on TV told her it was later in the afternoon than she'd realized. She walked through the empty living room to the kitchen and stopped in her tracks.

A showered but unshaven Ted Marsh sat at the kitchen counter, coffee cup in hand and a plate of beans and Vienna sausages in front of him. Henry the cat perched on the counter before his own plate, scarfing up beans as though he'd never seen a sardine in his life.

The thought occurred to Julia that they were two of a kind. The tough, wiry tom went his own way and touched her life only peripherally. The lean, self-contained investigator with the thatch of reddish-brown hair and shuttered gray eyes would do the same.

She cleared her throat. "I don't allow him on the counter."

Ted looked up, his gaze holding hers for a long

moment. Then he slanted his lunch companion a wry look. "How do you keep him off?"

"I start by putting his food on the floor."

"I tried that, but he seemed to prefer mine. So I gave him his own plate."

Whisking the dish out from under Henry's nose, Julia placed it in a far corner. The cat stared at her for several seconds, his breath rattling in something dangerously close to a hiss. Julia stared him down. With a final twitch of his tail he leaped off the counter.

Buoyed by the small victory, Julia poured herself a cup of coffee. When she leaned against the sink, the coffee cradled in both hands, she discovered that the need to talk to Ted about her dizziness last night had somehow gotten tangled up in a reluctance to talk about last night at all.

He'd warned her. He'd said that they'd both regret what had happened between them. She could sense his withdrawal already. Hiding her tiny niggle of hurt, she said what had to be said.

"Thank you for last night. For coming when I called, I mean. I was sick and scared and knew I could trust you."

"Because I already know the worst about you?"

The hurt became an ache. Her chin lifted. "No. Because I'd been drugged, and I knew you'd help me through it."

"Were you drugged, Julia?"

She set the mug aside, afraid that her hands

would start shaking. He had to believe her. No one else would.

"Yes, I was. I went to a restaurant on King Street. I had two glasses of wine. I started getting dizzy at the restaurant and came home. I knew before I reached my front door that I'd done it to myself again."

His brows slashed down. "What do you mean?"

"I was stupid. So *stupid*! Just like with Gabe."

"What the hell are you talking about?"

Balling her fists at her side, Julia got the words out through clenched teeth. "I met a man at the restaurant, okay? He seemed nice enough. I suggested going to the Pickford Theater. He must have thought I was coming on to him. Maybe . . . maybe I was."

This was harder, a lot harder, than she'd thought it would be. Shame coursed through her, along with a biting, corrosive anger at her sheer bad judgment.

"He must have slipped something in my wine when I went to the ladies' room. I heard a news report last week about a new . . . a new date drug . . ."

Ted cursed and shoved the stool back. He came around the counter, his face flat and hard. "A new date-rape pill? Is that what you're trying to say? It's called Rohypnol, Julia. Rossie, as it's known on the streets. It's not new. It's been around for years. It's also illegal as hell in this country, but any college kid knows how to get his hands on a bottle or two. You think this guy you tried to pick up at the restaurant slipped some in your drink?"

The lash in his voice added to her stinging hurt. He couldn't feel any more disgust for her than she felt herself.

"That's the only explanation I can come up with! I don't take drugs. I never have. And when that car followed me home, I thought it was him."

He gripped her arms. "What car?"

"It was just a car. It trailed behind me on Fairfax Street for a block or two. He must have wanted to see if his pills worked."

"Did you get this man's name?"

"No." She hated him for the doubt in his eyes, and herself for putting it there. Her lips curled in a faint sneer. "I didn't even get his telephone number, Ted. So I called you instead. I have to admit, this—this Rossie or whatever is pretty potent stuff."

She expected anger, or a fresh flare of disgust. To her considerable surprise, he displayed neither. His brow creasing, he stared down at her for several tense moments.

With lightning swiftness Ted weighed the odds. It could have happened the way she described it. She was lonely, frightened. She went to a bar and struck up a conversation. He shoved aside the jealousy that spiked through him, and the savage regret that she'd had to turn to a stranger for comfort.

The guy could have followed her home. Or someone else could have . . .

His stomach twisted into a tight, hard knot. Julia

had castigated herself for her stupidity. Ted could go her one better than that. He'd been more than stupid. Instead of listening to his suspect and hearing what she was saying, he'd taken advantage of her confused, weakened state and compromised the hell out of himself and his investigation. In the process he'd let the lead she'd given him grow stone cold.

He should have tried to track that car down last night. He should have sent Barbara or another agent to the restaurant and tried to verify just whom Julia had talked to—or hadn't talked to. He'd let her desperate plea that he not take her to the emergency room and get the incident recorded blind him to the fact that it could work for her as well as against her.

A voice far back in the corner of his mind reminded him that he had no proof Julia had been drugged and followed. Only her word. She could have doped herself up. Could have planned that desperate, pleading scene—and the bedroom scene that followed.

He stared at her, absorbing the clean skin and soft, silky hair. As quickly as the thought had come to him, Ted dismissed it. Every instinct he possessed told him her need last night had been real. Still, he couldn't request protection for Julia without explaining why he wanted it, and the explanations

were going to get sticky as hell. First, though, he had
to follow up on the only lead he had.

"I have to go back to the office," he told her, his
voice tight. "I want to check Dean Lassiter's whereabouts last night."

She sucked in a sharp breath.

"Stay inside," he instructed tersely. "Call me if
you need me."

"I will." Her mouth edged into a tremulous
smile. "I did."

EIGHTEEN

The last of the afternoon sunlight was slanting between Old Town's tall, narrow buildings when Ted Marsh drove back through its streets. Despite the late Sunday afternoon hour, the sidewalks on Duke Street were crowded. Even the blustery wind off the Potomac couldn't keep the tourists from snapping a few more pictures or picking up just one more souvenir from the trendy boutiques and bookstores.

In the bright light of day he found Julia's house on Queen Street easily enough. Squeezing his Camaro into an empty space a half block from Julia's town house, he slammed the door behind him without bothering to lock it. In its primed and unpainted state, no one would want to steal the car. Ted had been restoring it for several years now and wasn't in any hurry to finish the job. As his ex-wife had acidly observed, he enjoyed tearing things apart far more than putting them together. That particular deplorable habit had ranked number eleven or twelve on her list, he remembered.

Carlene had been right, he thought with a twinge of self-disgust. He had a knack for tearing things apart. He'd certainly done a helluva job on this investigation. He'd compromised himself and his case. He'd come up empty-handed after a futile attempt to chase down the only solid lead that could have pointed to someone other than Julia as the killer. And he'd just about run out of time. He squinted at the low-hanging sun and cursed.

Julia answered his ring and greeted him with a determined smile. "You don't have to tell me. Dean Lassiter attended a dinner at the White House last night."

"How did you know?"

"I saw a clip on CNN."

"CNN, huh?" Marsh followed her up the short flight of stairs to the living room. "It took me four phone calls and an outright threat to his obnoxious assistant to get the same information."

She hung his jacket in a hall closet, leaving him to wander into the airy living room. He'd explored the room earlier that morning, while he was waiting for Julia to come out of her exhausted sleep. Not a book out of place or an unread newspaper anywhere, but the clean, open feel to the room appealed to Ted. Julia had decorated her home for comfort as well as beauty. Like her, the white leather furnishings carried an air of cool sophistication, yet the armchair he sank into welcomed his weight—much as Julia herself had earlier.

To distract himself from the instant erotic image that leaped into his mind, Ted sniffed the tantalizing scent drifting in from the kitchen.

"Is that by any chance food?" he inquired hopefully as she folded her legs under her on the sofa.

"After I saw that news clip, I needed something to cheer me up. I called the market on King Street and ordered grilled porcini mushrooms and pasta."

"Mushrooms cheer you up?"

"Well . . . I ordered a triple chocolate torte, too," she admitted. "Are you hungry?"

"I'm always hungry."

They were dancing around the subject that hovered in both their minds like a gathering black thundercloud. Ted knew he'd have to broach it sooner or later. Sooner was more his style.

"I'm sorry, Julia. I shouldn't have leaped to the conclusion that Lassiter was the one who drugged you last night. Granted, he got all tight-jawed when I questioned him about his arrival at Yakota. Granted, he formed some kind of partnership with Hunter while he was in Vietnam that I don't quite understand yet. But I'm damned if I can find any connection between him and Hunter's murder."

"So . . ." She drew in a deep breath. "So you think my friend at the restaurant slipped me that little surprise in my wine?"

"Right now we can't prove that anyone did."

Julia fought to keep the fluttering panic his words raised from showing in her face. She'd run a tortuous gamut of emotions since stumbling across that seeming discrepancy in Dean Lassiter's travel dates. From nervous, tingling excitement she'd progressed to guilty hope, then to a crushing disappointment at the glimpse of Lassiter at the White House dinner last night. Now she faced only the bleak, stomach-clenching prospect of a trial by court-martial.

Tomorrow, she decided fiercely. She'd deal with that tomorrow. Tonight, she'd share a dinner and maybe . . .

She yanked in her wandering thoughts. She wouldn't plan beyond dinner. Ted had warned her that they'd regret what happened last night. He already felt the weight of that regret. She'd seen it in his eyes that morning, and felt it in the way he'd reverted to the roles they each played in the investigation. Once again he was the investigator. Once more she was the subject of his investigation.

Uncurling her legs, she started to invite him to join her in the kitchen when the faint clink of coins caught her attention.

"Do you have Claire Hunter's phone number?" he asked suddenly.

"Of course. We talked to each other at least once every few weeks until . . ." Her shoulders lifted in a small shrug. "Until recently."

"Is there a possibility Claire would know something about her husband's association with Dean Lassiter?"

Julia searched her memory. "I doubt it. Claire only met Dean once or twice."

"She was Hunter's wife. He might have told her something, or written her about Lassiter."

"Gabe? He wasn't the sharing, caring type."

"He married her. He must have felt something for her."

Had he? Julia glanced down at her hands. She had to get past her own feelings about Gabe Hunter, still so intense after all these years. Had he loved his wife? Claire believed he had. In his own way, she'd always insisted, Gabe had loved her.

Julia had done everything she could to protect her friend's illusions about her husband. Until this investigation forced the truth out of her, she'd never told anyone about Gabe's crude propositions. She'd never talked about that deserted stretch of perimeter road and the rape attempt. She'd kept that night bottled inside her, along with her rage and her self-blame. She'd let Gabe Hunter dominate her even from the grave.

How ironic, she thought. Only after she'd been accused of Hunter's murder had she been able to throw off his dominance.

"I don't know if Claire will speak with me," Julia warned as she eased off the sofa. "This investigation has hurt her. I've hurt her."

Ted rose slowly. "I'll talk to her, but it's probably better if I do it in person. If you'll get me the number, I'll call and ask if she can see me tonight."

"Tonight?"

Julia grimaced at the note of disappointment in her voice. Dammit, she'd warned herself not to think beyond dinner!

Ted didn't try to soften the blow. "If Claire's available, I'd better skip the mushrooms and cut right to the triple chocolate torte. I have to talk to her tonight. If I don't find some reason to extend the investigation, it's over."

Ever after, Julia would feel a small dart of pride that she managed something close to a smile. "Then I guess you'd better get on the phone and I'd better dish up the torte."

She prayed that her shaky legs would get her out of the living room. She'd sobbed in Ted's arms already once today. She refused to do it again. Her throat tight, she pushed through the swinging door to the kitchen.

From the top of the fridge, Henry the cat sat watching the simmering pots on the cooktop. His hooked tail swished back and forth patiently.

"I hope you like mushrooms as much as sardines and Vienna sausage," Julia muttered.

Like most Washington residents, Ted Marsh often drove miles out of his way to avoid the crush of late weekend traffic on I-95 south of the beltway.

Even with the weekenders clogging the lanes, however, the interstate still offered the fastest route to Claire Hunter's home in southern Virginia.

He used the long drive to ease the tight, aching regret that had grabbed him when he'd walked out of Julia's house. He didn't like leaving her with only that awful cat for company, although he had to admit Henry's disreputable appearance had started to grow on him. He disliked even more the idea of Julia slipping into that wide, empty bed upstairs.

He could have shared the bed with her tonight. He could have convinced her to put off her misgivings for one more day. He'd felt her need when she'd welcomed him into her body early this morning.

Ted didn't try to kid himself that she had craved anything more than the most basic human contact. She'd needed help and comforting, and had called the one man who'd understand why better than anyone else. He'd provided what help and comfort he could. He'd also broken every rule in the book, he reminded himself grimly.

Whatever Claire Hunter came up with tonight, Ted knew he'd be off the case tomorrow.

A deep, starry darkness had fallen by the time Claire Hunter greeted him at the door to her colonial brick home and showed him into the living room. Brass lamps spilled circles of light onto the thick carpet and chased the shadows in the room to the far corners.

Ted knew as little about decorating as he did about porcini mushrooms, but it struck him that women expressed themselves in their homes far more than men did. Julia tended toward smooth, polished hardwood floors, tall ceilings, and light colors. Claire Hunter preferred rich, wine-colored wing-backed chairs and rose potpourri. Ted didn't want to think what the week-old newspapers, scattered car parts, and comfortable brown recliner in his apartment said about his personality.

Claire gestured him to a chair and took the one opposite. When he explained his mission, she shook her head.

"I don't have much. Only a few letters Gabe wrote after I left Vietnam."

"Did he make any reference to Dean Lassiter in those letters?"

"Not that I remember."

"May I see them?"

Her reluctance showed clearly in her face. Ted understood. The few letters she'd hoarded all these years constituted her only link to her husband and the father of her son.

"Why are you asking about Dean? What has he to do with your investigation?"

"Maybe nothing. I'm just following up on a question Colonel Endicott raised."

Her dark brows feathered together. "Julia raised a question about Gabe and Dean? What kind of question?"

"She pointed out a possible discrepancy in the date Mr. Lassiter left Vietnam. He supposedly left the day before your husband disappeared, but a news story puts him arriving in Japan the day after."

Claire stared at him; then her eyes slowly widened. "Does—does Julia think Dean Lassiter might have killed Gabe?"

"She hasn't made any accusations. She simply brought a discrepancy in the date to my attention, and I'm—"

She surged to her feet, cutting him off. "Why would Dean kill my husband?"

Ted scrambled up. "I'm not saying he did, Mrs. Hunter."

"Someone did, and it wasn't Julia!"

He countered with a swift question of his own: "How do you know Julia didn't kill him?"

Bright spots of color rose in her cheeks. "I was in love with my husband, Mr. Marsh, but I wasn't blind. He was aptly named. He loved the thrill of the chase. I surrendered the first time he snared me with one of his grins, but Julia resisted. Whatever she gave him, she gave him unwillingly, even that damned kiss at Christmas. I know that. It took me awhile to work through my hurt over that kiss, but I know that."

Ted kept silent. When—if—the case against Julia went to trial, Claire Hunter would discover the truth of her assessment. Julia hadn't given Gabe Hunter a damned thing willingly.

"Whatever happened between them, Julia Endicott didn't kill my husband," the widow asserted unequivocally. "She wouldn't have done that to me. Nor would she have stood godmother to my son if she'd killed his father. If you don't realize that by now, I question your investigative and intuitive skills."

Ted lifted a brow. "I'm beginning to question them myself."

"I'll go get the letters."

She swept out of the room, leaving her visitor to revise his estimate of Claire Hunter. She was smart and loyal and not at all weak.

She returned a few moments later with a small box embroidered on the top and sides with fanciful red dragons and gold Chinese characters. Placing the box on the coffee table, she traced a finger over one of the characters that decorated the lid.

"Gabe bought me this box in Hong Kong. During our honeymoon. The shopkeeper said that this symbol means happiness." When her gaze lifted, her brown eyes held a hard-won peace. "Gabe made me happy those days. Without even trying it, he gave me enough happiness to last a lifetime."

Ted had no answer to that one. He'd need a far greater knowledge of human nature to understand how the same man could inspire such love in one woman and such hate in another.

She handed him a thin stack of envelopes tied with a purple ribbon. Ted slipped the bow and read the three short letters Gabe Hunter had sent his wife.

In the first, he asked about her flight home. Told her about the air strikes over Hanoi that appeared to have broken the back of the Easter offensive. Suggested she follow up his letter to his father with a phone call, just to assure the old man that his youngest and wildest offspring had finally gotten married.

In the second, he related that the Shadows had transferred their assets to the Vietnamese Air Force, and answered her question about a name for the baby.

In the last, he mentioned that his commander had recommended him for a Silver Star, which wouldn't amount to beans when he got back to the rule-crazy, cover-your-ass peacetime Air Force.

Given Hunter's poor record of performance between his two assignments to Vietnam, Ted suspected he'd been right. He would've had a hard time making it in a peacetime Air Force, even with a silver star.

Ted folded the last letter and slipped it back into its envelope, disappointed at the meager content. Claire retied the purple ribbon with an ease that said she'd done it many times before. Obviously, she treasured the letters. Just as obviously, she read more into the casual endearments than Ted had.

"I didn't think there was anything in them about Dean."

"I just wanted to check it out. Thanks for letting me look at them."

Returning the letters to their box, she rose and walked him to the door. Her fingers curved over the brass latch.

"Is there anything I can do to help Julia?" she asked hesitantly.

He answered her question with blunt honesty. "You might call her. She still thinks of you as her friend, and she needs all her friends right now."

Turning up the collar on his jacket against the icy cold that had come with the night, he walked the curving drive to his car. The stripped-down Camaro looked out of place in the neat suburban setting, like a poor relative come to call. It moved like a prince, though. Its retooled engine purring, it negotiated the bend in the drive and turned onto the road. Ted had just put his foot to the gas when Claire came running out of the house behind him.

"Mr. Marsh! Wait!"

He jammed on the brakes and shoved the gear shift into park. She was beside the Camaro by the time he got the door open.

"I'm glad I caught you," she gasped, her breath frosting on the night air. "I just remembered something. There was an envelope in the box with Gabe's personal things. The envelope has some clippings or something in it."

"Do you still have it?"

She nodded, her eyes excited in the glow from the car's door light. "I put the box away somewhere. Can you wait while I look for it? It might take me awhile to track it down."

"I'll wait."

There was no way in hell she was getting rid of him until she found that box.

They searched the garage, the attic, and the storage closet under the stairs. Finally, Claire remembered that she'd moved some boxes into her son's room when he moved out. Triumphant, she pointed at a dusty carton on the top shelf of the boy's closet. Ted lifted it down and set it on the floor.

Claire knelt beside him as he slit the sealing tape. Ignoring her swift indrawn breath, he lifted out neatly folded uniforms and a number of squadron plaques.

"There," she murmured a moment later. "That brown envelope."

His pulse racing, Ted slid a finger under the flap and turned the envelope upside down. Three newspaper articles fluttered to the floor. Two he recognized immediately from the grainy black-and-white pictures. The DaNang article he could almost recite by heart. He'd spent hours poring over these articles, all written before Hunter's death. If there was anything significant in them, Ted sure couldn't see it.

Claire must have seen the bitter disappointment in his face. "Don't these help?"

"I've read them before," he replied, refolding the yellowed newspaper. He started to slide them back into the manila envelope when he noticed a hand-written note on the back of one.

One-way ticket to the big time!

The handwriting looked like Hunter's, but Ted asked Claire for the letters again for verification. She retrieved the Chinese box and compared the scribbled note with the addresses on the envelopes.

"Isn't that the article that won a Pulitzer for Dean?" Claire asked.

"Yes. It was awarded in the spring of '73."

"I guess Gabe recognized the story as a winner right from the start."

"I guess. May I borrow this?"

"Will it help Julia?"

He couldn't lie. "I don't see how, but I'd like her to take a look at it."

"If there's even the slightest chance that article will help her, Mr. Marsh, you can dissect it, chemical-test it, or fricassee it." She pushed herself to her feet. "Please tell Julia I'll call her tomorrow. I think it's time I came up to the city. We both could probably use a facial and a body massage at Elizabeth Arden's."

Ted went back out into the frosty night, the clipping tucked in his shirt pocket and Claire's words ringing in his mind. He doubted Julia would glean anything more from Hunter's note than his wife had, but it gave Ted a reason to swing back by her place tonight.

He occupied himself during the long drive back to D.C. by thinking alternately about the scribbled note, his unfinished investigation, and giving Julia a body massage.

The moment she opened the door, he stopped kidding himself. He hadn't needed any other reason to swing back by her place than her warm, sleepy smile. She leaned against the doorjamb, her hair mussed and her terry-cloth robe tight against the cold air.

"I hope you're not expecting any mushrooms. Henry took care of them all."

"No, I just wanted to bring this by. Hunter's commander sent it to his wife along with his personal effects."

She examined the article in the light from the landing behind her, then started to hand it back to Marsh.

"Look on the back."

Holding the scrap of newsprint up to the light, she studied the note. "Gabe was more astute than I sometimes give him credit for. He was right, this article was certainly Dean's ticket to the big time."

There was more to it. There had to be. Ted raked

a hand through his hair, frustrated and unwilling to let go.

"I'm missing something. My gut tells me that article links Hunter and Lassiter in some way I haven't figured out yet."

She stared at him for long moments, then rose up on tiptoe and brushed his mouth with hers.

"Thank you," she said softly. "Whatever happens tomorrow or next week or next month, you believed in me today. I won't forget that."

"Julia . . ."

"It's all right. I'm not frightened or lonely, as I was last night."

"I know. But—"

She stopped his response with another light kiss. "You helped me through a rough time, and I appreciate it. I won't embarrass you or myself by asking for more."

She was right. Ted knew she was right. Better to end it now, clearly, since things would start to get real messy tomorrow. Knowing she was right and turning away from her were two different matters, however.

She was the one who pulled back. With a final good night, she closed the door. Ted waited until he heard the dead bolt slide into place before he tucked the article in his pocket and walked back to the Camaro.

NINETEEN

"You slept with her?" Bob Pfligerman's voice rose to a roar. "You slept with the primary suspect in a goddamned murder case? You're nuts, you hear me? You're goddamned nuts!"

Ted didn't bother to point out to his boss that half the headquarters could hear his bull-like bellow. Instead, he stood at a loose parade rest in front of the colonel's desk and waited for him to vent his temper. Pfligerman always needed a venting period.

Ted had met him for the first time during their early days in OSI, when Pfligerman was a captain and Ted a ten-year veteran with a brand-new officer's commission and shiny second lieutenant's bars. Ted had recognized immediately that the big, brawny captain with the white-walled crew cut and foghorn voice possessed one of the keenest minds in the business. Pfligerman in turn had shamelessly exploited Ted's experience as a cop. In the months they worked together, he'd also gained a healthy respect for Ted's instincts. Their paths had crossed off and on throughout their Air Force careers. Bob's had culminated in his assignment as chief of the Criminal Division. Ted's could very likely culminate right here in Pfligerman's office.

"Let me get this straight," the colonel boomed. "You drag out an open-and-shut investigation to follow some dead-end leads the suspect herself hands you! You go rushing over to her house, find her stoned out of her gourd, and don't even get her to the hospital for a blood test! You swallow in one gulp her story about someone drugging her, and then you sleep with her! Jesus H. Christ, Marsh, why didn't you just hand her your badge with your balls? She's gonna cost you both."

"She didn't kill Hunter."

"Oh, right!" His bellow bounced off the walls. "She didn't kill him! Did she let that little piece of information drop when she was whispering sweet nothings in your ear? I don't suppose it even crossed your mind that the colonel might have enticed you into her bed to compromise you and your investigation?"

It had crossed his mind—for all of ten seconds. Maybe twenty. He would have to be an idiot not to think about the possibility. Another woman might have been able to pull off a deliberate seduction that night. Not Julia. She'd stripped her emotions down to the core.

"She didn't shoot Hunter, Bob."

"Dammit, that's not for you to decide! Your job is to collect the evidence and present it to her commander. He and the judge advocate will decide whether the evidence is sufficient to present to a trial by court-martial, in which case the *court* will decide if she did it!"

"I need more time."

Pfligerman's fleshy face turned brick red. His cheeks puffed as though he were about to explode. Then he caught Ted's eye and deflated like a punctured blowfish.

"I can't give you any more, Ted." He rubbed a hand across what remained of his flat top. "The White House is breathing down the chief's neck about this goddamn trade mission in Vietnam. Now we're hearing rumors that this journalist you've managed to royally piss off is planning an exposé on the military's inability to police itself. When word gets out that you've slept with Endicott, my ass is grass right along with yours."

"I know. I'm sorry about that part."

Pfligerman's big shoulders rolled in a shrug. "I can handle it."

From long experience Ted knew that the man who was more his friend than his superior had passed his flash point. Bob turned hot, but he burned fast. Sure enough, Pfligerman waved him to a chair, then slumped his heavy-set body in the seat behind his desk.

"I have to relieve you, Ted. I have no choice.

You've compromised yourself and your investigation."

Ted had expected to hear the words, but they still stung. He'd spent most of the early hours before dawn in his office, weighing the pros and cons of telling his boss about his time with Julia.

Common sense had told him to just keep his mouth shut. If neither he nor Julia talked about what had happened, chances were that their secret wouldn't leak out for a while, if at all. His edgy, uneasy instincts urged otherwise, however. He couldn't protect Julia while he was prosecuting her, and he refused to ask her to hoard another dark secret. She'd borne too many, for too long.

He'd expected Pfligerman to relieve him. He would have done the same if one of his subordinates had come to him in a similar situation. Still, the reality of it left Ted a little shaky around the edges.

"Look, Bob, I understand your decision to take me off the investigation. You have no choice. But I'm not giving up on this case or on Colonel Endicott. I'm going to keep asking questions . . . on my own, if necessary."

Pfligerman's color started to rise again. "Don't put me in the position of having to suspend you permanently."

"That's your decision."

"Why don't you ever make things easy?" his boss asked resignedly.

Ted grinned. "Easy isn't my style. I thought you found that out when we worked our first undercover gig at Eglin."

Pfligerman shuddered at the memory of the weeks they'd spent masquerading as marijuana cultivators at the huge base in the Florida panhandle. They'd battled mosquitoes the size of B-52s, trigger-happy deer hunters, and the occasional overzealous local law enforcement type to tend their five-acre patch. In the process they'd infiltrated the drug underground and, eventually, helped bust a sales and distribution network that stretched clear across the southeastern United States.

Pfligerman leaned forward. "Look, this is the best I can do. You're officially off the Hunter case as of now. Lyles will take over as lead investigator. You'll work any questions you want asked through her, got that?"

"Fair enough."

"Now get the hell out of here. I've got to make some phone calls," he said glumly.

Ted didn't move. "I want some electronic surveillance for Colonel Endicott."

"What?" Pfligerman's voice rocketed off the walls. "You want me to plant a bug on her? Are you out of your frigging—"

Ruthlessly Ted cut him off. "I'll get her consent. It's just for a few weeks, until this case is resolved one way or another."

"It could be months before a court is convened!" the colonel exploded.

"Not with the pressure from the White House and Lassiter. The case is going to move fast from here on out, and you know it."

"Yeah, right. It would have moved faster if persons unnamed hadn't dragged their feet!"

Ted ignored his sarcastic comment. "I'm asking for this as a personal favor, Bob. I don't know how or why the colonel was drugged, but I'm convinced she was. I want some surveillance for her."

The OSI commander glared at him for several seconds. "All right, all right. I'll sign the authorization. Now get the hell out of my office."

Ted received more than one sideways glance as he left Pfligerman's office. The rumor mill would spread the word that he'd been relieved around the headquarters faster than a Pentium processor, but he knew the tight, close-mouthed OSI community would keep that fact within these walls. He wouldn't see his fate announced in the newspapers, as Julia had. Unless, of course, Lassiter got hold of the information.

Frowning, Ted climbed the stairs to his office and gathered the notes he'd made during the long, eventful weekend. Then he strode down the hall to Barbara Lyles's office. Smaller and far neater than his, the cubbyhole reflected Barbara's personality. A huge, framed poster of modernistic pyramids shading from red to purple dominated one wall.

Disgustingly organized bookcases marched along the other. Her desk was bare except for the report she was currently working on.

"You've got the Hunter investigation," Ted told her by way of greeting. "Pfligerman will make it official as soon as he's finished explaining to the chief how his chief investigator compromised himself."

Barbara swiveled her chair around and steepled her long, perfectly shaped nails. A striking picture in gold and onyx, she surveyed her partner coolly. Her former partner, Ted amended.

"Just how did his chief investigator compromise himself?"

Hitching a chair over to her desk, Ted recounted the events that occurred after Barbara had departed the office Saturday afternoon. She didn't comment or interrupt, but her brows soared at several points.

"So we're back to where we were a week ago," she summarized when he finished. "We've collected a whole pile of evidence that suggests the colonel had the means, the opportunity, and a good reason to drill a couple of holes in Hunter, and a gut feel that she didn't. Unfortunately, the gut feel doesn't go into the report."

"I know."

"I'll have to finalize the report, Ted," she said quietly. "I don't see where else I can go from here."

"You can try to track down the maintenance tech who figured in Lassiter's DaNang story." He spread the folded news clipping on her desk, along with the notes he'd made Saturday afternoon. "All we've got on him is name, rank, and the fact that he served in Vietnam in 1972."

"Not a problem," Barbara replied, scribbling the details on a notepad. "I'll access the personnel data files."

"Good. While you do that, I'm going to check out this Italian photographer, Remo D'Agustino."

To her credit, Barbara didn't question or object to his plan. Since Ted had been pulled from the case, he couldn't access official Air Force files. He could, however, make a few phone calls to non–Air Force sources. The distinction was a fine one, but neither of them worried about it.

Barbara strolled into his office a half hour later, her gold bracelets clanking as she held up a single typed sheet.

"Staff Sergeant Scott Forbes separated from the Air Force two years after his tour in Vietnam. I plugged his Social Security number into a couple of credit bureaus and tracked him down to Salina, Kansas. He bought a big-screen TV last month," she reported with a smug smile. "A Christmas present for his wife."

"Did you get a phone number?"

She looked offended. "Of course. No one was home when I tried it, though. What about you?"

"I struck out."

"You couldn't find D'Agustino?"

"Oh, I found him." Ted tossed his pencil into the morass of paperwork on his desk. "It took half a dozen phone calls to the National Press Association, the International Society of Photographers, and the Italian consulate, but I found him. He's buried in a village a few miles north of Florence."

"Ouch."

"It was a long shot. So is this Sergeant Forbes, but I'm asking you to follow up on him, Barbara."

"You know I will."

"Good." Pushing away from his desk, he lifted his suit coat from the back of his chair. "Call me on my beeper if you get anything."

"Where are you going?"

"I'm heading over to FAA headquarters to give Lassiter's PanAm flight one more shot. Then . . ." Common sense waged a short, fierce battle with instinct. "I might go buy some mushrooms."

Julia caught the phone on the fifth ring. Tossing her car keys and her Air Force purse onto the kitchen counter with one hand, she snatched up the receiver with the other.

"Colonel Endicott," she answered breathlessly.

"Is this a bad time?"

She sagged against the counter, surprised at the pleasure that percolated through her at the sound of Ted's voice. "Bad is a relative term these days, but on the whole I'd say this is a pretty good time."

"Good enough for a picnic?"

"A picnic?"

"You know, as in tables in the park and containers of food."

Her eyes flew to the darkened kitchen window. "Isn't it a little late in the day and a little early in the year for park benches?"

"We need to talk, Julia, and you need fresh air. I'll pick you up in twenty minutes. Oh, and bring the cat."

"Henry? You expect him to go out in the cold?"

"I need him for backup," Ted said. "In case these mushrooms taste as awful as they look."

Julia hung up laughing. The sound surprised her. She couldn't remember the last time she'd laughed. No, that wasn't true. She *could* remember. She'd giggled like a silly schoolgirl in Ted's office the day he'd surprised them both by inviting her for a meatball sub.

She folded her arms, staring at the light reflecting off the darkened kitchen window. Her strange relationship with Ted Marsh was like the window, she decided. In the darkest moment of her life, he'd provided her a glimmer of light. He'd interrogated her, pulled secrets out of her she'd never intended to reveal, comforted her, and made her laugh.

Shrinks could probably put a precise clinical term to the complex, convoluted association between Ted and her. Cops probably experienced it every day. Criminal co-dependency or something.

Julia chewed her lower lip. She had to remember

Ted's duty put him on the opposite side of the table. She couldn't let her laughter or his sympathy blind her to that fact. Nor could he.

She kept that sobering thought in mind as she changed out of her uniform and into a warm sweater, slacks, and boots. Stuffing a pair of gloves and some ear muffs into the pocket of her fleece-lined down jacket, she gingerly scooped Henry the cat from his boneless position on the leather sofa. He eyed her narrowly, as though he suspected the reason behind this sudden attention, but allowed himself to be carried to the front door.

Ted drove up just as she stepped outside. Depositing Henry on the backseat, Julia lifted a shopping bag filled with cartons out of the animal's reach and slid into the passenger seat.

"Interesting car," she commented, placing the shopping bag on the floor beside her. "Does it come with a heater?"

"It did originally. I disassembled the blower when I reworked the engine and haven't gotten around to reconnecting it yet."

"I hope we're not driving far," she murmured.

"Just down to Founders Point."

Wonderful. Darkness, cold, and the wind off the Potomac. Ted really knew how to treat a lady.

To her surprise, the chill night air gave her appetite a sharp edge, and the view from the picnic table they perched on side by side proved spectacular. Lights twinkled on the Maryland shore across the broad, black Potomac. An occasional barge cut through the inky river waters, and, once, a dinner boat strung with lights, the lively strains of an old-fashioned big band floating from it. The Woodrow Wilson Bridge formed another string of lights against the night sky to the south. To the north, the tip of the Washington Monument flashed a red warning to aircraft approaching National Airport.

Ear-muffed and gloved, Julia dug a plastic spoon into the deli cartons Ted passed her. He tucked the disgruntled Henry inside his sheepskin jacket and fed him the leftovers, eating little himself. From Ted's lack of appetite Julia guessed what had brought them to the park. She waited until he'd poured them both some coffee into a foam cup before broaching the subject.

"You've finalized the investigation, haven't you?"

"Barbara Lyles finalized it. I'm off the case as of this morning."

Julia swung around to face him. "Why?"

He rubbed a knuckle absently over the cat's head. Henry hissed at the rough caress and pulled his head inside the jacket.

"I told my boss what happened between us Saturday night."

She went still. "I . . . see."

"I wasn't covering my ass, Julia. I was trying to cover yours."

She lifted her chin. "You'd better clue me in. I'm

having a little trouble understanding how telling your boss has helped either of us in any way."

"I told you. I'm off the investigation. I'm not caught in a conflict of interest anymore."

Reason finally penetrated. Ted had wanted himself taken off the case and, she realized belatedly, put his own career on the line to help her. The street lamps scattered through the park cast enough light for her to see the dead seriousness in his eyes.

"I don't believe you killed Hunter," he told her, "but I'm not the one who'll make that determination. You're going to need someone in your corner."

"That someone can't be you. You'll put your career in jeopardy."

"It's my career, and my decision."

"Why? What do you want from me?"

She knew she'd said the wrong thing the moment the words were out. His face went hard for a moment, and Julia felt as though the temperature around her had dropped another ten degrees.

"I don't remember asking for anything from you, Colonel."

Despite the cold she felt a flush climb up her neck. "I'm sorry. I didn't mean to insult you or impugn your motives."

The stiffness left his shoulders. "And I'm sorry I threw your question back in your face. It's a legitimate question, and I'll give you an answer as soon as I figure one out. Then we'll talk about what we want from each other. For now, why don't we just concentrate on the immediate future?"

Biting back the observation that she might not have any other kind of a future, Julia listened while he related the dead end at the FAA and Barbara Lyles's brief conversation with former Air Force staff sergeant Scott Forbes.

"Forbes remembers that night at DaNang in exact detail. He's promised to jot down his thoughts and fax them within a day or two. In the meantime you can expect the case file to be forwarded through the Eleventh Wing Commander to the court-martial convening authority. The general will—"

"I know the process," she reminded him gently.

"I guess you do." He hesitated, then slipped his hand into his pocket and drew out a small black case the size of a matchbox. "Carry this with you for the next few weeks."

She turned the case over in her hands. "What is it, a high-tech pager?"

"Close. It's a miniaturized transponder. It sends out a steady, low-frequency signal. If you need help at any time, just close your fist around it. The pressure and heat will activate an emergency signal."

She stared down at the small black box, both relieved and repelled. The idea that she might need help worried her, but having help at hand was infinitely reassuring. She glanced up to find Ted's eyes on her face.

"I'll come if you need me, Julia. Anytime you need me."

His words echoed in her mind when she received the call two days later to report to the vice chief's office. For a half heartbeat her hand hovered over the phone. Resolutely she pulled it back. She couldn't rely on Ted or anyone else for moral support. She had to face this session with General Titus on her own.

Pulling on her dark blue service dress jacket, she picked up her purse and informed the chief of the Issues Group of her summons to General Titus's office. He nodded, his face as solemn as Julia knew hers must be.

Her heels echoed hollowly on the marble floors as she took the bisecting corridor to E-Ring. She made the turn, then stopped abruptly. Her jaw set, she retraced her steps to the ladies' room. General Titus could wait. Julia refused to face him looking pale and frightened.

She pushed open the door to the ladies' room and plunked her purse on one of the sinks. Originally conceived and designed as a hospital, the Pentagon boasted cavernous bathrooms with long rows of stalls and equally long rows of sinks topped by stainless steel mirrors. The harsh light above the mirrors leached what little color was left from Julia's face. Grimacing, she flipped open the purse flap and reached for her makeup bag. Suddenly, her hand froze. For long seconds, she stared down at the small, silver oak leaf pinned to the inside lining.

Agony seared through her. For the father she'd lost so long ago. For his dreams for her, and her dreams for herself. As she had so many times in the past, Julia brushed the oak leaf with the tip of one finger. Slowly, her agony subsided. In its place came a grim determination to meet her fate head-on. Her mouth firming, she applied a layer of lip gloss and a sweep of blush across her cheekbones.

Squaring her shoulders, she checked the fit of her uniform. The silver U.S. insignias were perfectly aligned on her jacket lapels. Her shiny silver eagles sat at ninety-degree angles to her shoulder seams. The nickel-and-gold badge earned during a tour on the Joint Staff years ago gleamed above her right breast pocket. Above the left she wore six rows of ribbons, legacy of her years of service and out-standing performance.

Her eyes lingered on the blue-striped longevity ribbon with its row of oak leaf clusters. The basic ribbon represented four years of service. Each cluster represented another four. She'd served more than half her life in the military. All her life, really, since she'd grown up as an Air Force brat. In another few months she would have added another oak leaf cluster to the row.

Now Julia knew she'd never add that cluster.

Whatever happened in the next few minutes, her career had ended the day General Titus had called her into his office to inform her she was under investigation. She'd come to terms with that fact, but she wouldn't go down without a fight. Iron Man Endicott's daughter didn't intend to walk meekly to her fate. If and when she went before a court-martial board, she'd give the prosecutors one hell of a run for their money. If she didn't go before a court-martial . . .

Her gaze drifted to her purse and the small black box hooked to its strap. Maybe, just maybe, she'd take Ted Marsh up on his offer to call him. Anytime.

Five minutes later, she stood at rigid attention before General Titus. Chin high, shoulders back, hands curled into loose fists at her sides, she listened impassively as he summarized the evidence against her. Then his frosty blue eyes locked with hers.

"Based on this preliminary report, I'm appointing an officer to conduct a formal inquiry under Article 32 of the Uniform Code of Military Justice. The inquiry will determine whether the facts as presented in the OSI report warrant a formal charge of murder, a lesser charge of wrongful death, or no charge at all. I'll advise you of the inquiry results and my decision within seventy-two hours."

Having braced herself for the worst, Julia

couldn't decide whether she was more relieved or disappointed at the delay.

"Do you have any questions, Colonel?"

"No, sir."

"That's all."

Her arm whipped up in a smart salute; then she spun on one heel and headed for the door.

"Julia."

Surprised, she turned to face the general. He regarded her steadily for a moment, then walked from behind his desk. In the bright overhead lighting his face showed tired creases around the mouth and eyes.

"When I learned that Special Agent Marsh had been removed from the investigation, I called him in. I wanted to hear from him what the hell happened."

Julia's stomach knotted. She'd come to terms with the termination of her own career, but guilt riddled her at the thought that she might have ruined Ted's, too.

"I don't trust myself to tell you what I think about this business between you two, but I will tell you this. That idiocy aside, Marsh is a good man. One of our best. He asked for more time. Seventy-two hours is all I can give him, or you."

The general's gruff concession eased a small weight from Julia's heart. She'd always respected this man, and his recent coldness had hurt more than she wanted to admit.

"I understand, sir."

She plucked her purse from the chair in the vice chief's outer office and tipped a nod to the exec and the secretary. Her walk brisk, she headed back to her temporary office.

Seventy-two hours. Three more days. She didn't know what, if anything, she could accomplish in three days, but she didn't plan on wasting them. Nor, it appeared from the general's comment, did Ted Marsh. He hadn't left any doubt that he and Julia were on the same side of the table now.

Full of anticipation and energy for the first time in weeks, Julia didn't even blink at the new set of claw marks in the white leather living room sofa arm. Tossing her purse onto the cushions beside an indolent Henry, she slipped out of her heels and crossed to the entertainment center.

"It's been too gloomy around here," she told the disinterested cat. "We need something joyous to liven this place up."

Flipping through the plastic CD cases, she pulled out her favorite recording of gospel classics. The soaring strains of the Athenium Church Choir's rendition of "Take My Hand, Precious Lord" filled the room.

"Now, cat, I'm going to take a shower. Then we'll see what gourmet delicacies we can scrounge up for your supper tonight."

Some twenty minutes later, she pulled on her terry-cloth robe and started back down the stairs.

Hungry for a few gourmet delicacies herself, she decided to call the deli. Her hand slid along the smooth oak railing as she joined in the choir's rhythmic, pulse-pounding version of "When I Walk This Way Again."

She was halfway down the stairs when her front door crashed open. Choking off the refrain, Julia gaped at the figure who burst in and dropped into a crouch, his snub-nosed revolver aimed directly at her midsection.

TWENTY

"Get down!"

With the finale of the gospel classic thundering in her ears, Julia barely heard Ted Marsh's shouted command. She stood rooted in surprise as he pounded up the stairs. Her breath left with a whoosh as he flattened her against the wall with his body. Holding his weapon double-fisted in his hands, he swept the living room below and the stairs above.

"Where is he?" Ted yelled over his shoulder.

Breathless from the force of his weight jamming her to the wall, Julia could only shout back stupidly, "Who?"

For several tense seconds he didn't reply or lessen his rigid stance. Julia's heart thumped in her ears, even more loudly than the music. Finally, he eased the pressure that held her pinned to the wall. His face taut and his gun at the ready, he edged down a half step.

"What happened?"

She barely heard him over the singing.

"Nothing," she yelled.

"Why did you signal?'

"I didn't!"

Frowning, he lowered the weapon. "We got a signal and . . . Damn, can't you turn off that noise?"

"I could if you'd get out of my way!"

He detoured to the downstairs landing and kicked the splintered front door shut, then followed her into the living room. Julia punched the off button on the CD player. Blessed silence instantly descended. Her heart still hammering, she turned to face Ted.

He looked like he'd just run a marathon. Literally. Sweat glistened on arms left bare by a sweatshirt with gaping, ragged armholes. A pair of yellow shorts skimmed hard, corded thighs. His damp hair fell across his forehead, showing red tints in its brown depths, and his chest rose and fell as rapidly as Julia's. He'd obviously come straight from working out at the gym.

"What's this all about?" she demanded.

He fingered the safety catch on his weapon. "We got an emergency signal from your transponder. When you didn't answer the phone, the guys on the desk called me."

"I didn't hear the phone."

He sent her a disgusted look. "No kidding! You didn't hear the doorbell, either. When I saw all your lights blazing and got no answer, I could only assume you were in distress."

"Hey, don't lay this one on me." Her adrenaline was still pumping as hard and as fast as his. "It was your little piece of electronic gadgetry that malfunctioned."

"Those transponders went through rigorous field tests," he snapped. "They don't malfunction."

"Oh, yeah?" Julia pointed out the obvious. "This one did."

"Where is it?"

She had to think. "Attached to my purse strap. The purse is on the couch."

"Smart, lady. Real smart. The damn thing's going to do you a lot of good if you're upstairs and it's—" He broke off, his mouth twisting downward. "Well, the mystery's solved."

"What?" she demanded, moving to peer around him. "Oh."

Her purse lay where she'd tossed it on the sofa cushion. Henry occupied the same cushion, his tough, wiry body planted solidly on the purse strap. Ted's precipitate entrance had brought his head up in wide-eyed alarm, but he was still sprawled in his usual indolent state across the unit. His weight and body heat had set off the emergency signal.

"Oh?" Ted repeated. "That's all you have to say?"

His sarcastic drawl ignited a small flare of temper. Folding her arms, Julia glared at him.

"What do you want, an apology? All right, I'm sorry my cat activated your high-tech, state-of-the-art, oh-so-infallible transponder." In her irritation she didn't even notice that she'd claimed possession of Henry. "And since we're talking sorry, you might give a thought to my front door."

The snide comment earned her another disgusted look. Realizing that she should show a little more gratitude for his mad dash to her side, Julia reined in her temper.

"I've already apologized. What more can I say?"

"You can say that you'll keep the damned transponder *with* you!"

"All right! Fine! I'll keep it with me!"

He rubbed a hand over his face, obviously battling with the surging emotions that had sent him careening through the night to protect her from Henry the cat. Julia couldn't help but notice the ripple of slick muscle the movement caused . . . and the wide stance to his thighs. A small dart of sensual awareness spiked into her belly.

A few nights ago she'd asked for comfort, and he'd given her so much more. Now comfort was the last thing on Julia's mind. She wanted to spark tiny fires under his skin. She wanted to make him burn with the same heat he'd ignited in her. Impatient, she waited for him to control the coiled tension that had made him snap at her.

He must have lost his inner battle, because he

turned without a word and headed for the door. Disappointment crashed through Julia.

"Ted!"

"What?"

"Let's talk, calm down a little."

Not bothering to reply, he took the short flight of stairs to the front door. Angry all over again at his intransigence and more frustrated than she wanted to admit, Julia started to follow. She'd apologized, but she was damned if she'd grovel. Jaw tight, she watched while he examined the damaged door.

"Christ! You didn't even have the dead bolt on. No wonder I got through so easily."

With a muttered curse he stepped outside and scooped a shoulder holster from the front stoop. He checked the safety, then shoved the revolver into its leather nest. Returning inside, he put a shoulder to the door to jimmy it back into place and test the dead bolt.

While he worked, Julia made a serious effort to swallow her irritation. He'd come charging to her rescue, she reminded herself. He'd thought she was in distress and kicked the door down to get to her.

She worked up a tight, grateful smile and had it firmly in place when he came back upstairs and strode across the room toward her. Her smile slipped into open-mouthed surprise as he slid his hands into her hair and tipped her head back.

"I—I thought you were leaving," she said, suddenly, embarrassingly flushed.

"Not tonight. My heart couldn't take another wild ride through the night if your cat decides to sit on the transponder again."

"Is that right?"

"That's right."

Julia's still erratic pulse skittered wildly at the steel glint in his eyes.

"Then you'd better understand something. If you stay, I refuse to regret what happens."

"I'm past the point of regrets, Julia."

His fingers tightened almost painfully in her hair, as if anchoring her in place. She had no intention of moving, but didn't say so. The fierce expression on his face held her in thrall.

"I didn't want to put any more pressure on you," he told her, his voice rough. "You've got enough to worry about without the added complication of an investigator who can't keep his damned hands off you."

Her palms slid over the bunched muscles of his upper arms. The husky scent of male sweat teased her nostrils.

"Right now," she murmured, "my only worry is that he *will* take his hands off me."

This time she didn't have to urge him to love her. This time their joining didn't start slow and end fast. His mouth came down on hers with hot, driving greed. Her hands were frantic on his body.

Panting, they scattered her robe and his clothes across the living room. Intent only on each other, they displaced an indignant Henry and tumbled to the sofa cushions. Cool, smooth leather kissed Julia's back and buttocks. Ted kissed her throat, her breasts, her belly. Then he spread her legs and kissed her heat.

His fingers dug into her bottom and lifted her hips to his mouth. Gasping, Julia closed her eyes and gave herself up to the sucking, soothing, exquisite sensation. He took her up, and up, until her only thought was that she didn't want to take and not give. Pushing his shoulders with both hands, she wiggled backward.

"Ted! Let me touch you. Let me feel you inside me."

He knelt between her legs, his chest heaving, and held her in place with hard hands. "No! No more unprotected sex between us, Julia. You're too important to me."

"But ... but ..."

Twisting on the buttery soft leather, she tried to find the courage to tell him that she wanted him desperately—unprotected or otherwise.

"Tomorrow I'm going to stock up on a year's supply of condoms," he growled, lifting one of her legs to drape it over his shoulder. "Tonight I'm going to bring you to pleasure this way."

She gasped, arching her neck against his assault. "Is ... that ... right?"

"That's ... right."

Later, she promised silently, feverishly. Later

she'd give him the same pleasure he was giving her. At that moment all she could do was anchor both hands on the arm of the sofa and lose herself in the heat streaking through her belly.

The shrill of the telephone brought them out of the stupor that comes with total and repeated satisfaction.

Ted grunted and jerked awake. Julia started, her backside bumping the leg of the coffee table. She wasn't quite sure when or how they'd ended up on the floor. Wincing, she decided that they'd expend the year's supply of condoms Ted intended to procure upstairs, in bed. Hardwood flooring and such energetic activity didn't mix.

Levering herself up on one elbow, she groped for the phone on the table beside the sofa. Her mumbled greeting brought a sharp response.

"Colonel Endicott? Are you all right?"

Frowning, Julia swiped her tongue over swollen, tender lips. "Who is this?"

"Special Agent Lyles. Where's Ted?"

"He's, ah, right beside me."

"What the hell's going on there?"

"I beg your pardon?"

Julia's clipped retort drew a more moderate reply from the investigator.

"I've got the lead now on the Hunter case," Lyles said crisply, "but the duty officer forgot that pertinent fact until a few moments ago. He just got around to advising me that Special Agent Marsh responded to an emergency signal at your residence. All you all right?"

"I'm fine. It was a false alarm. My cat sat on the transponder."

Ted groaned and covered his eyes with one hand. Julia suspected his buddies at the headquarters would have a field day with that one.

"Your cat?" Lyles sounded slightly stunned.

"My cat," Julia confirmed, grinning.

The agent cleared her throat. "May I speak to my partner, please? My former partner," she amended.

Ted took the receiver from Julia's sweaty palm. Naked and far more casual about it than she was, he pushed himself up to a sitting position.

"Everything's secure here," he assured Lyles.

Julia had no idea what his former partner said in reply, but she watched, fascinated, as the tips of Marsh's ears turned a dull red. Suddenly he surged to his feet.

"When?" he barked. He listened for a moment, then nodded. "I'll be there in fifteen minutes."

Slamming the phone onto the cradle, he grabbed for his clothes. Julia scrambled up, snatching her robe as well.

"What's going on?"

"We just got a fax." He yanked on his sleeveless sweatshirt. "From Sergeant Forbes."

"Who in the world is . . . ?" Her hands tightened

the terry-cloth belt. "You mean the Sergeant Forbes in Dean Lassiter's story?"

"The one and the only." Marsh hopped on one foot, jamming his other into a high-top sneaker. "Look, I'll call you as soon as I take a look at—"

"Oh, no! You're not leaving me here to wait and wonder! I'm coming with you."

"Julia . . ."

"You will *not* leave without me, mister!" She raced for the stairs. "In case you have trouble recognizing it, that's a direct order!"

He snapped her a salute. "Yes, ma'am."

She was back downstairs in less than five minutes. Snatching up her purse, she headed for the kitchen. "We'll take my car. It has a heater."

He matched her stride. "This giving orders comes easy to you, doesn't it?"

"It's all part of being a colonel," she threw at him with a grin.

She refused to let the thought that she might not be a colonel for much longer worry her.

They found Barbara Lyles with her palms flat on a worktable in a small conference room. Frowning, she was studying the three pages spread across the table. Julia had time to admire the woman's classy style, even in jeans, before her head jerked up. The frustration in her face sent Julia's stomach plunging.

Beside her, Ted tensed. "Nothing?"

The agent shook her head. "Nothing that makes any difference to our investigation."

She stood aside to give Ted and Julia access to the table. Julia didn't stop to think about the propriety of a suspect reviewing evidence hot off the wires. Lyles would have provided her and her lawyer copies of the documents eventually.

She skimmed Forbes's handwritten account of that night in DaNang that Dean Lassiter had captured so graphically in his story. Disappointment sat like a stone in the center of her chest by the time she got to the end. Swallowing hard, she started again.

The sergeant recalled his exhaustion after a long drive into DaNang with his counterpart, Sergeant Troung Doc Li. They'd waited several hours for their transport to Saigon, only to be told they'd been bumped and would have to catch a flight the next morning. Too tired to fuss with the folks at the billeting office, they'd gotten word of an empty hootch from one of the supply sergeants, then bedded down for the night.

Forbes had been sound asleep when the siren went off. His months in Vietnam had made the routine second nature to him. He'd rolled off his bunk, pulled on his flak vest, then squeezed under the bunk. Sergeant Li did the same. Forbes remembered hearing the shrill, whistling sound of the rocket and, he thought, a distant thud. When no explosion occurred, he and Li crawled back into their bunks.

They were both asleep when the rocket detonated and took a small ammo-storage facility with it. The explosion threw Forbes off his cot and across the hootch. Flames ignited the wooden structure. He stumbled outside and discovered Li hadn't emerged. He went back into the hootch to get him.

Despite her crushing disappointment, Julia couldn't help being moved by Forbes's courage and loyalty to his friend. For a moment she was back in Vietnam, remembering the men and women she'd shared those desperate days with. Most of them hadn't understood the politics of the war or of the prolonged, painful peace process. Most, like Julia, had served out of a sense of duty. Some, like Sergeant Forbes, had gone beyond duty and achieved honor.

She'd forgotten the simple, uncomplicated concepts of duty and honor during the past weeks. She'd let Gabe's ghost haunt her and tarnish her memories of her own service in Vietnam. Sergeant Forbes's account helped restore balance to those distant days.

She straightened, her breath easing out, and turned to Barbara Lyles. "Ted . . . Special Agent Marsh told me that you were the one who tracked Sergeant Forbes down. I want to thank you for—"

Ted interrupted unceremoniously, "What kind of rockets hit DaNang that night?"

When both women stared at him blankly, he thumped a knuckle on one of the faxed sheets.

"Forbes was back in his bunk and sound asleep again by the time the thing detonated. I don't know much about the artillery used during the Vietnam War era, but that seems like one helluva long time for a delayed fuse to detonate."

Barbara shrugged. "Vietnam was before my time."

"It wasn't before yours, Julia. How long a delay could you expect between impact and detonation?"

"I don't know. I only went through a couple of rocket attacks, and only that one hit close."

"Get Lassiter's article," Ted barked at Lyles. "I want to see if he mentions the type of rocket."

"Get it yourself," she replied with a hitch of one brow.

Muttering something about women who give orders but sure didn't know how to follow them, he stalked out of the conference room. He returned a few moments later with the yellowed clipping Claire had found among Gabe's personal effects. Holding the article up to the light, he skimmed the opening paragraph.

ROCKETS HIT DANANG

DaNang Air Base, South Vietnam, Mar. 29

A barrage of 107mm rockets rained down on the base last night, destroying an ammunition-storage facility.

"According to Lassiter, it was a 107mm," he told Julia. "Does that have a delayed fuse?"

"I don't know. My specialty is public affairs, not munitions. Why does it matter?"

He stared at the article, collecting his thoughts. "Suppose this rocket didn't go off. Suppose . . . Just suppose, now, it hit the ground and someone set it off."

"Why?"

The question came from Barbara Lyles. Ted didn't answer, deferring instead to a suddenly thoughtful Julia.

"Suppose Dean went outside with Gabe after the attack," she said slowly. "Suppose there wasn't any damage, no story for him to write or pictures for D'Agustino to take. The rocket was a dud. Or it buried itself in soft earth beside the ammo shed. Suppose—"

"You're crazy!" Barbara exclaimed. "Both of you! Lassiter wouldn't purposely set off an explosion just to get a story or a picture. He's not that stupid, for one thing, and for another, he doesn't have the balls!"

"No," Julia replied, her whole body vibrating with tension, "but Gabe did."

"Bingo," Ted said softly.

Their eyes locked across the conference table, his hard and flinty, hers leaping with hope and dismay.

"That's what Gabe's note on the back of the

article refers to. He was talking about a one-way ticket to the big time—for himself as well as Lassiter."

Barbara stared at them both, doubt and disbelief on her face, then snatched the article from Ted's hand and turned it over. Scowling, she studied the hand-scribbled note.

"Okay, okay! Just *suppose* for a moment that Hunter stage-managed this rocket attack. Why would Lassiter then kill him? They were in it together, pals, buds, co-conspirators, if you will."

"Maybe Lassiter decided he had to keep his accomplice quiet," Ted theorized.

Barbara splayed her hands on her hips. "Then why wait almost two months to do it? Why not kill him sooner, to make sure he didn't brag about the setup to his hootch mate or to his wife?"

"It must have been a matter of timing. Maybe Hunter didn't have time to brag to anyone." Ted appealed to Julia. "Didn't you say he stayed at DaNang after the rocket attack and Lassiter came back to Saigon with you?"

Julia bit her lip, trying desperately to remember a sequence of events that had happened more than two decades ago. "The Easter offensive was still making things hot for us. I remember that Gabe remained in DaNang a couple of weeks, flying for the undermanned Stinger squadron up there. I don't know if he talked to Lassiter after he came back to Saigon or not."

"We know he talked to him on the night of May thirteenth," Ted reminded her.

Julia forced down her instinctive sweep of anger at the memory of that night. She refused to dwell on the party at the Caravalle Hotel, or her struggle with Gabe afterward.

"Let me think a minute," she said, forcing mind past May 13. "Maybe Gabe didn't realize the impact of the DaNang story until it was nominated for a Pulitzer. Maybe . . . maybe he started thinking about how he could benefit from the prize as much as Lassiter."

Ted piggybacked on her thoughts. "Hunter was getting close to his rotation back to the States. He'd been recommended for a Silver Star, but he wrote his wife that even an award as prestigious as that wouldn't help him in the pansy-assed peacetime Air Force. Maybe he started putting pressure on Lassiter, who—"

"Hold it!" Barbara lifted both palms. "Let's get a grip here. We can suppose all night long, but how do we prove any of this? Hunter's dead. The photographer's dead. That leaves Lassiter, and he isn't going to admit he staged the story that catapulted him to fame."

"So we find a way to get him to admit it," Ted said, his eyes glinting.

Lyles shook her head. "For pity's sake, we don't even know that the 107mm rocket didn't go off on its own! It could very well have been triggered by some kind of a delayed fuse!"

He reached for the conference room phone. "That's easy enough to verify."

Julia crowded beside him. "Who are you calling?"

"I'm going to track down an ordnance expert. There's got to be someone in this town full of military personnel who can give up the specifics on Vietnam–era rockets."

"There is."

She took the phone out of his hand and punched in a number. Foot tapping, she waited impatiently through four rings. She'd almost given up when a calm, cultured voice answered.

"Jonas? This is Julia. May I ask a favor?" She paused for his reply, then said, "We're on our way."

"The type 63 107mm rocket was a primitive instrument," Jonas Moreton advised calmly a half hour later.

Dressed in a crisp white shirt, black tie, and his trademark gray wool sweater with the patches at the elbows, the historian glanced from his computer screen to the group hovering at his shoulder.

"Constructed by the People's Republic of China and provided to their allies in North Vietnam, it was a simple aim-and-shoot device. The rocket was fired from a twelve-tube, spin-stabilized launcher mounted on a two-wheeled cart. The NVA also used a smaller, single-tube launcher that could be backpacked into the field."

"What about the fuse?" Ted asked. "How long after the rocket was fired would it detonate?"

"The maximum range was ten to twelve kilometers, which would give it a flight time of"—Jonas did a swift mental calculation—"eighteen to twenty seconds."

"Could it have been triggered to detonate some time after impact, say fifteen or twenty minutes?"

"No, Mr. Marsh, it could not."

Ted straightened, his face hard and more dangerous than Julia had ever seen it. "I think I'll have another chat with Mr. Lassiter. Maybe he can explain how a primitive, unguided rocket detonated some fifteen to twenty minutes after it impacted the ground, taking an ammo-storage facility with it."

"You're off the investigation," Barbara reminded him pointedly. "If anyone's going to chat with Lassiter, I will."

"No," Julia said, her voice tight. "I think it's time I talked to Dean. Personally."

Ted vetoed her participation with a quick chop of one hand. "It's too risky. We don't know he had anything to do with Gabe Hunter's murder. We don't know if he got nervous after we questioned him about his departure date from Vietnam and subsequently tried to scare you out of the picture with drugs or worse. We *do* know how much he'd have to lose if we discredit his DaNang story and link him to Hunter's death."

"He doesn't have any more to lose than I do," Julia replied grimly.

TWENTY-ONE

Julia and Ted argued for a solid hour about whether she should confront Lassiter.

Barbara Lyles said nothing. Like Ted, she initially opposed Julia's involvement. She quieted, however, when the colonel reminded her pointedly that the OSI had no jurisdiction over the journalist. To question him officially as a possible suspect in a murder case, they'd have to work through civilian counterparts. Given the purely speculative nature of their suspicions and Lassiter's high-level connections, a civilian inquiry could take weeks—if it happened at all.

Conceding the point, Lyles suggested that they wouldn't gain anything by arguing more tonight. With a gracious good night to Dr. Moreton, she led the exodus.

Julia and Ted returned to her town house well after midnight, each lost in their own thoughts. Only after Julia had pulled into the alleyway that led to her garage did she begin to wonder if Ted had meant what he'd said about not leaving her alone again.

He did, as she discovered when they walked into the kitchen and found a decidedly irritated Henry the cat waiting beside his empty dish. Slitted yellow eyes telegraphed baleful signals. The bent tail whipped right and left like a lash.

"What's the matter?" Ted asked, going down on one knee to knuckle the cat's head.

"You'd better watch your hand," Julia warned. "He's probably upset because he didn't get fed tonight."

She bridled at the two accusing stares directed her way.

"Hey, I was on my way downstairs to do just that when someone kicked down my front door."

Dragging out a can of sardines, she plopped them on the counter. Her nose wrinkled at the first whiff of Henry's dinner. "God, I hate these things."

"You go on upstairs," Ted said, relieving her of her smelly chore. "I'll feed Henry and join you later."

Julia carried the confirmation that he'd be spending the night with her up the stairs and into the bathroom. As late as it was, she turned on the taps to the tub and dumped a whole handful of bath oil into the water. Something told her she was in for a long night.

She was right. She and Ted spent the next hours alternately making love and arguing. Morning found them physically spent and still at odds. In the cold chill of the new day, they drove to the Pentagon to meet Barbara Lyles.

Strange, Julia mused as she threw her coat over the back of a chair in the small conference room. A few weeks ago Ted Marsh had escorted her to this room to interrogate her for the first time. Then his expression had remained carefully neutral as he faced her across the conference table. Now he didn't try to hide the disapproval that cut deep grooves on either side of his mouth.

"I don't like the idea of you confronting Lassiter," he repeated again some hours later. "I don't like tipping our hand, and I sure as hell don't like the idea of you setting yourself up as bait."

"I'm going to do this," Julia insisted stubbornly. "Gabe and Dean and I have come almost full circle. I want to close the loop and get on with my life."

"And what if Lassiter decides he wants to keep the loop open?"

"Then I convince him otherwise."

"How?" Ted pushed his hands into his pockets. Coins jangled noisily as he paced the room. "We don't have any hard evidence to link him to the murder, only supposition and speculation."

Julia's eyes hardened. "In my business, sometimes that's enough."

He stared at her, his eyes flinty. Julia took his silence for acquiescence, if not approval, and reached for the phone.

Despite her utter determination, the instrument felt slick and hot in her palm. She clutched it in a tight fist and tried to ignore the fluttering in her stomach as she punched in the number Barbara Lyles supplied. It rang twice before a female voice answered.

"This is Colonel Endicott. I'd like to speak to Mr. Lassiter."

"I'm sorry," the woman replied, sounding anything but. "Mr. Lassiter's working his final notes for this week's commentary. Give me your number and I'll see that he—"

"Interrupt him."

A distinct huff came over the line. "He gave me express instructions not to disturb him. Leave your number and I'll get it to him."

"Tell him Julia Endicott is on the line, and I'm offering him an exclusive on Gabe Hunter's murder. He takes my call now or not at all."

Julia wasn't about to be put off by an underling. She knew damn well Dean would talk to her. He was too much of a newsman not to.

The receptionist huffed again, then conceded with a snippy "Hold on."

Lassiter came on the line a few moments later. "Julia?"

She hadn't talked to Dean in almost a year, but she recognized his resonant, well-modulated voice immediately.

"What's this about an exclusive?"

"I thought that might get your attention. I need to talk to you, Dean. Today."

"About Gabe?"

"About Gabe." She dragged in a steadying breath. "They're going to bring court-martial charges against me. Once the charges are filed, the Air Force will do a public release about the case. You and I both know that I'll be tried and convicted by the press before I ever reach a courtroom—unless I sway public opinion first."

"How do you intend to do that?"

"I'm going to tell what happened at DaNang."

The tense silence lasted only a second or two. Julia hadn't realized that mere seconds could stretch into infinity.

"What Gabe Hunter did was unconscionable," she said softly. "I didn't shoot him, but whoever did deserves a medal."

"Julia . . ."

"Look, I can't talk about this over the phone. I'm at work. Meet me for lunch."

"Not lunch," Lassiter said after a short pause. "Dinner."

"All right. Dinner at Celine's, on Wisconsin Avenue. Eight-thirty tonight."

She hung up, taking care that her shaking hand didn't rattle the phone in the cradle. A half second later, Ted replaced the extension handset. His mouth hard and tight, he shook his head.

"I don't like this."

"I'm not real thrilled about it, either," Barbara Lyles said, interjecting herself in the tense silence. "But at least we've got some time to get you wired and get you some range time. Do you have a weapon of choice?"

"Yes." Julia's hands curled into fists at her side. "A Smith & Wesson .357 magnum. And I won't need any range time."

Rain drizzled down the windshield as Julia navigated the late-evening traffic clogging Georgetown's streets. Turning right onto Wisconsin, she drove the few blocks to the restaurant she and the OSI agents had chosen for her meeting with Lassiter.

Celine's high-backed booths would provide the privacy she'd need to draw the journalist out and still allow the team of agents they'd already put in place to keep her in sight at all times.

Julia managed a smile at the mental image of Barbara Lyles in the severe uniform worn by Celine's wait staff. As she recalled, it consisted of a black tuxedo jacket, white pleated shirtfront, long skirts or trousers, without a speck of color or chunky piece of jewelry allowed. The autocratic French restaurant owner believed her people should be dressed impeccably but also blend into the dimly lit background, allowing her customers to concentrate only on their food, their wine, and their conversation.

Barbara was already in place, having gone early to check the physical layout of the restaurant.

She'd stay in a separate dining room, as would Ted, who was following a short distance behind Julia in his own car. Two other agents whose faces were unknown to Lassiter would occupy the booth next to Julia's. They'd remain within shouting distance at all times, Ted promised grimly, although she wouldn't have to shout. He'd be listening to every word.

Julia lifted a hand from the wheel and tapped a nail against the tiny wireless receiver in her right ear. She'd worn her hair down in a smooth sweep to cover the flesh-colored device. Barbara had assured her that it was invisible, but it felt as huge as a boulder and all too obtrusive to Julia.

"What's wrong?"

She jumped as Marsh's voice barked in her ear. Resting her left hand at the top of the steering wheel, she spoke directly into the jeweled watch she'd been given a few hours earlier.

"Nothing's wrong. I was just adjusting the ear piece."

"Leave it alone," he ordered curtly. "It's working fine."

"Your high-tech transponder worked fine last night, too, when Henry sat on it. I just want to make sure I don't have to sit on my ear tonight."

Ted was tense and didn't appreciate her feeble attempt at humor. "Leave it alone. Isn't that Celine's up ahead?"

She peered through the swishing windshield

wipers at the ornate gold lettering on a rain-soaked awning.

"Remember the drill," Ted instructed. "Pull up and let the valet park your car. Walk slowly into the restaurant. I'll be right behind you."

"Right."

The patter of rain on the Mercedes' roof cut off abruptly as she drove under the awning. Her nerves tingling, Julia put the car in neutral and reached for the purse on the passenger seat. She had just lifted the strap to her shoulder when the passenger door opened and a trench-coated figure slid in beside her.

"We can't talk without interruption here. Too many people know me."

Julia froze, staring at Dean's styled gray hair and taut face.

"Drive," he instructed tersely. "Head south, to River Park."

"Get out of the car!" Marsh's voice came low and fast in her ear. *"Now!"*

She made her decision in a single heartbeat. Iron Man Endicott's daughter had never run from anything. She wouldn't allow Dean Lassiter to haunt her for the rest of her life, as Gabe Hunter had for so many years.

"All right. We'll go to River Park."

"Dammit, Julia, get out of the car!"

She was tempted to switch off the ear piece and shut out Ted's warnings.

366   *Merline Lovelace*

Her hand shaking, she placed her purse on the floor just under her knees and reached for the gear shift. The Mercedes eased into the stream of traffic. She clutched the top of the steering wheel with one hand, keeping the jeweled watch within easy speaking distance. The other hand stayed at the bottom of the wheel, a short grab from the leather purse on the floor.

Ted cursed viciously, then barked a series of commands to the listening agents. Julia thought she heard the screech of his car's tires as he whipped the vehicle around to follow hers.

Neither she nor Lassiter spoke during the three-block drive to the deserted park at the bottom of Wisconsin Avenue. On a summer day the tiny patch of greenery bordering the Potomac provided a shady spot to watch Georgetown University's rowers slice through the water. On a winter night the river flowed dark and silent and forbidding.

"Not here," Lassiter objected when she pulled into one of the parking stalls at the west end of the lot. "Someone might see us. Drive to the far end of the lot."

"Stay in the goddamned light!"

Julia nosed the Mercedes halfway down the empty lot, out of the circles of light from the overhead spots but not so far into the shadows that she couldn't see Lassiter's eyes as he turned and stared at her.

"All right, Julia. I canceled my dinner with the

White House chief of staff to meet with you tonight. What do have you to tell me about Gabe Hunter that the rest of the world doesn't already know?"

"I'm pulling up behind the warehouse at the west end of the park. I'll be in position in a few seconds."

"The world doesn't know Gabe raped me, or tried to," Julia began.

Dean's mouth twisted. "From where the rest of us stood, it didn't look like he'd have to resort to rape."

"But we both know appearances can be deceiving."

"Is that why you killed him?" Lassiter asked coolly.

"All right, I've got him in my line of fire. Julia, get the hell out of the car. Barbara, where are you?"

Julia reached for the door handle. "It's too hot in here. I'm sweating."

She shouldered open the door. Lassiter did the same on the passenger side. In the process of climbing out of the low-slung Mercedes, Julia unobtrusively transferred the Smith & Wesson from her purse to her coat pocket. Hooking her thumbs in the corners of her pockets, she steeled herself to face Dean.

She wasn't the only one who was sweating, she noted with a stab of fierce satisfaction. The glare of the headlights picked up a film of perspiration on the journalist's forehead. A bead of sweat trickled down his neck to disappear in the collar of his smartly pressed Burberry trench coat. The expensive coat ratcheted the tight coil in Julia's chest another notch.

They *had* come full circle, she realized. Dean and she and Gabe. The first time Julia had met the reporter, his pristine, unsullied bush jacket had telegraphed his neophyte war correspondent status like a flashing railroad signal. Now his tailored overcoat, carefully styled gray hair, and manicured nails bespoke a man at the peak of his profession. How far he'd come from those days in Saigon. How far she'd come.

Strangely unafraid, Julia faced the reporter. Her career shattered, her life in shambles, she knew the past twenty-four years had filtered down to this moment. She had to have the truth. Whatever the cost, she wanted Gabe's ghost laid to rest.

"I didn't kill Gabe Hunter, Dean. You did."

For several seconds no one spoke. Not Julia. Not Lassiter. Not even Ted in her ear.

"Interesting theory," the reporter said at last. "I suppose you're going to tell me how I accomplished that particular feat when I'd already left Saigon."

"You didn't leave Saigon until the eleventh, the day Gabe failed to report for his mission brief."

"I say I did. Can you prove otherwise?"

"Not yet," she admitted with unflinching honesty. Then, just as unflinchingly, she lied. "But I still have a few friends. One of them works for FAA.

He's located a box of microfiche records that include PanAm's flight data for the years 1970 to 1975. He called me this afternoon to tell me that he thinks he can trace your flight."

Lassiter's eyes narrowed to pale slits across the headlights' beam. "You're bluffing. There are no records."

"How do you know? Have you checked?"

"Yes, after Marsh relayed your wild accusations. I thought I might need backup." His mouth thinned. "Even if I'd been in Saigon that day, you have no proof, nothing to link me to Gabe's murder."

Julia had never learned to play poker. A few hours of gambling in a smoke-filled casino bored her to tears. Given the stakes, however, she had no difficulty taking her bluff to its final, deadly extreme.

"I don't have to prove you killed him. I just have to create enough doubt to acquit myself. In the process I'll take you down, Dean. I'll tell the world about DaNang and Gabe's 'one way ticket to easy street.' "

"I don't know what you're talking about."

"Gabe was blackmailing you, wasn't he? He set off the explosion the night of the rocket attack in DaNang, then decided to ride to glory on your coattails after you won the Pulitzer."

Lassiter leaned against the Mercedes' fender, a study in cynical amusement. "You must indeed be desperate, Julia. I expected better from you."

"The rocket that hit inside the compound was a dud," she continued slowly, deliberately, with absolute authority in her tone. "It buried itself in the mud beside the ammo-storage container. Accommodating and reckless as always, Gabe put a few rounds into the CONEX and lit up the sky for you. D'Agustino got his pictures. In the process he lost his arm."

"He got too close. He admitted that himself in his memoirs before he died."

"He got too close, and you got your story when Sergeant Forbes stumbled out of the hootch next door."

She watched his eyes. They never flickered. Never left hers.

"That hootch was supposed to be deserted, wasn't it? Even Gabe wouldn't have taken a chance like that if he'd known two men had bunked down next to the ammo-storage area. We both know he could be a bastard at times, but he wouldn't deliberately endanger two men's lives to provide you and D'Agustino with some local color."

Lassiter's lip curled. "Your story won't play on the nightly news, Julia. It's all speculation and no hard facts."

"I have enough facts for *Sixty Minutes* to jump all over this story." Her voice taut, she laid them out. "The trajectory and detonation times for 107mm rockets. Statements from witnesses that the rocket hit without exploding. Sergeant Forbes's own testimony."

The reporter stiffened, so slightly the casual observer might not have noticed the small movement. Julia was far from a casual observer.

"Watch his hands! If he reaches for his coat pocket, I'm coming in."

"What testimony?" Dean asked.

"Sergeant Forbes gave me a written deposition. In it he states that he'd crawled back into his bunk and was sound asleep when the explosion threw him across the hootch."

Her throat tight with suffocating tension, Julia waited for Lassiter to comment. He regarded her, his face unreadable for long, endless seconds. Then slowly, so slowly, his gaze dropped. It caught on the bulge in her pocket for an infinitessimal second, before snaring hers once more.

"Are you wired, Julia?" he asked, so softly she almost missed the question.

"What?"

"Is that what this is all about? Are you taping this little conversation, trying to set me up to incriminate myself?"

"I don't need to set you up. You and Gabe set yourselves up in DaNang."

"We're back to square one. Even with this deposition from Forbes, you can't prove anything. This is all still speculation."

"I know. But think what fascinating copy my

speculation will make, Dean. Think how easily your associates can spin supposition into damning fact." She leaned forward, her body taut. "How many toes have you stepped on to get where you are today? How many of your peers will grin gleefully when you stand accused in print with me?"

"Get back, Julia. You're in my line of fire."

"How many will dance in the newsroom aisles when the Pulitzer committee strips your prize from you?"

The skin across his cheekbones whitened. Julia coolly played her last, desperate hand.

"Gabe reached out from the grave to destroy me, but I'm not going down alone. I'm taking his killer with me, one way or another."

Lassiter's eyes burned into her. Suddenly he jerked upright, his whole body tensing. "Don't do it, Julia! Don't shoot!"

"What?"

Startled, she peered into his face for a blank second—just long enough for Lassiter's right hand to dive into her coat pocket and whip out the Smith & Wesson.

"Jesus!" he shouted, throwing himself into her. "Don't shoot!"

She went down under his crushing weight. Her back slammed into the pavement. The breath left her lungs. One arm was pinned under her. A vicious grip caught her other wrist and twisted it to the ground. A gun barrel dug into her ribs.

Gasping, she stared up into Dean's glittering eyes. Her skin went ice cold.

The reporter was staging her death, just as he and Gabe had staged the rocket attack. Lassiter saw the acknowledgment in her eyes. The weapon dug deeper into her ribs.

"Let go of the gun!" His hoarse cry was for the benefit of the wire he'd guessed she was wearing. "Let—"

The sound of a weapon being cocked cut through Lassiter's harsh breathing and Julia's frantic struggle. She caught a glint of blue steel as a gun barrel indented the skin at Dean's temple.

"Get off her!" Ted's low, deadly command cut through the roaring in Julia's ears. "Now! Or I'll put a bullet through your skull the same way you put one through Hunter's."

The reporter froze, his weight sprawled atop Julia in an obscene intimacy.

"If the gun in your hand goes off," Ted warned, "you're a dead man."

For a heart-stopping eternity Lassiter didn't move. Then carefully, very carefully, he eased himself up a few inches.

"Isn't this what they call a Mexican stand-off?" he snarled over his shoulder. "You can't shoot me without taking the chance that I'll blow a hole through your lover's gut."

He grunted as Ted's gun barrel cut into his temple. Then his lips turned back in a sneer.

"Was she worth it, Marsh? Oh, I heard she screwed you, just like she did Gabe. She spread her legs and compromised the hell out of you. Now you're both trying to pin Hunter's murder on me to clear yourselves."

He was still playing for the wire, Julia realized. He didn't know who was listening. Desperate now, he was going to kill her, then go for Marsh.

"It won't work," Lassiter went on. "I've got her gun in my hand. I'm not letting either of you take me down without a fight. Back off! Back off or she's dead! I've got nothing to lose. The two of you are going to ruin me anyway."

"Don't do it!" Julia cried. "He's setting us up."

"Don't do anything stupid," Ted ground out. "I'm pulling back."

"No! No, Ted! Don't!"

Ted's gun barrel withdrew, millimeter by millimeter.

"Now drop it and kick it out of reach," Lassiter said.

She wanted to sob with fear and frustration as Ted's gun snickered across the pavement. She clawed Lassiter's arm, fighting the choke hold he used to drag her to her feet, fighting the pain that pinched her side from the steel barrel in her ribs. If she threw herself sideways, maybe she could—

"All right, Lyles," Ted said, his voice low and careful. "He's on his feet. We can see the weapon in his hand. Come out. Slowly."

The reporter jerked his head around as Barbara Lyles emerged from the shadows, her weapon at the ready. A second agent showed himself and the pistol he held pointed at Lassiter's head.

Hands out, jaw granite hard, Ted faced the reporter. "You might have been able to stage Julia's death and mine. But not Special Agent Lyles' or Jordan's, or the others who will be here in the next few seconds. Let her go, Lassiter. The story's over. You wrote the final copy when you pulled that gun on Julia."

Julia couldn't move. Didn't breathe. The acrid scent of fear rose in waves around her. She didn't know if it came from her or Dean. Didn't care. Closing her eyes, she fought her way through the black, swirling vortex that threatened to consume her.

"They're . . ." She dragged in a rasping breath. "They're not worth it, Dean. All these secrets we've carried . . . I've found out these past weeks, they're not worth what Gabe made us pay for them. I've let go of his ghost. You've got to let go, too."

His breathing was harsh and ragged in her ear. Julia could hear its frantic rhythm, feel its hot wash on her cheek.

"I understand how Gabe was," she said bitterly, her fingers tearing at his rigid arm. "God, I understand! He made me despise myself for wanting him and laughed at me the entire time. He could—"

She broke off, gasping, as the forearm around her throat tightened.

"It's over, Lassiter." Low, calming, implacable, Ted's voice carried through the frozen stillness. "Let her go."

"You're wrong," the reporter said hoarsely. "I haven't written the final copy yet."

The barrel jabbed Julia's ribs a last time, then jerked upward. She grasped his intent instantly.

"Don't do it! Dean, listen to me. I've lost my career, my pride, and I survived. You can . . . Dean! Oh, God! *Don't!*"

She screamed as the sound of the gunshot exploded in her eardrum. Lassiter jerked back, dragging her with him. With superhuman strength Julia tore out of his arms and threw herself at Ted.

TWENTY-TWO

Julia stood alone, her fist locked around the silver oak leaf cluster she'd yanked out of her purse. The sharp metal stem cut into her palm as she stared into the night. This time, her father's rank insignia couldn't give her comfort.

Before her stretched the flat darkness of the Potomac. Behind her, intermittent red and blue flashes from emergency vehicles pierced the night. She strained to hear the calming rush of the river over the cackle of police radios and the muted voices of an ambulance crew.

Ted had wanted her to leave the scene after she'd given the D.C. police her statement, or at least wait in the warmth of a car. Julia couldn't bear to sit inside the suffocating confines of a closed vehicle. She had to feel the cold air in her face. Had to listen for the sounds of the river as the ringing in her ears gradually disappeared. Had to believe the nightmare was truly over.

It was, she realized wearily . . . and it wasn't.

Dean Lassiter had died without confessing to Gabe's murder or to rigging the story at DaNang. His death hadn't exonerated Julia. That would come eventually, though. No court-martial board could now determine beyond a shadow of a doubt that she had killed Gabe. Nor would anyone ever know if Lassiter had. Gabriel Hunter would always remain an elusive ghost.

She could almost see him out there in the darkness beyond the river. A mocking grin tipped up his mustache. His eyes glinted as he laughed at her. At them all.

She wanted to curse him, and discovered that she didn't have the anger left in her to do it. She closed her eyes and let the night take her back a final time to a land of purple mountains and green checkerboard paddies.

Lieutenant Julia Endicott had left Vietnam on a day much like the one she'd arrived. Dark thunderclouds piled up on the horizon. Puddles shimmered on the runway. The acrid scent of jet fuel hung like a heavy, muggy blanket over all.

She stepped off the bus that had transported the departing passengers from the aerial port to planeside and glanced around. Somewhere in the deepest recesses of her mind she half expected to hear a jeep roaring up and watch while a rakish, grinning Gabe clambered out.

Hunter wouldn't come to see her off, as he'd

come to greet her a year ago. He was missing in action. He had been for several months. And Julia wasn't the same woman who'd let a man like Gabriel Hunter sweep into her life and leave it in shambles. Not again. Never again.

Slowly, she climbed the steps to the plane, following the file of jubilant troops heading home. She paused at the top of the steps. As it had a year ago, her gaze settled on the distant line of peaks. Misty clouds obscured the scars. From here the mountains looked so beautiful, so serene.

Swallowing, Julia stepped inside the 747 and let the raucous excitement of the returning soldiers claim her.

Her war was over.

"Julia?"

Ted's voice pulled her from the past. The mountains faded, and there was only the swift, rushing river. He came to stand behind her, a solid presence in a dark world eerily pierced by red and blue beams.

"We have everything on tape," he told her quietly. "With that, and the circumstantial evidence against Lassiter, it's unlikely you'll even stand trial."

"I know."

"I'll make sure the transcript of the tape gets to General Titus tomorrow. He'll see that you get a swift decision."

"I know."

Ted moved closer, his body shielding hers from the business of death taking place behind them.

"No court-martial will convict you."

She nodded, her eyes on the dark river. They watched it in silence for a while. Then Ted asked the same question that was echoing in her mind.

"What will you do now?"

She didn't answer right away. Letting go of Colonel Julia Endicott was both easier and more difficult than she'd imagined it would be.

"I think . . . No, I know. I'm going to hang up my uniform and find out what life is like outside the Air Force."

His arms came around her. She leaned back.

"I've spent my whole life in the military," she murmured. "Either as a dependent or an officer. I've done my duty as best I could, and served with honor."

Ted was there behind her, his breath on her temple.

"Now," she mused, "I'm going to let my hair down. I'm going to give up wearing panty hose for the foreseeable future, and I'm going to lie in the sun with Henry the cat if I feel like it."

His chin rested on the top of her head. "Sounds like a good plan to me. You and Henry want some company?"

She smiled into the darkness. "I can't speak for him, but I wouldn't mind sharing a beach towel."

He didn't speak for long, soothing moments. A

sense of rightness drifted through Julia. She laid her head against Ted's shoulder.

He held her. Just held her.

The rightness flowed into peace, and the beginnings of wonder.

"I think . . . no, I know." He echoed her words. "I want to share more than a beach towel with you, Julia. I want to share your bed and your laughter and your life."

"Are you sure you want me?" she asked softly. "Or are you confusing the woman I am with the girl in the picture taped to your wall?"

"They're one and the same in my mind," he said simply. "They always will be."

She closed her eyes. She knew, if Ted didn't, how different she was from the young lieutenant who'd set off for Vietnam, determined to serve out the tour her father had never finished. She'd been so sure of herself then. So confident in her abilities and the profession she'd chosen for herself. Gabe's betrayal had changed that. And Ted's love.

"The day we met," she confessed, "I felt as though you had brought my world crashing down around my ears."

"And now?"

She twisted in his arms, turning her back on the darkness. "Now . . . Now I think I might be on the point of exploring a whole new universe."

His mouth came down on hers, and Julia took her first step into a future unshadowed by her past.

ᐯ TOPAZ

WONDERFUL LOVE STORIES

☐ **SECRET NIGHTS by Anita Mills.** Elise Rand had once been humiliated by her father's attempt to arrange a marriage for her with London's most brilliant and ambitious criminal lawyer, Patrick Hamilton. Hamilton wanted her, but as a mistress, not a wife. Now she was committed to a desperate act—giving her body to Hamilton if he would defend her father in a scandalous case of murder.
(404815—$4.99)

☐ **A LIGHT FOR MY LOVE by Alexis Harrington.** Determined to make the beautiful China Sullivan forget the lonely hellion he'd once been, Jake Chastaine must make her see the new man he'd become. But even as love begins to heal the wounds of the past, Jake must battle a new obstacle—a danger that threatens to destroy all they hold dear.
(405013—$4.99)

☐ **IN A PIRATE'S ARMS by Mary Kingsley.** They call him the Raven. His pirate ship swoops down on English frigates in tropical seas and he takes what he wishes. Taken captive while accompanying her beautiful sister on a voyage to London, spinster Rebecca Talbot is stunned when the handsome buccaneer winks at her and presses her wrist to his lips. She daringly offers to be the Raven's mistress if he will keep her sister safe.
(406443—$5.50)

*Prices slightly higher in Canada

Buy them at your local bookstore or use this convenient coupon for ordering.

PENGUIN USA
P.O. Box 999 — Dept. #17109
Bergenfield, New Jersey 07621

Please send me the books I have checked above.
I am enclosing $_____ (please add $2.00 to cover postage and handling). Send check or money order (no cash or C.O.D.'s) or charge by Mastercard or VISA (with a $15.00 minimum). Prices and numbers are subject to change without notice.

Card #_____ Exp. Date _____
Signature_____
Name_____
Address_____
City _____ State _____ Zip Code _____

For faster service when ordering by credit card call 1-800-253-6476
Allow a minimum of 4-6 weeks for delivery. This offer is subject to change without notice.